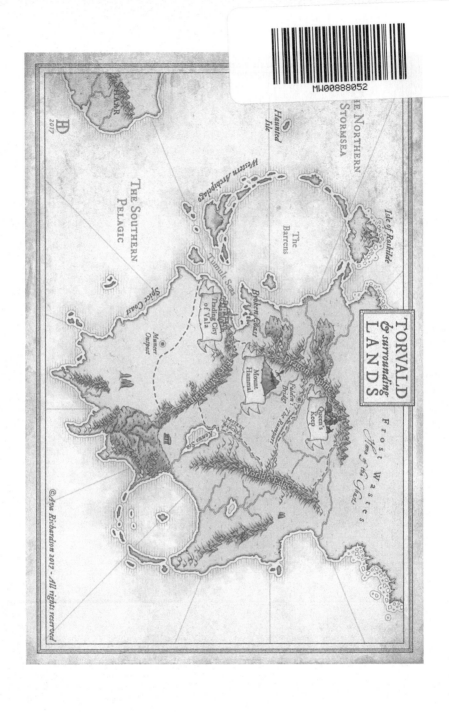

TORVALD
& surrounding
LANDS

THE NORTHERN
STORMSEA

Haunted
Isle

Western Archipelago

THE SOUTHERN
PELAGIC

The
Barrens

Isle of Rakkilde

Frost Wastes
Home of the Ghosts

Tumult Seas

Spice Coast

Bakers Gaar

Trading City
of Vala

Mount
Hammal

Dragon Spine

Paldin's
Bridge

The Ramparts

Queen's
Keep

Mancer
Outpost

Selapion Mountains

World's Edge

THE RETURN OF THE DARKENING SERIES

Dragon Trials

Dragon Legends

Dragon Bonds

Cover Art by Joemel Requeza.

www.relaypub.com

DRAGON LEGENDS

Return of the Darkening Series Book Two

AVA RICHARDSON

BLURB

Ever since scruffy Sebastian Smith and Lady Thea Flamma were paired as Dragon Riders, their lives have been forever changed. The unlikely duo forged an unbreakable bond, but now with dark stirrings in the south their bond will be put to the ultimate test.

Seb discovers Lord Vincent has returned and he wants to unleash an ancient evil that will destroy the lives of everyone in the kingdom – The Darkening. In order to defend the realm against unspeakable foes, Seb, Thea, and their shared dragon, Kalax, set out on an arduous journey to find the sacred Dragon Stones – before their dark power ends up in the wrong hands.

But to conquer an old enemy, Thea must find a way to overcome her own inner demons, and Seb has to muster the courage to become the brave leader his kingdom needs . . .

MAILING LIST

Thank you for purchasing 'Dragon Legends'
(The Return of the Darkening Series Book Two)

I would like to thank you for purchasing this book. If you would like to hear more about what I am up to, or continue to follow the stories set in this world with these characters—then please take a look at:

AvaRichardsonBooks.com

You can also find me on me on
www.facebook.com/AvaRichardsonBooks

Or sign up to my mailing list:
AvaRichardsonBooks.com/mailing-list/

CONTENTS

CHAPTER 1
ATTACK ON HIGH ROAD

The wind screamed past me, tugging at my armour and pulling at the goggles on my face as Kalax fell in a dive, straight for the bare earth.

"Seb!" Thea gasped the word and grabbed the back of my harness. I could feel tension and anxiety thrum through her body and into mine.

"Hold," I shouted with my mind and voice, leaning low over the long neck of our red dragon. Kalax's excitement, her eagerness for this fight, trickled up through the connection I had with her. But I had to concentrate. We had only one shot at this, and I had to be sure we didn't miss.

The ground grew larger, filling my sight. In a matter of seconds, the straight road that ran north to south from Torvald had turned from a faint, ochre line to a lane and I could make out the way markers on either side. The mounted figures beside the burning house looked like large dolls, but they glanced up and I could see their harsh faces.

"Now!" Kicking forward, I used the stirrups to activate the levers and pulleys that fed back to Thea.

Kalax roared, unfurling her wings in a sudden snap, catching the wind and sending a beat of air as powerful as a gale down on the bandits below. She roared again, the muscles of her wings and shoulders trembling under the strain of slowing her descent. I knew she could do this tricky maneuver—there were times when we were flying that Kalax and I became one body, one mind in flight.

The thunderclap of air swept in down at the bandits, startling their horses, sending two men sprawling to the ground and blowing apart bits of burning thatch before they could catch onto the rest of the structure. The smell of soot and smoke wafted up, as did the screams.

"Hyah!" Thea stood up in her saddle and fired down at the bandits. One arrow hit the side of the building, the other found its mark and the bandit who was attempting to mount his terrified steed fell.

"Up," I whispered to Kalax. Her excitement and thirst for the hunt bubbled up inside me. She could smell the terrified horses, and hadn't eaten anything all day except for a skinny old sheep this morning.

Hunt? The word appeared in my mind, flowing through the warm scales under my hands and blossoming with an accompanying desire for the thrill of the chase. Kalax was sharing her thoughts more and more with me now, rather than just listening to mine. Commander Hegarty had said it was because we were becoming more attuned to each other—but Merik, who I had told about it, thought it was a Dragon Affinity—an extra strong connection that I had with dragons.

No, I thought back at her. *Wait.*

Kalax was puzzled and I could sense her disappointment. But she rose into the air and circled.

"I've still got another shot," Thea shouted.

I glanced back at her. Some of her flame-red hair had come out of her helmet and she scowled, as fierce as the bandits. Two of the bandits below were carrying short crossbows—they could fire much quicker than Thea could draw her long bow. As the Navigator, it was my duty to choose the lines of attack and escape, and to keep Kalax out of danger. And Thea.

I didn't want to admit it, but I was afraid for her. The memory of her, lying on the floor of that cavern, blood seeping from the wound in her side as she lay dying, chased a shiver through me. I wasn't going to let that happen again.

The bandits below were screaming now, shouting to run even as another of them tried to call the others back. Three were fleeing on their mounts, headed south and into the wilds. *We'll leave them to the King's Patrol,* I thought, wheeling Kalax around in a wide arc to come back to the remaining four.

Small, black bolts sped past Kalax. One thudded into her scales, causing her to roar. I leaned to the side, wanting her to veer out of the way. The bolt had done her no harm, but I didn't want a lucky shot piercing her wing. My order confused Kalax

3

for a second, making her spin in mid-air, before she turned and headed at the remaining bandits.

Thea shouted a war cry, and a flush of panic doused me in chill sweat. *What if they've had time to reload?*

But Kalax was fast. She fell on them, her forward claws seizing two bandits. She swooped past the half-demolished building and released them into the brambles. They'd be battered and bruised, and probably happy to give themselves up to anyone.

Standing in her stirrups, Thea shouted down at the bandit who seemed to be the leader. "Halt in the name of the king!"

One bandit turned and ran, leaving the last man—the biggest one—on his own against one of the kingdom's fiercest defenses—a Dragon Rider of Torvald. I wheeled Kalax around, preparing for another swoop. The man threw his sword onto the ground and raised his hands in the air.

With a triumphant roar, Kalax skimmed over his head a little lower than was necessary, knocking him flat. I had to grin. We had driven off the bandits and fulfilled our mission. And we had survived.

⚜

The King's Patrol arrived just in time to see Kalax land on the road, flattening the grass with the beat of her wings. I knew they had ridden out from the capital at the same time Commander Hegarty dispatched us, but no horse could match the speed of a dragon, especially not Kalax.

She was a red, meaning that some of the old bloodlines had resurfaced. Kalax had a long neck, tail and wings big enough to wrap around an entire house. She wasn't as sinuous as the blue dragons or as strong as the short-necked greens, or as fast as one of the wild blacks, but to me she was the perfect mix of all of their best skills. She had barbs that she could flare from around her face and along her tail if she ever needed to, and had teeth as long as my forearm.

At the moment, she was happily preening her thick wing like a bird, obviously happy with the day's work.

I swung off Kalax and glanced around.

The captain of the patrol looked to be a woman with a square jaw and fair hair scraped back into a thick braid. She wore leather armour, like most riders, but also wore a long sword and had a banner of the Middle Kingdom fixed to her saddle. Her warhorse was large dark grey, but seemed a little skittish, snorting as if it didn't trust Kalax.

Kalax huffed out a warm breath and the captain had to hang onto her mount.

She glanced at me and said, "Captain Lacee. This is the leader, huh?" She nodded to where her men were tying up the last bandit who'd surrendered.

Thea unclipped her harness and jumping down. "Three more are fleeing southwards."

"We'll get them, no fear. As for these, they'll be taken back to the city. A year and a day of working on the high pastures or something and they'll rethink a career of theft."

Thea shook her head, crossed her arms and faced the bandit. "You're lucky. My father, Lord Flamma, would have had you whipped and thrown into chains."

I winced at the comment. As much as Thea had changed, sometimes the fact that she was from a noble house still came out at the worst times. Oh, sure she knew which knives and spoons to use at dinner, or how to address a lord or a captain or an ambassador correctly, but she also could stick that upturned nose of hers in the air and act like a snob.

It was different for me.

The only time I'd ever had to address someone of rank had been to say 'sorry sir' for an order that was late. I'd come from the poorest part of Torvald, and becoming a navigator and partner to Agathea Flamma was something I still wondered at. There were times I thought I'd wake and find this was a dream —or a nightmare, for rumours of war were still as thick on the ground as fallen leaves in autumn.

Thea turned away from the bandit, but I kept staring at him.

I was no expert on bandits, but this lot didn't look the type to be out for an easy gold mark. Most bandits I'd ever seen looked a lot like the people I'd grown up with in Monger's Lane, with dirty, patched tunics and cloaks that could hide their faces. They'd pushed through hard times. These fellows looked more like warriors. They could afford crossbows and swords, and wore stiffened leather armour, dyed red. They also wore their hair in an unfamiliar fashion with a braid running the length of their scalps and either side shaved. Tattoos covered their arms and necks.

"Captain Lacee?" I asked. "Where would you say these bandits are from?"

The captain turned to look at the man and nodded. "From a long way off. Up from the Southern Reaches, maybe."

That was an awful long way away. The maps I'd seen at the academy had shown the Southern Reaches were weeks away by horseback, and days even by dragon. Due to recent troubles, that would also take them through hostile regions.

Why come all this way to burn down a few houses?

"Don't worry, lad. Just bandits." The captain signaled for her men to mount and move off. "We'll be sending a team down to deal with those that fled." She threw a quick salute, mounted and rode off.

Thea leaned against Kalax and I scratched below Kalax's jaw at the spot she liked itched. "Let's allow Kalax to get her breath before we return." Thea nodded, but she seemed to stare at the horizon, as if she saw something I couldn't make out.

She didn't say anything, so I headed over the where the bandits had dropped their weapons. The long sword and the crossbows were all well-made. I'd learned enough of a smith's work from my father to know when a weapon was a costly piece, and these were worth more than any bandit would have found in this small village.

Something didn't feel right. Glancing at the ground I saw a leather pouch that one of the bandits must have dropped. Opening it, I found a shark's tooth, a few gold marks and a few beads. Keepsakes of a man whose life was on the road?

"Hey!" Thea walked up to me. "What are you doing?"

"Look at these." I showed her the items from the pouch. "A shark's tooth means from the sea—or the coast at the very least."

She shrugged. "So? It's not where they came from that matters, it's that we finished the battle in what, two minutes? Come on, Seb, we've rested enough. And you're looking for more trouble where there's none to be found."

She headed back to Kalax and I put the items back in the pouch and left it by the half-ruined house.

The truth was, I was worried about trouble—and feared it would find us before we were ready to be found.

We had defeated Lord Vincent and the Darkening once—but it hadn't been a full victory. Lord Vincent managed to escape and the rumours of the Darkening—of villages where everyone forgot their lives and simply disappeared—were still surfacing.

That meant the Darkening was still out there, probably regrouping to come at us again. And we still had no real idea how to defeat the Darkening for good—or even if we could.

CHAPTER 2
NOBLESSE OBLIGE

"Riders, stow those saddles and get off my platform." Commander Hegarty barked out orders. He was looking pretty annoyed, his eyes a darker grey than usual, his hands on his hips and his face red. He was a short man with a wiry strength, and he always looked in control, but right now he kept smoothing his mustache as if he was worried it would start twitching and betray some emotion.

"What's got him so riled up?" Seb asked. Kalax had just alighted on the landing platform and we hadn't even had time to dismount. Kalax grumbled—even I knew that tone of her voice—and I shrugged. Then a word popped into my head.

Fish!

I laughed and Seb turned in his saddle to look at me. "Did you hear that? Kalax saying fish?" he grinned.

"Of course," I muttered. "You're not the only one that Kalax talks to."

"But it shows you're getting better at it."

"Riders—move!" Hegarty yelled again.

Seb unclipped his harness and slid to the wooden platform below. I did the same.

We stood on one of the several large platforms that sat atop the walls of the Dragon Academy, overlooking the training ground, barracks, keep and lodgings. This was our home. From here, we could even see the tiered levels of Torvald spread out below the walls. I loved it up here where I could feel the wind in my hair and hear the banners snap. It was a place where I felt I belonged.

But the commander was glaring at everyone—not just us, other riders, too. We quickly started to unharness Kalax.

"Didn't you hear me? Not three months out of training and you think you're above taking orders? Let me remind you, you haven't been assigned to a squadron yet. You're late, and I've important visitors coming in."

Seb rubbed Kalax's nose, but I turned to the commander. "Sorry, Commander Hegarty, but we had to escort the captured bandits to the citadel for trial, sir."

The commander shook his head and moved off.

Nudging my elbow, Seb said, "Come on, give me those saddles. I'll take them down to the kit shed."

I shook my head. "You're the one with the special connection to Kalax. You look after her, I'll take the saddles. I'll meet you down in the keep later."

"Want to head into the city to eat tonight?" Seb asked, sliding onto the broad neck of Kalax. Not many could ride their dragons without a saddle, but Seb was getting better and better at it. He also seemed to be enjoying the fact that as riders—and not just cadets—we could come and go as we liked and didn't have to sneak out like we used to.

"Sure, whatever," I waved Seb off. He had to get Kalax back to the enclosure and I wanted our gear put away.

Heading down the wide, stone stairs to the equipment shed, I wondered why my mood had soured. Usually a fight got my blood flowing. Today, I just wished I could head up into the hills and not have anyone around. Was it due to Seb acting odd today—almost trying to keep us out of combat with those bandits? I didn't know.

The equipment shed was busy with other riders cleaning and oiling their harnesses. The floor had been scrubbed by someone unlucky enough to get that job and smelled faintly of lavender and meadowsweet, and the dirt of the practice yards had been raked. Obviously, Commander Hegarty had wanted the academy looking great.

Grabbing a brush and a pot of leather oils, I set to work cleaning our gear.

The Dragon Horns sounded, a light fanfare. Someone was arriving and a ripple of excitement spread through the shed. Everyone moved fast, putting away gear and cleaning up.

How times had changed since I was a cadet.

I had the weight of a sword at my hip, a long bow and quiver of steel-tipped arrows that I could hang next to my saddle. And Seb and I were given missions now—even if some were simply to scare local bandits.

Heading outside, I saw shadows flicker over the ground. The cries of approaching dragons shook the air. I heard others muttering and looked up to see the very large and very ancient royal dragon Erufon. He was easy to spot for he was a very rare gold, his scales a deep yellow-orange. Erufon was also big. He'd once been the mount of King Durance, before the king himself had to give up riding due to injury and to losing his navigator. But Erufon never left the royal enclosure, so it was unusual to see him.

I quickly realized why the gold was here. Other dragons were landing on the platforms. The platforms filled with dragons. I recognized the green dragon of Prince Justin and my brother, Ryan, and the large blue of my eldest brother, Reynalt and his navigator. Beside them a host of smaller dragons—all the mounts of senior riders, captains and even an ambassador—crowded the platforms.

The horn sounded again. Commander Hegarty and Instructor Mordecai moved forward to greet the royals and other guests who'd flown to the academy. I was glad that I didn't see Seb and Kalax still on the platforms—that would have brought the wrath of Mordecai down on both of us and we'd end up raking the practice yard.

Large and hunched over, Mordecai seemed a twisted man—at least on the outside. He had a sharp nose and stringy grey hair.

Almost everyone disliked him. I'd heard he had been a Dragon Rider a long time ago, but his dragon had died, and his partner, unable to take the loss, had thrown himself from the observation tower. I didn't know if that was true, but what was true was that he was a bitter man.

Leaning against the shed wall, I tried to stay out of Mordecai's sight and wondered if I could catch a moment with either of my brothers. One of them might tell me why there was all this fuss. Obviously, these were important matters at hand.

I waited by the door to the equipment shed until I saw the commander and the others head inside the keep, then I waved to Ryan and headed to his side.

Grinning, he caught me up in a hug.

I punched his arm. "What, the navigator to none other than Prince Justin himself is going to be seen hugging his sister?"

Ryan set me on my feet again. "What trouble are you getting into, Thea?"

I shook my head. "None at all."

He gave me a sideways look. "This is Ryan, not Reynalt you're talking to. Our older brother might believe your stories, but I don't. Come on—tell me."

"Just cleaning my harness. After catching some bandits."

Frowning, he let out a breath. "Don't tell Mother."

"Mother should have seen me shooting bandits."

Ryan groaned. "And don't tell her that. Ever!"

"What? Are you ashamed of me being a rider…a protector?" The itch under my skin clawed at me, making me want to claw back at Ryan.

He shook his head. "Of course not. Nothing as close as a Flamma and his dragon, right? Well, her dragon." Ryan looked earnestly sincere, his eyes soft and warm and his eyebrows flattened. I knew the look well. It was the same one that he had used ever since he had been a child stealing apple tarts.

"Bad enough that I have to put up with all the looks from the other senior riders—a girl as protector, Lady Agathea not acting much of a lady. As if I did nothing to prove myself by saving King's Village. No…it was my dragon, Kalax, who did the deed. Even Seb's been looking at me as if I'm made of porcelain!"

Ryan shook his head and held up his hands in front of him. "It's not like that."

Punching a finger into his armour, I told him, "No Ryan, I've had enough. Everyone knows I'm one of the best fighters, but Commander Hegarty has us chasing bandits and watching the roads. The Darkening is still out there…and trouble is coming. You know that. Is that why the prince is here? To talk to Hegarty about that?"

"Agathea!" Ryan said, his tone sharp.

His good humour had vanished. Standing before me wasn't my fun-loving brother, but a serious commander. He shook his head and said a little more gently, "You were told to not talk about that. Remember? Not at all. Not to anyone. There are enough stories about the Darkening without more being added. Do you want to create a panic?"

Mouth pressed tight, I shook my head.

Ryan put a hand on my shoulder. "I know you have questions, Thea, and I know you're better than what the commander has you doing right now. But you have to trust him—and trust in Reynalt, Prince Justin and me."

"Something's happening, hasn't it? I can see it in your eyes. Something important. That's why all of you are here." I stepped closer and dropped my voice lower. "It's to do with the Darkening isn't it? Lord Vincent and the Dragon Egg Stones?" It had to be. Why else would they all be here, and why would Commander Hegarty be so short with everyone if he wasn't worried?

My brother sighed and glanced around as if to make certain we weren't overheard. But almost everyone else had gone into the keep for the evening meal. Ryan wet his lips and said, his voice fierce, "You died in that cavern. If it hadn't been for Commander Hegarty and Seb, you wouldn't be here. You of all people know the danger we face. And that we cannot alarm Torvald with rumours and tales."

Sudden, quick memories came back—a stabbing pain, the glint of light on Lord Vincent's sword, a cloying, suffocating darkness and a sensation like falling. I shook my head. "I didn't die, Ryan."

"Only because of the Healing Stone. Hegarty used it to bring you back. But even that is something not to be spoken of. The Dragon Egg Stones are—"

15

"A myth. A story. So powerful they must be guarded. I know all that. You don't need to treat me like a child. But because I know, those are all the reasons to tell me why you're here and what's going on."

He pressed his mouth closed and his stare slid away. "We're bringing Erufon to the main enclosure. The king himself ordered it, saying that it was unfair to keep Erufon alone. It's hoped he may even breed and we'll have a new line of golds."

"Dragon poop!" I hissed. I could always tell when he was lying because he wouldn't look at me. "You and the prince have been away for a long time. Why, in the last three months I've hardly seen you, but I have seen riders coming back saddle-sore and looking as though they've been flying for weeks. Do you think we're all blind here?"

Ryan frowned again.

I grabbed his arm. "You're out looking for the Darkening and the other Dragon Egg Stone. King's Village was saved, but you've been trying to find Lord Vincent—and discover if he has new forces in the north or the wild lands and the mountains."

"Agathea Flamma!" Ryan snapped out the words and drew himself up. He knocked away my hand. "I am going to give you two bits of advice, one as your senior officer and one as your brother, and you probably won't like either of them but that's your problem. As your senior, I am saying you need to let this go. Ever since that...well, you know what, you've become...I don't know, more eager to throw yourself into harm's way. You need to stop. Give yourself time to heal. And leave the business of the senior riders to them. As your brother,

I am going to only say this—our mother is worried for you as is our father."

"When are they not?" I muttered.

He gave me another sharp, disapproving look. "We didn't tell Mother what happened to you in King's Village. Father knows. But both have been talking about how important it is to have a stable family—as you would know if you ever visited home. But no…you want danger and you court disaster."

I shook my head.

Ryan shrugged. "Mother's been arguing with Father about what's best for the family as a whole. And she's swaying him. They look to the future for the name Flamma."

"Fine—if they are worried, *you* marry. I've no interest. I'm a Dragon Rider!"

Ryan looked away. "What if the prince agrees with them?"

I laughed, but Ryan didn't. "Please…I've known Prince Justin since…well, forever."

"I know. We've shared nurseries and tutors. The prince wants what is not just best for you, but for a royal house as well." Ryan put a hand on my shoulder again. "It's all a part of being a noble and being a rider. You must walk in two worlds. So keep yourself safe. Make Mother and Father happy. Wear a dress every now and again and don't give anyone a reason to petition the king for your removal."

Waves of rage and terror battled inside me. Ryan patted my shoulder and moved away, but I could only stand there, sucking in huge breaths of air, my skin hot and my fists clenched. We were the king's riders—we were here to do his bidding, so if he asked any of us to step down, we must. That would leave Seb without a protector—he would have to stop being a rider, too. And Kalax...I would never see Kalax again. I'd never fly the skies, I'd never stand on the landing platforms and turn my face to the wind, and I'd never fight for my country and king.

I headed back into the shed to scrub the dragon harness and fight off my frustrations. They would do me no good. I needed my wits about me to fight this new enemy—my own family.

CHAPTER 3
THE TROLL'S HEAD

Laughter. Loud talk. Then the smell of ale and unwashed bodies hit me as soon as I opened the door to the Troll's Head. I'd sent word to Thea to meet me there, but I hadn't seen her since we'd parted ways on the landing platform. I'd flown Kalax to the enclosure, and by the time I walked back, Thea was gone from the equipment shed. I couldn't find her in the keep, so I asked Varla to tell Thea I'd meet her at the Troll's Head.

I slid into a seat at a table in the back. The noise, the bustle of serving maids and the crowd of workers at the bar stirred memories of my dad. Mostly, I remembered him coming home, stinking of strong ale. If we were lucky, he was too drunk for anything more than stew out of the kettle and falling asleep in front of the hearth. If we were unlucky, he would start shouting about whatever imagined slight he'd suffered that day, working himself into a fit.

That's not me.

I looked at the tankard of cheap mead that sat before me—it no longer seemed a tasty drink.

Someone banged against the table and I looked up. A large man in a dirty, grey cloak was weaving his way through the crowd. I glimpsed a hint of a beard speckled with gray. Ripples of annoyance followed the man and voices around the bar turned to grumbling.

The mood in here tonight was bad, and I wondered why.

The Troll's Head stood at the top of Torvald, near Hammal Mountain itself, and only a short walk from the academy. Over the years, it had acquired bits and pieces from various Dragon Riders—banners, or a tooth from a famous dragon, broken harnesses and worn saddles. I had even found three items from Flamma history—Thea always hated it whenever anyone pointed them.

Oh yeah, that was Grandfather Brutus' armour, and Great-Great Uncle Marcosia used that saddle.

She shrugged it off that some of the bravest and most well-known Dragon Riders in Torvald history were of her blood. I thought she was worried she wouldn't live up to their reputations, but why did she worry so much? I shook my head. Who would have thought that the son of a smith from Monger's Lane and a noble with the best training money could buy would be matched by a dragon's choice. Kalax had picked each of us.

I sipped my mead and looked around the tavern.

A few riders were here, both the warrior protectors and their pilot navigators, along with soldiers. Their tunics gave away their trade. So did the rough wool jerkins of the woodcutters and the dusty clothes of the stone masons. From the looks of some of the riders, they'd been doing a lot of hard flying. The faces I could see looked drawn and pale, and the riders were leaning back in their seats as if exhausted. Some still had on dusty tunics, and I pitied them if Commander Hegarty ever saw them—not that he'd ever come to the Troll's Head that I knew of.

One young rider raised his tankard and muttered, "To the campaign!"

An older rider slapped him on the leg. "Get down with your nonsense and hush."

I frowned—what campaign was that?

A voice pulled me from my thoughts. "Drinking alone, are we, Sebastian?" Turning, I saw Beris with his navigator, Syl and Shakasta behind them. That lot never went anywhere without each other. And Beris drew out my name like it was an insult. He still seemed to think no one from Monger's Lane had any right to be a rider—or maybe he just didn't like me.

"I'm waiting for Thea," I said and instantly cursed myself for even responding to him.

Beris waved at my mug. "Looks like you've been left to your cups. What's wrong—everyone tired of your company?"

Behind him, Shakasta snickered. The surrounding noise level had gone up, so no one noticed—except me.

I stared at the three of them. I was a Dragon Rider now. I didn't care what they thought.

Beris smiled and leaned a hand on the rough wood of my table. "Don't you know why the commander has you out on patrol? Why you are just flying around and around and aren't out with a real squadron?"

I gritted my teeth. It was true. We'd had constant road-patrol duties of late—that and more training. We hadn't been assigned a squadron yet. And we hadn't been asked to protect our borders. I didn't mind, but Thea did. And I was sure the commander was worried for us.

What effect does nearly dying have on someone? And is Thea really fully healed? At times, I was sure she was, but at other times, I thought she looked pale and she tired more easily. Sometimes it just seemed her mind was somewhere else a long way off.

Of course, the events that had led to Lord Vincent's defeat were known to only a very few. Commander Hegarty himself had sworn us to secrecy. I couldn't talk about them now.

Staring up at Beris, I shrugged. "Protecting the king's roads is as important as his borders. We stopped some bandits today. That's probably more action than any of you've seen."

Beris's face reddened. He straightened. "Been fighting bandits? A dragon against what—a few old men with sticks and bare fists?"

Now Syl laughed too. I gritted my teeth. Anger uncoiled in my gut.

Enemy? Fight? In my mind I could see Kalax stirring in her cave.

No. It's okay.

It hadn't occurred to me that I could be sharing my feelings with Kalax—not at this distance. Something new to worry about. I sighed and bit back on everything I was feeling.

Grinning, Beris said, "Well, when you're done with the petty criminals, Seb, you can think about us. We're the ones dealing with wild dragons up in the Leviathan Mountains!" Beris and his friends moved away and I stared at my drink.

What if Beris is right? The commander had once thought well of Thea, Kalax and me, but we'd also done a lot of things that were against orders. Those wild dragons Beris mentioned might be the same ones that fled after we routed the Darkening. Was that the campaign that young rider just mentioned? Were those dragons still causing trouble?

Jensen and Wil slid into the seats opposite me. Jensen was one of the best protectors. He was another noble, but he never reminded anyone of that. "Beris is a fool."

My face warmed. So they'd heard everything that had been said. I shrugged and asked, "Is it true? Are squadrons chasing wild dragons?"

Jensen's gaze slid away. "Between you and me, it's wasted effort. They're just chasing cattle and the odd flock of sheep. They're not much use—or much of a danger."

I frowned—I remembered wild dragons, black ones that were a danger. A very big danger.

Merik and Varla headed over to our table. Tall and thin, Merik stood out with his dark skin and even blacker hair. He wore special optics to see, and right now he pushed them up on his nose. Varla also stood out with her pale skin and the long, red hair she wore pulled back into a braid. They were flying partners, along with Jensen and Wil. I was the only rider here alone. But I didn't want to think about that, so I asked Jensen what he'd been doing.

Jensen shifted in his seat. He'd been letting his brown hair grow long and it was getting shaggy. He pushed a hand through it now. "Our captain just has us chasing after wild beasts that threaten farmers. Anyway—you never heard that from me." He stood, and he and Wil, who seemed like Jensen's shadow these days, walked away to find their own table.

Merik and Varla sat, Varla ordering broth and Merik stew. Merik didn't like strong drink and neither did Varla. Like Thea, Varla was a protector. Her dragon, Ferdinania had accepted Merik as navigator and as a second choice. That hardly ever happened, but the three made a good team. Varla also shared a room with Thea, so I asked, "Seen Thea?"

"She was hanging around the practice yard," Varla said and dug into her bowl of broth. "Her brothers are here."

"She's been pretty annoyed these days," Merik said.

I nodded. In some ways I wondered if the Healing Stone had changed her. I didn't really trust magic—you never really knew what it was going to cost. My old man had always said you never get something for nothing, and now I knew what he'd meant.

"So—she's visiting her brothers?" I was still annoyed with Beris and I knew it came out in my voice.

Merik opened his mouth as if he were about to say something. He gave a muffled grunt and Varla shifted like she'd just kicked him under the table. She said, "They're bringing old Erufon to the enclosure." She glanced around and leaned closer. "But I think something else is up."

"I don't think it's just chasing after wild dragons." Merik lowered his voice, "I think they're looking for something…for the Armour Stone."

Someone bumped into the table and I looked up to see the same old man in the tattered, grey cloak that I'd seen earlier. He spilled a little of his beer on the table, waved an apology and headed back into the crowds.

Perhaps it was just my suspicious mind, but I wondered if we should be worried about spies, I glanced at Merik. "Let's not talk about that here."

"Talk about what?" Thea said, sitting down next to me. She ordered food, discarded her cloak and smiled.

I didn't trust that smile—I'd seen it too many times and knew what it meant. I didn't want to ask about it. But she leaned her elbows on the table and said, "I saw my brother Ryan today. Something's up with the Darkening. I'm sure of it. I think they're having a council of war at the academy." Her cheeks warmed as she talked, as if she was only too happy at the prospect of a blood-curdling battle.

Varla told her about the wild dragons being chased, and Thea nodded. "We might be going to war again. Soon."

I sipped my mead and told her, "That's not a good thing."

"If we defeated Lord Vincent once, we can do it again," Thea said.

Someone started to play a guitar. Others started to sing. I was glad of it. We could more easily talk without being heard. Turning to Thea, I told her, "He doesn't have the Memory Stone—we took it. So how could he still be turning villages into his army?"

She rolled her eyes. Her stew came. She poked at it with a spoon. "I don't know—we don't even know where the Memory Stone is now. Commander Hegarty took it. The question is, what are we going to do about this trouble that's brewing?"

I glanced at Merik and Varla. They swapped a glance, and then Varla leaned in. "We were looking around the old library…just for any old tales about…well, you know. Some stories refer to the three stones separately. That this great king had the Armour Stone, and so defeated the Wildmen of J'hul, or that the Healing Stone was used to save some princess or another. The trouble is that none of these legends match up. It's like they were written by someone who only heard the tales. But…the stones are always large and egg-shaped…sometimes they glow, sometimes they crack open—other times they even make a noise."

I frowned. "Like what?"

Varla made a face. "That doesn't matter. What does matter is that the oldest story has two clues…armour was used at a battle high up on Leviathan Mountain but a monk took the Armour

Stone afterwards to Wychwood." She went back to eating her broth.

I stared at her. "Do you know how big Leviathan Mountain is? And Wychwood? That's nowhere near there and even bigger."

Merik nodded. "My old gran used to tell me stories that the last time the Darkening rose, the Armour Stone made the king's gold dragon invincible as he fought the final battle above Leviathan Mountain."

Thea thumped the table. "So we go there."

Merik glanced around and shook his head. "That's not the story Varla dug up. In that, the stone went to a princess to keep her safe as she led her own forces to Wychwood. And then a monk took it after the king died and fled to some far off monastery to keep it safe."

Thea growled. I stared at my mead. "On a mountainside or in a forest…it's obvious no one wanted it found."

"It's got to be. There are three stones—we know that for a fact. The commander has one - hidden. Lord Vincent had one, and we can't let him get something like perfect armour. We need to get the third stone," Thea said, shooting me an annoyed glance. "The next free day we have, Seb and I will search Leviathan Mountain. Varla, you and Merik take Wychwood."

"You're forgetting other Dragon Riders are out there on patrol. We'll end up on report," I told her.

"We have to do something," Thea said.

I started to tell her we could wait—that waiting wasn't always a bad thing. But an uneasy sense of being watched came over me. I shivered and looked up. The old man in the grey cloak was watching our table. He ducked his head and turned as if I'd caught him in the act.

Frowning, I stood. The old man made for the door. At the door, he threw a glance back over his shoulder and straight at our table. For a brief moment our eyes locked, and I could see sharp eyes peering out from the hood. These were not the signs of drunkenness I knew so well, having seen them in my father —and that man was not drunk.

Jumping up from the table, I started after him.

"Hey!" Varla said.

"What is it?" Thea asked.

I pushed through the crowd. *Why is that man watching us, who is he?* I wanted answers. The tavern door swung closed behind the cloaked figure. Bursting out into the cold night after him, I looked up and down the cobbled road. He seemed to have vanished. I couldn't hear footsteps or see his grey cloak.

Heading around the back of the tavern, I glanced into the stables, my heart hammering. Nothing. Hearing footsteps behind me, I turned to see Thea dragging on her cloak. "What is it?"

"We were being watched."

Thea looked at me warily. "Who was it?"

"An old man in a cloak. I'm sure he was spying on us."

She pulled her cloak tighter. "Do you think…do you think he's part of the Darkening? One of…of Lord Vincent's agents?"

I stared into the night, but there was no sign of anyone. "I don't know. But if I see him again, I'm going to make certain I get a few answers."

CHAPTER 4
A SENSE OF DISQUIET

F*alling...falling...darkness...cold...who am I? What...? Pain...spreading...so cold...*

With a shout, I opened my eyes and sat up.

My bedsprings squeaked and the covers tangled around my feet. No wonder I'd been cold. I heard the strike of a flint against steel and a light flared. The yellow glow of a lamp lit the room and Varla's pale face appeared out of the darkness, her eyebrows pulled tight and her hair a mess around her face. "Thea, what's wrong—you were mumbling and groaning in your sleep as if something awful was happening."

Annoyance bit into me. "Nothing wrong. Just bad dreams." Grabbing the covers, I pulled them back up over me. But my muscles were aching and I still felt dizzy as if I really had been falling. Why was it that bad dreams could sometimes make you feel worse after they had gone? Dread itched at the back of my skull and sat on my chest like a weight. Seeing Varla's kind eyes just made me feel worse. "Sorry," I muttered.

Varla shrugged. "Might as well get up. It's almost time anyway." She threw off her covers and started to dress, brushing her hair and braiding it, then pulling on her tunic and pants, and finally the quilted jerkin that went over them.

I climbed out of bed. The thick, colourful carpet didn't seem to do anything to make the stone floor seem warmer. Varla was right to dress so fast. I did the same and stepped over to help her with the straps on the back of her jerkin. "Here, let me do that," I said, trying to make up for my earlier bad temper.

"Thanks." Varla lifted her arms, letting me tighten her training gear.

Finished, I slapped her on the back. "There. Good as any of the best." I was trying hard to sound chipper, but it was more than difficult. That dream was hanging onto me, and today was going to be a hard day for all of us. What I really wanted to do was crawl back into my bed and sleep another hour. That wasn't like me and I tried to shake off the mood.

Varla frowned at her image in the long mirror my mother had sent me for the room. The rest of the room was pretty bare. We had our two narrow beds, two chests for our clothes, the mirror and the carpet. Varla's mother had sent that to her—I knew it was a tempting reminder of the luxury back at Varla's home. I'd have the same at House Flamma—poor Varla got letters every other day from her parents, urging her to return, telling all she was missing by not acting like every other noble girl in Torvald. Varla wasn't like me in many ways—she was skinny, awkward at times and liked books better than people. But she was a Dragon Rider—we had that in common.

Turning to me, Varla shrugged. "I just wish…well, I'm glad Ferdinania was okay with choosing Merik instead of going back to the enclosure. But sometimes, I just wish I was like any other rider on any other team. Everyone's always pointing us out—like we're the odd ones here. 'Oh, look, there's one of the few girls here, and she's the one whose dragon had to make a second choice.'"

I nodded. Varla and I were the only two female riders right now —that was why we roomed together. It was enough to make us feel like we didn't really belong here. I also knew Varla's folks were still pressuring her to give this up and go back home where she could marry and raise kids. I shivered—and it wasn't just from the cold. At least my father had seemed proud that I was following Flamma tradition by becoming a rider.

But one of the other problems of a second choosing was that the dragon and its riders didn't often have the same connection as from a first choice rider. I knew Varla always worried about that when she flew.

"Cheer up. Merik is a good navigator. He's the best at signals, better even than the senior riders. Besides, today is practice tournaments, all padded weapons—and no one's in danger of being sent home. We're not cadets anymore. And it's the sort of training that might just save us in a real battle."

Varla grumbled, but she helped me get ready.

We headed down to the keep to break our fast of the night. Our boots clumped on the stone stairs.

Out in the practice yard, the sun had just cleared the walls. A chill hung in the air, stinging my cheeks and burning my lungs. I headed over to Seb—who was looking worried as usual and probably thinking about the Armour Stone. Sometimes he thought way too much. We fell in step and headed for the keep, falling in line with the other riders to get our meal.

"Tomorrow," Seb whispered to me. The heavy, padded woolen tunic we all had to wear for today's training made him look broader than I knew he was. However, he had filled out over the last year. He was no longer the skinny boy I'd first met on choosing day. "I was talking to Merik and he says that we might be able to get a day off tomorrow."

I nodded. The unease from my dream hadn't left me. The morning light seemed a little too bright, too washed out. *Am I coming down with something?*

Not feeling hungry, I settled for bread and a small bowl of porridge. Merik joined us and the talk shifted to the training for the day. We were all looking forward to some action—at least I was.

After clearing the tables, we headed out of the keep and assembled in the practice yard. The Dragon Horns—the great, brass horns that shaped our lives—blew to announce the start of the day's training.

Shifting on my feet, I heard boot steps behind us and the instructors—all senior riders—and Commander Hegarty strode forward. Instructor Mordecai was with them—not my favorite instructor. He limped, and as usual a scowl pulled down his face. Sometimes I thought he'd prefer to have the academy kept empty and all to himself. The feeling of unease from my dream returned—as if the world was still not right and I was still dreaming. I pinched myself to check—it hurt, so I knew I was awake.

I could also see my brother Reynalt with them. Although Ryan flew with Prince Justin, it was Reynalt who was one of the senior captains. He was almost on an even footing with Commander Hegarty—and while Hegarty was entrusted with the academy to train all riders, Reynalt was our tactical leader out in the air.

I heard Wil whisper to Jensen, "What is he doing here?"

"Evaluations," Jensen whispered back.

I frowned at them, but kept facing forward. When we'd been recruits, evaluations could mean getting kicked out of the academy entirely if we proved we weren't good enough to be Dragon Riders. These evaluations could only mean it was time to find out what squadron we'd fly with, and what our roles would be.

Dragon Riders from the academy would defend the city. The King's Own, which Erufon had once led, was down to Prince Justin and Ryan—just one dragon. The Black Claws—Reynalt's squadron—was always the first into battle and had the fiercest fighters. But some dragons were heavier and better suited to transporting heavy loads. And the Green Flags acted as messengers, traveling vast distances—they were also usually made up of the skinnier, green marsh dragons.

Kalax was a crimson red—strong and fast and a natural candidate for frontline duty, so I was hoping we were to become Black Claws.

"Today you will be conducting a series of practice drills," Commander Hegarty barked. It was odd. Every time I looked at him the feeling that something wasn't quite right came back. Now I knew I should have eaten more at breakfast. I should be looking forward to the day and not worrying about stupid dreams.

"It's going to be a long, hard day in the saddle, ladies and gents! Your first mission is to fly to Ghastion Point and back. First team back is the winner!"

A moment of stilled amazement held everyone. Unless it was an emergency situation, Hegarty was a stickler for flight proto-col. He wanted the flights to be logged, the correct flags to be produced to be able to signal the approaches of each dragon, the kits inspected before they went out. He never just announced a scramble like this.

"It's a combat-response practice," Jensen said, already breaking rank and dragging Wil with him to the equipment sheds.

I started running as well. If the commander wanted to see how fast we could get in the air and deploy, I was going to show him we could be the fastest. At the equipment sheds, riders jammed in, everyone trying to grab their harnesses and saddles.

Seb got his saddle and ducked out. A nudge lifted in the back of my mind—an urge to get to the platforms. I knew he was calling Kalax. Unlike the others, his Dragon Affinity meant he didn't need to have a special dragon whistle to call our dragon. I could even feel a shiver as he touched minds with Kalax. Seb had been trying to teach me to do this, but it seemed to me that his Dragon Affinity was more than rubbing off on me lately.

"Get off!" Shakasta shouted, pushing one of the younger riders out of the way.

"Out of the way," Beris snarled, pushing Merik to one side and grabbing his saddle. Beris ran for the platform, but Jensen was reaching up for saddles and harness, throwing them to whom they belonged. "We'll all get out quicker this way," he said.

I caught my saddle and heard Kalax's roar from above. A flicker of pride stirred. She was the first dragon to arrive; none of the others had started calling their mounts yet. Seeing Merik fumbling with his saddle, I stopped to help him. He wore special goggles for his bad eyesight and hadn't put them on yet. Varla grimaced and stopped too, picking up the saddle and putting it into his hands. I grabbed my bow, practice arrows and the jousting staffs we used in practice.

Heading outside, I saw Seb waving to me from the landing platform where Kalax sat, snuffing the air. Hefting my saddle, I ran up the stairs. Kalax greeted me with a bird-like chirrup, and we set about getting the saddles and harness in place.

With a roar, Beris and Syl's dragon launched into the air. Their bully-tactics had given them an advantage, it seemed.

Is this what we're being taught? That sometimes, in the heat of battle you had to put yourself and your team first?

"Clips secure," Seb shouted, cinching the leather straps that held his saddle. He worked fast, and Kalax seemed eager to fly. She kept stretching her wings as if to ask now...now...now? Climbing onto Kalax, I yelled at Seb to get moving. He jumped into his saddle, fastened his harness and leaned down to whisper to Kalax. She swung around and hurled herself from the platform with a roar.

That familiar sensation of panic and of my stomach trying to force its way up through my throat spread through me. The ground spun in shades of brown and green. Then Kalax spread her wings and we were flying—swooping low over the road and the trees, heading after Beris and Syl. Behind us, other dragons were noisily arriving to the calls of their riders' whistles. We were second in the air. Kalax, her nose twitching, gave a thrumming roar that I felt underneath me.

Turning, Seb grinned at me. "She wants to hunt...and fight."

I matched his grin with one of my own. It felt good to have an eager dragon. All too soon, Kalax seemed to realize we weren't on patrol or on a mission at all. She soared up into the sky and began to glide.

Kalax—come on. We have to win. We've got to earn a spot in the Black Claw squadron.

I could have almost cried with frustration. "Seb, you've got to tell Kalax this is a race." He nodded and leaned over Kalax again. She turned her head to the south where I could see the sparkle of sun on water.

"She's bored," Seb yelled back at me. "She just wants to hunt, not practice."

I knew how she felt, but now was not the time for Kalax to play. Glancing back, I saw Jensen and Wil's dragon up in the air and gaining on us. I turned to Seb. "Tell Kalax if we don't do well in this, we'll be stuck carrying sacks of grain from one dreary village market to another for the rest of our lives."

Seb didn't have to tell Kalax—she seemed to figure it out from what I'd said. She trilled and picked up speed. She still wasn't going flat-out, but she pulled ahead of Jensen and Wil.

We passed over the city and now were out over the fields. Kalax flew high, using the air currents to carry her as she swooped down over some low mountains. Ghastion Point was hours away by horse, but a dragon could fly there in a fairly short time—and Seb needed to keep Kalax interested.

Beris and Syl and their stocky blue dragon, Gaxtal, were far ahead now. I gripped my flight harness, thinking there wouldn't be much for a protector to do on this challenge. I was also thinking about beating Beris in single combat—I'd done that before and it would be a pleasure now to do that again. But even though we were in second, a sense of peace welled up through me. This was where I belonged—in the air with my dragon and a navigator.

Kalax seemed to agree with me, for she gave a soft cry.

Why spend time on silly things, when there are enemies to fight?

Seb turned around to look at me, his eyes wide with surprise. "Was that you talking to Kalax?"

I shrugged. "I—I don't know."

Seb nodded. "Can you sense any other dragons? The others behind us maybe?"

"Seb, we've tried that before. You have the affinity. I'm barely able to get through to Kalax." But I realized there was something else pulling at my senses, too. It felt like something was pulling me back to the academy...and something further south.

Is this what it is like to feel the dragons? Is this what Seb feels —a tug?

The strange pull started to fade, leaving me confused. I was about to tell Seb about it when Jensen and Wil on their sinuous, green dragon dove past us, both of them yelling. They'd obviously caught a higher and more powerful air current and used it to shoot past us.

"Kalax!" Seb shouted.

Kalax seemed to decide this was a game she might be interested in. She flapped her powerful wings and started to close the gap with Jensen and Wil's green dragon, Dellos.

Ghastion Point was approaching. I could see the higher mountains and the land sloped up from the moors to the cliffs. The tallest point had an old, white watchtower, and the stones lay tumbled around the tower's base. It was one of the old watchtowers from the days when big beacon fires had been lit to warn of impending attack. I could see Jensen and Wil rounding the tower, turning on a wingtip of their slinky green up ahead as we followed them in.

"Head's up!" Seb yelled.

I looked up to see Beris and Syl on their stocky blue sweep down out of the sky above us. Syl was sending Gaxtal straight at us, and the dragon had his claws extended. I ducked and reached a hand for my sword, but Seb and Kalax worked together to duck the move. Kalax pulled in one wing in, twisted and fell in a roll, out of the way of the oncoming claws.

My stomach jumped and I shouted at Seb, "What does he think he's doing?"

Kalax grumbled and glanced back at them like she wanted to go after Gaxtal, but Seb was urging her to fly around the point. "We'll get them. Don't worry, we'll get them," Seb called out.

They must have been waiting up there for us," I shouted and pointed to the top of the old watchtower. Anger was burning in my stomach, or maybe I was just picking up Kalax's anger. With a roar Kalax reached out and nipped Dellos' tail. Jensen and Wil's green twisted and turned in mid-air, snarling. The dragon fell two lengths down and I could see Jensen and Wil struggling to get the dragon back on course.

"Kalax," Seb reproached, but I whooped out a yell and shook a fist in the air. That had been a great move. Glancing back at me, Seb shook his head. "Thea, rein it in! You're picking up too much from Kalax, and you're only making each other worse."

"Worse? That's your problem, Seb—you're worrying and thinking too much, and we need to win! I'm not letting your weakness hurt our chances of being Black Claw." My anger leapt up hotter than before, beating inside me like a fist, making my heart pound and starting a headache behind my eyes.

"Thea, you'll lose us the competition!" Seb yelled.

Another voice echoed in my head. *Seb not weak. Seb strong.* It was Kalax, and I could feel her disapproval of my judgment.

My anger evaporated in a moment, leaving me feeling shamed and small. What was upsetting me so much? Why was I so angry at the world? Was it the thought of losing the competition, of not doing my name and my brothers proud? Or was I just pushing too hard to be the best protector there ever was—and even the best Dragon Rider ever. I wasn't sure.

For the rest of the flight, I kept quiet, keeping my thoughts to myself and concentrating on matching my moves to Seb's to help Kalax gain speed. I wasn't going to feel anything—not anger or happiness.

We headed toward Hammal Mountain from the south, over the tiered city of Torvald. I could see flags bright and fluttering above the landing platforms of the academy. Red flags.

"Combat?" I yelled at Seb. "Are we under attack? The Darkening?"

Seb shook his head. He pulled out his periscope viewing glass to read the flags. "One red, barred, and the training flag is up. Non-lethal training." Seb put away his scope. "We're supposed to pair off and fight."

The only other riders around were Beris and Syl on Gaxtal, so I was going to get my chance to smack Beris. Maybe. Usually, the Dragon Horns would sound to start a bout, but we were also expected to practice on our own time—and everything was obviously going to be a surprise today.

"The commander did say that today was going to be tough," Seb said. He settled lower into his flying saddle. I glanced around, looking for Gaxtal. I didn't see him around, so I knew what that meant.

Looking up I saw Gaxtal screaming out of the heavens in an attacking dive, the sun behind him to try and blind us.

"Turn now!" I shouted, grabbing hold of my harness.

Kalax knew what to do. She twisted and rolled. Seb grunted as he was thrown to the side and then backwards in his harness. The turn was so fast that the wind tore at my face and goggles, pushing me backwards. I had to struggle to get to my bow and the wrapped practice arrows.

Gaxtal shot past us again. I could see Beris grinning. He wasn't holding a bow, but held a wooden practice lance, one end padded with leather. But they could still leave a bruise or leave your ears ringing if they hit an unpadded leg or hit your helmet. Syl had Gaxtal dive past again, and I knew Beris was aiming for Seb. He threw the lance.

With a snarl, Kalax flipped and seized the wooden staff with her claws, snapping and dropping the shards. She hadn't forgotten that Gaxtal had recently come at her. I glanced over and thought I saw a flicker of fear on Beris's face. Was he worried? Scared at how far he had pushed us? I couldn't be sure.

Notching an arrow, I took aim and pulled in a breath. But Gaxtal flapped his wings, and air displacement sent my arrow off course, making it spiral down into the trees below. Cursing, I reaching for another practice arrow and Gaxtal headed back into the sky.

Seb urged Kalax to follow the blue. She flew after Gaxtal, winding around one of the academy towers and then sprinting over the landing platforms. Gaxtal was fast, but not as fast as Kalax. We were gaining on them.

Bent over Kalax's neck, Seb pointed. He was lining me up for a perfect shot, one that would send an arrow right between the shoulder blades of the dragon and at Beris's chest. I aimed. Syl was trying to get Gaxtal to work harder and race out of our way. But the blue dragon turned with a shriek—Syl had flown Gaxtal straight into another dragon fight: Jensen and Wil on Dellos against Merik and Varla on Ferdinania. The three dragons tangled and struggled not to hit into each other, which could send any of them falling to the ground.

"Pull back," Seb yelled, shouting at Syl, Beris's navigator.

Gaxtal plunged between the two other dragons. Kalax followed, but it was too confusing. Wings flapped, colours flew past. I heard shouts and dragons let out unhappy belches of smoke and gave sharp, warning cries. Seb found a space at last and got us out of the dangerous encounter before anyone could clip Kalax's wings or bump into her.

Kalax spun and then pulled up to level out. I pressed a hand to my stomach, my head spinning from the move. Something bounced off Seb's chest and I heard him grunt. The Dragon Horns blew one short, sharp sound to indicate a bout had been won. I knew then what had happened. That had been Beris's practice arrow that hit Seb. If this had been real combat, I would have lost my navigator.

As it was, we'd lost the bout.

Kalax gave a low growl and Seb glanced back at me, his face pale. I couldn't see much more with those goggles on his face, but Kalax clacked her jaws together, spitting and hissing which told me Seb probably felt about the same.

Syl, Beris and Gaxtal settled on a landing platform, and Seb wheeled us around just as the gold winner flag was pulled over Gaxtal. Now I wanted to growl.

More flags went up—we were all to come in and take a break. I glanced at the sun. It was almost mid-day and we'd lost not only the race but the combat, too. On the platform, I slid off Kalax, my cheeks hot. I could see Reynalt talking with the other captains.

Kalax was grumpy—you didn't need Dragon Affinity to know that. Her claws raked the landing platform and she barely waited for us take the saddles and harness off before she leapt into the air, shooting over to the enclosure without even waiting for Seb to give her the order to do so.

That wasn't going to look good, either. I sighed. They were going to think Seb—the best navigator around—couldn't control his dragon. And that I couldn't fight.

Pulling off his helmet, Seb kicked at a loose pebble on the platform. "She can annoy the hell out of me sometimes," he whispered to me. "She hasn't been right all day. It's like...well, it's not like her." He shook his head, picked up his harness and saddle, and we headed for the equipment shed.

The Dragon Horns sounded again—another bout had been won by someone. I didn't care who since it wasn't us. As frustrated as I was with what had just happened, I had to agree with our dragon. This was silly. This wasn't real. Seb and I had already proven ourselves in a very real battle, but no one seemed to want to remember that.

In fact, no one seemed to want to remember the Darkening was still out there, Lord Vincent was still a danger, and the threat was a lot more real than all this.

I scowled at Beris and Syl who were standing around, chests puffed out like they'd won a real battle. They were going to gloat for days.

"Just ignore them," Seb said. But I couldn't. They'd won and we'd lost.

We waited for the other riders to return from Ghastion Point and then watched as they were thrown into immediate battles. I could see the reason for the practice—it was like being ambushed. The commander must want to see how we would react when we were tired from a flight and suddenly had to face battle.

Well, we reacted like untrained cadets.

Commander Hegarty and the instructors strolled over to us, but they were busy watching the sky. The headache I'd had earlier came back, pressed against my eyeballs and pounded in my head.

After another hour of roaring, swooping, curses and cheers, all the bouts had been fought. Jensen and Wil won. Varla and Merik joined us in kicking the dirt.

Stepping in front of us, Commander Hegarty scanned every-one's face. "Attention!" he bellowed. We all jumped into order, everything else forgotten. "And I thought you were Dragon Riders. I've seen cadets do better!" Commander Hegarty sounded in full military mode today, his voice sharp and his eyes even sharper. "Do you think the king will thank you for dying so quickly? Or for flying so slowly? Some of you can barely even seem to control your dragons." I winced and glanced at Seb, but he just kept watching the commander.

"Your performance was terrible. I expect you to be faster, tougher, meaner. I expect your battles to be longer, for it to be more difficult for anyone to get the advantage of any of you! I also declared a race to Ghastion Point, and the first thing I see is all of you squabbling as if you are all children! Did none of you want a fair race or a fair fight?" His stare traveled over the group. No one moved—I think we were all afraid to even breathe. Hegarty snapped his stare to Beris and Syl. "Riders, you two were first back, but it appeared that you won your combat more by luck, and so you may spend the rest of the afternoon practicing your skills in the yard."

Beris and Syl nodded and strode away.

"For the rest of you—physical training. Clean up and come back for a run," Hegarty barked.

A groan burst out of the collected ranks.

I kicked a stone. It had been a test, all of it. And we had all failed. I glanced up and saw Reynalt on the landing platforms. He stood where he was, arms folded and stone-faced, staring into the skies. Was he wondering what we'd do if this had been real combat? Was he thinking that the Darkening might attack us soon? Had Lord Vincent grown strong enough to try and take the city? Or was there something else on his mind?

CHAPTER 5
LEVIATHAN

I woke with everything hurting, and wondered if Thea was feeling about the same. My legs seemed sore and limp, like I'd run miles and miles, which I guess we had, and my back ached even more than it had when I'd had to help my dad with the forge. Even my hair seemed to hurt.

I hope that you're happy about this—this is what we get for not doing our best all the time. I sent the thought to Kalax, and got back a disgusted snort in response. She thought running was for sheep and didn't understand why we'd ever want to do anything but fly. She was curled up, deep in her cave and warm in the enclosure. But she knew we had plans for the day and I could tell she was looking forward to it. For now, though, she was happy to rest and wait for my call.

With a groan, I rolled off the bed and lit the lamp. It was still dark outside. Merik's snores echoed from the stone walls. I wasn't surprised. We'd had the worst practice of our lives and I was still wondering just how we were going to get over it. Thea had been angry with me, and with herself for not doing better. I couldn't blame her. I'd been more worried about her than I had been focused on the race and the battle. I kept thinking how she'd looked when she'd almost died, how warm and slick her blood had felt on my hands. I'd been thinking about all the wrong things.

Letting out a breath, I dressed quickly. We'd all been given the day off and it had been strongly recommended we use it for studying tactics and strategies. However, Thea had other plans in mind, and those plans kept my stomach churning this morning. She wanted us to fly to the Leviathan Mountains. The largest peak in the range was the one she was sure had to be the resting place of the Armour Stone. I wasn't sure why she felt so certain about it. It was a huge area to cover. But if we went and saw nothing was there, at least she'd feel better.

With my tunic, pants and boots on, I headed to the kitchens to see if I could pick up some food that we could take with us for the day. The smell of warm bread rolled over me, warm and encouraging.

Peeking into the kitchen, I saw Margaret the academy cook, working at one of the long tables in the huge space. She looked up from her bowl and grinned at me. She already had her sleeves rolled up and flour dusted her arms and nose, and a large tray stood on the table near her, stacked with bowls. The kitchen smelled of meat roasting and I could hear something bubbling as it sat over the fire. "Sebastian Smith, you're up early," she said.

"Morning, Margaret," I said and tried to look like I didn't have anything planned—like flying off to the Leviathan Mountains.

"Might as well make yourself useful." Margaret gestured to the tray. "Take this to the keep for morning meal."

I nodded, feeling a flush of warmth. I always felt more comfortable around Margaret. Like me, she wasn't a noble. She worked with her hands for a living just as I had before coming here, and she always knew the goings-on of Monger's Lane. If hanging out with Kalax in the enclosure was my number one place to be, in the kitchens with Margaret was the second.

I took the bowls into the keep. It was early enough that the girls who worked under Margaret were already there, sweeping the stone floors and cleaning last night's ashes from the hearth. I headed back to the kitchens.

"Thank you, Seb," Margaret said. "I guess you're down here for a bite to eat?"

"I wouldn't say no." I grinned and sat down at the table, where fruit sat stacked high in huge wooden bowls and fresh loaves of bread cooled under linen towels. "Thea and I might take Kalax to fish in Hammal Lake."

"Ah, well, there's a stack of meat pies on the shelf, and apples in the bin. Take as many as you need."

Helping myself to three meat pies, two for me and one for Thea, I watched Margaret work. There was something off about her—a small frown pulled her eyebrows tight and I thought she'd sounded a little worried. I wrapped the pies in a cloth and asked, "What's the bother?"

She let out a sigh and turned to face me, flour on her hands. She was about the age my mother would have been, and I sometimes wondered if she saw me as rather like a son to her. Wiping her hands on her apron, she came over and sat down. "Well, I can't say that there's nothing wrong—but I was begged to not say anything."

I rolled my eyes. She could no more keep a secret than I could stay away from dragons. "Margaret, you know me. I won't tell a soul."

She gave me a sideways glance. "Actually Seb, it was about you. I saw your step-ma the other day, down in the market when we were putting in orders for supplies."

"Is she well?" I wet my lips. My da had remarried after we'd lost my mother. She was a good woman, and I worried about her and my sister. I knew they were proud I'd become a Dragon Rider, but I also knew my da had no help now with the smithy.

"She's fine, lad." Margaret sighed and put her hand over mine. "She just misses you, is all. She heard about that fuss in King's Village and she asked me how you were doing, and promised me not to tell you of it."

"Margaret, there's something else. I can see it in your eyes."

"I wasn't going to tell—but your father's been poorly."

"Drunk you mean?" Margaret knew my father's reputation. It often seemed like half the city knew.

Margaret shook her head. "It's not the drink. It's a cough that won't leave him. He's not been able to work."

I gave a snort. "Not been wanting to work is more than likely."

She slapped my arm. "Seb, have a little respect! That man is your father!"

"He was never much of one to me. But…yes, I know he's blood. What if I happen by, and maybe take them some of your soup with me?"

She nodded. "Good. You do just that. And not a word of our little chat," Margaret said, fixing me with a stern glare.

I nodded and headed back to my room, both worried now and wondering if that cough was something worse.

Merik was up and dressed and doing his stretching exercises. Tall and thin, he could always outrun any of us and he looked now as if yesterday had been no effort at all for him. The sun was still more of a promise—the sky had lightened to grey, but it was still far too early for almost anyone else to be up.

Slipping on the optics that helped him see better, Merik peered at the cloth in my hands. "What's that? Breakfast?"

I slapped his hand away. "Hands off. You get your own."

Kalax grumbled over me doing that as she stretched. Bad moods seemed to be catching of late. But Merik only laughed. "So…are you ready?" I knew what he was talking about—our search for the Armour Stone. But I didn't want to say anything. Every time we mentioned the stone, it felt odd—as if we were poking at something we should leave alone.

Merik turned to his small bedside table where he had a stack of scrolls. He'd been reading them last night by the light of a lamp when I'd fallen asleep. His long fingers flickered over them, opening their bindings with practiced ease, checking until he found the roll he was looking for. He presented it to me. "I found this last night."

The roll of yellowing paper looked old. Faded ink crossed it like a spider web. I couldn't even read what language it was in. "What am I looking at?" I asked.

Merik snapped his fingers. "That is the script of Zholar. In fact, it is a copy of a fragment of a letter sent by a Zholar merchant to his lord—sent long ago in the time of the first Dragon Riders."

I glanced at Merik. "What does it say? Weather's fine, the food it terrible, I wish you were here?"

"Ha, no. The Zholar merchant was trying to impress his lord, and so it details the fabulous Dragon Riders he saw and their dragons, as well as strange stones he called magic eggs."

"The Dragon Egg Stones?" I glanced at the writing and wished I was as clever as Merik and could read far better than I did. I had trouble reading just one language.

Merik opened the scroll. I was almost afraid it would fall into dust, but Merik didn't seem worried. "He writes that a white one seemed to glow like moonlight."

"The Healing Stone—the one that Commander Hegarty has," I said.

"Another was black, about the size of a man's hand, and gave protection—that's the Armour Stone."

"Great! A description at last."

"That is not the most interesting thing—this merchant seems to suggest the stones can call to each other, or they're connected with each other."

"What?" I looked at him in confusion.

Sitting down on the edge of his bed, Merik shrugged. "It's... well, the writing is difficult to make out in spots. But there's mention of how he saw a group of people gathering and that all had been touched by the magic."

"Touched? What, like they were now in a special club?"

"I don't know. But it's clear that the stones weren't secret like they are now. The way this guy writes, I think everyone knew about them and thought they were special, so anyone who came into contact with them also becomes special—revered even. History is full of weird things like that. You wouldn't believe what other people used to believe."

In a way, it sounded like the way we kept the dragons together in the enclosure. And a little like how my Dragon Affinity worked better when I was near Kalax. And Thea...her Dragon Affinity worked better when she was near me.

I plucked at my lower lip.

Are we all connected? The Dragon Affinity...the stones...*do the* stones *allow dragons and people to work together somehow?* But I'd never had a stone used on me—that wasn't where my Dragon Affinity came from. Or was it?

"Hello! Seb?" Merik waved his hand in front of my face. "I lost you there."

"I was just thinking that maybe they knew things about the dragons that we have forgotten. And the stones too. Maybe the way people and dragons get on with each other, what if it's tied to the Dragon Stones? What if my Dragon Affinity is getting stronger because the stones are turning up again? And maybe Thea..." I let the words trail...*Thea what?*

Merik frowned. "What are you suggesting? That somehow we're fated to find the stones? That this is our destiny or something? Or that now the Darkening is rising, that it's waking up the stones? Maybe making them choose people the way dragons choose riders?"

"I don't know." I shook my head. "It's just that life...well, doesn't it feel a little like everything is about to spiral out of control at any moment. Maybe we're picking up on the distress the dragons are feeling, or maybe the Darkening is spreading that feeling through the stones to confuse us."

Merik stared at me. "Kind of the way the Memory Stone can take someone's memory—leave them blank so the Darkening can control them?"

I let out a breath.

If this was true...well, Thea had had more contact with both Lord Vincent and the stones. She had been acting strange ever since she had been healed—it was as if she was always more angry, or more easily upset, or was trying to be braver and fiercer than anyone. Now it was like she was being compelled to find the Armour Stone. She couldn't let go of that idea.

I didn't like where that idea was headed, because it meant Thea might not really be Thea anymore.

It was still early when I left the academy with Thea. The sky was greying with early dawn and the sun was a touch of gold along the ridgeline of Hammal Mountain. Thea and I made our way up to the dragon enclosure, which was really a large crater. Walking behind me, Thea seemed lost in thought as she so often was these days. After talking to Merik, I was worried that maybe it wasn't such a good idea to find these Dragon Egg Stones. But if we didn't find them, Lord Vincent might, and he could use them to bring the Darkening to power. There didn't seem to be any good choices.

At the lip of the enclosure, I could see down into the wide, tiered crater with the caves where the dragons nested. Kalax rested on a ledge in front of her cave, her red hue almost blending with the rocks.

Behind me, Thea hitched up the harness and saddle she was carrying. As Dragon Riders we could leave the academy when we wanted to, for the most part. But if we were gone for a long time, there would be questions to answer. I wanted to leave early and be back soon.

A low, throaty moan split the air and I froze. That had definitely come from a dragon, but it was unlike any sound I'd heard them make. I opened my mind to the dragons and sensed an unease.

"Seb?" Thea asked. She nudged me with an elbow. "What is it?"

"I think—something might be wrong." I gripped my own saddle and harness tight, and quickened my steps. We headed down along narrow goat trails that led into the enclosure.

Most of the dragons were still asleep. A few were out sunning themselves on the warm slabs of rock at the bottom of the enclosure, soaking up the heat of the hot springs below the earth.

"Erufon," I whispered, pointing to where the vast bulk of golden scales spread out on one of the stones. I held my breath, worried for a moment, before I saw his sides heave up and down with the deep breathing of sleep. But something else was bothering me. Reaching out with all of my senses, I felt what seemed to be something hovering over Erufon.

A shadow fell over us. Looking up, I saw that Kalax had come down to land on the rock next to us. She purred at us in her throaty voice. She knew we would be flying today.

Reaching up to touch her nose, I asked, "What's wrong with Erufon, Kalax?"

Beside me, Thea dropped her saddle and stared at me. I could still sense something odd about Erufon—there was something wrong with his belly.

Bad fish, Kalax thought at me. I was inclined to agree.

I said the same to Thea and told her, "We'll have to tell the commander about Erufon when we get back." Kalax dropped her shoulder to allow us to attach the saddles. On the other side of the enclosure, Erufon turned over onto his side and opened a lazy eye to stare at us.

"Is he going to be alright?" Thea asked.

"I think so." I cast my mind over Erufon once again, and could find nothing else wrong except for that vague discomfort. "Maybe he's not used to the simple, wild food they have here," I said. I whistled to Kalax, who stuck her head up and gave back a rumble.

The Leviathan Mountains. "Yep, that's it Kalax—that's where we're going."

⚘

The Leviathan Mountains ran down the world like a scar. On one side, extending right down past the end, stood the Middle Kingdom of Torvald. Beyond the mountains lay the southern reaches, the pirate islands, the archipelago, and the hot and burnt lands. On the northwestern side of the mountains, the wild lands stretched out, home to bandits, tribes and the fierce, wild black dragons that raided our crops and fields every summer.

They were the largest mountains in the world, or so Merik told me, and he would know. The foothills spread out for leagues. The mountaintops were almost always dusted with snow and a bluish haze spread out from the constant cooling winds that came off the hills.

Kalax did a flyover of the full range, and then we headed to the highest, sharpest, conical peak. To one side stood Winter's Pass, a deep cut that was one of the only routes for wagons and caravans. It looked like a natural site for a battle. Large armies could have met in the pass and dragons could have found shelter on the slopes or up in the sky.

I tried to imagine what it must have been like back in the time of heroes, when the sky was split by flights of dragons, the peal of their war horns, their banners fluttering in the air above, and the Darkening forces rising up, only to be struck down by the Dragon Riders and the Dragon Egg Stones.

Behind me I heard Thea laugh. I looked back to see her spread her arms out, and I knew she was feeling the same thing I was. To fly like the heroes of legend ... deep down that was what every Dragon Rider longed for.

Kalax, too, seemed to be enjoying herself. She called to the winds and soared over the mountains below, her head twisting as she scanned the landscape. We could make out the occasional shepherd's hut. Flocks of hardy sheep scattered, terrified, over the green grass as Kalax flew over them.

Mutton, Kalax thought at me. She tasted the air with her tongue, then caught the warm updrafts that buffeted the side of a mountain, using them to fly even higher. The air started to get colder, to burn my lungs and sting my cheeks, but I wasn't afraid. Kalax knew what she was doing. And dragons have wild hearts that need the open sky.

Flying up even higher, it seemed as if I could see to the very ends of the earth. I pulled in a ragged breath. We were almost level with the highest, icicle-sharp peak. Before long, my head started to spin. Ice caked Kalax's wings. She screeched a triumphant call at the top of the world and dove downwards. The ice patches shattered from her wings, flying behind us in a dazzling, crystal haze. The wind caught at my face, pulling at my helmet and goggles, rattling and pulling on my jacket as we swept like a bolt of lightning toward the sloping mountains.

"The battle between the Dragon Riders of old and the Darkening must have been fought here," Thea shouted.

I shrugged. I hadn't grown up hearing all the old stories that she had. I knew most of them now, but to me it just looked like lots of rocks and snow and more rocks. I couldn't help but think some of those old stories had been made up. How could anyone find anything here? And why hadn't someone been here to search before now? But I knew the answer to that—the only way to reach this spot was by dragon. There was no way to climb up, and no way to climb down from the top of the peak, even if you could get there to start with. This one spot seemed surrounded by sheer drops.

Leaning over to one side on Kalax, Thea kept scanning the mountain as if she knew just what she was looking for. She swung out an arm, pointed and waved at one slightly flatter set of rocks that looked almost like giants. "Goblin Rocks. My family has an old painting of the battle, and it was said to have ended here."

That was as good as any place to start. I steered Kalax to the site, which was like a low cliff, its walls like fingers of rock sticking up. If you squinted and were wearing goggles, they did look a little like goblins peering down the slopes. It was also sheltered from the cold wind and one of the few places on the mountain where you could hold a duel—as the legends said had happened.

Kalax circled the site and dropped down onto the cliff.

"Thank you, Kalax." I unclipped my harness and dismounted. Pulling one of the meat pies from my bag, I threw it to Kalax. She snapped it up and tipped her head to one side, asking for more. I shook my head.

Thea had already jumped down and was lifting her pack off the back of her saddle. She'd had the sense to bring a few tools—a pick and a trowel. "Right, we'd better get started then," she said.

The ground looked as though it had been used by wild dragons —only dragon claws could dig that deep into rock, leaving deep ruts. Old sheep bones, a horse's skull, and a collection of scales, half burnished, lay scattered over the uneven rock as well. All signs of dragons. No wonder everyone left this spot alone—wild dragons usually didn't eat people, but they had been known to defend their territory. Often that meant picking someone up and dropping them back onto the ground from a great height.

Kalax sniffed the air and I could sense she was on alert, but she was also certain the site hadn't been used recently.

After a few hours of searching and finding nothing but rocks, Thea crouched down. Her voice lifted with excitement. "Seb! Look!"

I turned to see her pull up a rusted lump of metal. It was worn by time, but you could still make out faint designs of whorls and lines. This wasn't a naturally occurring metal. I took it from her. "It's an axe head. But any of the Wildmen could have dropped this up here." I ran my thumb over the blade and wondered what smithy had made it. I also pointed to the marks on the blade. "It was well-made at one time." Sunlight glinted on the dull metal. I bent down and found a rusted shard in the shape of an arrow point. Before long we even found a scrap of metal from a ruined breastplate.

But no Armour Stone—nothing that even came close to a Dragon's Egg Stone.

Thea kicked at a rock. It didn't move. "Okay, so a battle was fought here. But the legend said that the king offered a duel, and it was the power of the Armour Stone that saved his life." She huffed out a breath. "It's just…I don't feel it's here." She looked at me, her mouth pulled down and a hard expression in her eyes, almost as if she was daring me not to believe her. "It's hard to explain."

"Well, you're the one who wanted to come here." I kicked at the dirt and a faintly irregular black stone tumbled free. Grabbing it, I saw it had a crack on one side and was slightly larger than any Dragon's Egg that I'd ever seen. "What about this?"

"Too big, isn't it?" Thea pointed to where similar bits of black obsidian lay. "That looks like the other rock you all around here."

Large and small bits of the shiny, black stone—some roughly egg-shaped and others no bigger than a thumbnail—littered the ground. I collected any that were both black and more or less egg-shaped, but I wasn't sure I had found anything.

"What did the Healing Stone look like?" I asked. I was trying to think back to it myself. I remembered the light spilling out of Commander Hegarty's hands, and I remembered the tingle of power and energy that had flowing over me. "The light—it was so bright it blinded me. I don't even remember its outline.

The Memory Stone—all I remember about that was that Lord Vincent wore it around his neck on a chain."

Thea turned away and mumbled, "Don't know."

"You didn't see the Healing Stone at all?"

"I said no," she snapped, her voice flat. She sounded so lost. She also shivered.

Looking up, I saw that we'd been here most of the day. Striding back to where Kalax sat in the sun, trying to catch any warmth, I told her, "Come on. Let's go."

I couldn't help but feel this had been a wasted journey.

We flew back in silence, my saddle-bags full of clinking, egg-shaped rocks.

CHAPTER 6
THE FIGHT

"They're just a big old bunch of rocks!" I looked at Seb and then at Merik and finally at Varla.

Seb and I had returned from the Leviathan Mountains cold and tired. I wasn't hungry, but Seb brought me up a hot drink from the kitchen. I hadn't wanted it, but once I had it in my hands, I'd drunk it down. I had hoped that Merik and Varla would at least return from Wynchwood with better news. But they'd brought back their own collection of cracked, worn and roughened black stones even more useless than Seb's collection.

We'd gathered in my room—boys weren't supposed to be here, but Matron wouldn't do a room check until after dinner. Varla pulled in a low table from another room and everyone spread out their rocks.

Nothing on the low table looked like any kind of stone of power.

Seb's rocks looked like they'd come out of a volcano at some point—they were rough and sharp-edged. Merik and Varla's rocks looked like darkened river rocks—they were smooth and looked more like what I thought the Armour Stone should look like, but nothing…nothing felt right.

Seb stared at me, his arms folded across his chest. "How do you know? How do any of us know what the Armour Stone is going to look like?"

Getting up, I stared out the window. *How can I explain I am certain I will know it the instant I see it? Why do I even think this?* I bit my lip. It was like with Seb and his Dragon Affinity —it was just something he knew how to do. No one had taught him. I felt like I'd recognize the Armour Stone. Perhaps I was just fooling myself. But I'd seen and touched the Memory Stone—I'd had the Healing Stone used on me to save my life. Those weren't things you ever forgot.

I cleared my throat and turned to face Seb—and the others. They were all looking at me with worried frowns. "There's a feeling. Like…well, like I get whenever I remember what happened. I've been getting that same feeling whenever I see Commander Hegarty—so I think it must be from his connection to the Healing Stone. And maybe also the Memory Stone that we took from Lord Vincent."

An image flashed—*a pale face flashing above mine: empty, dark eyes, a mouth pulled down and tight.*

I shook my head and pushed it away. I didn't want to think about Lord Vincent or that awful sensation of falling into darkness I'd had after he'd struck me down. Blinking, I focused again on Seb, Varla and Merik.

Merik stood with his shoulders against the door, looking serious. Seb had his legs braced wide and his arms crossed. Varla sat cross-legged on her bed, her braid pulled over one shoulder. All of them looked worried for me—and I hated that.

Don't feel sorry for me!

Annoyance flash through me. I wasn't weak. I wasn't crazy. "Stop it," I said and stared at them. "Stop thinking I'm making this up."

Seb let his arms drop to his sides. "Thea, I think you're right. I think that there is something about the stones." He nodded at Merik and told me about the old scroll Merik had found.

"So...they used to keep all of the people who had used a Dragon Egg Stone together? Like they were—special?" I asked.

Seb nodded. "What if you can sense the other stones? What if you have...well, a Stone Affinity now?"

I nodded. "But how does it help us? It didn't help today."

"We just need to get you close to the stone." Varla tapped a finger on her chin. "You said that you got an odd feeling around Commander Hegarty? Maybe we should try to ask him about the stones?"

Seb gave a snort. "Commander Hegarty swore us all to secrecy. He said the stones can do good, but they've caused a lot of trouble. Any Dragon Rider trusted with the secret that the stones even exist is supposed to swear an oath not to talk about them, so I think if we start asking about them, he's going to want to throw us into the darkest hole he can find."

"But what has he has done with the Memory Stone? Could we use the two stones the commander has to find the Armour Stone?" Merik asked.

I pushed out a breath. "Maybe that is what he's doing with the patrol he's been sending out. But he said the stones were too powerful to be used all together. That's why they were split up. So he might not want them together. And he said the one Dragon Stone—all of them together as one or one that could control them all—was an impossible myth."

Varla pulled out a box of books from under her bed. "I can tell you for certain that the Dragon Stone—the one that has all of the powers—there's evidence it really exists." She leafed through the books until she found the page she was looking for. She spread out the book on our low table of rocks.

On the page a drawing of all of the Dragon Egg Stones jumped out at us, all looking exactly like eggs, but with different colours.

"Where did you find this?" Merik grinned like a fool.

"You're not the only one who's good in a library." Varla pointed to the drawings. "As we know, the grey is for memory, black for armour and white for healing. That—the one with a rainbow of swirling colours is the Dragon Stone. It's supposed to be slightly larger than the others, with inscriptions around the sides. And why would anyone bother to go into this much detail for a myth?" Varla folded her arms.

Cold trickled down my spine. "We have to make sure Lord Vincent and the Darkening don't get the Dragon Stone."

Seb nodded. "One thing at a time. We have no clue about the whereabouts of the Dragon Stone, but we know one thing—the Armour Stone wasn't at the Leviathan Mountains or in Wychwood, so the last story of the wandering monk must be true."

"There's a map of the old monastery networks in the map room," Merik said. "We studied it a few years ago. Even the academy used to be a monastery at one time—an order of monks that communed with the dragons. So we have a few maps of the other ruins of monasteries of that order."

I nodded. "Tomorrow, you two find the monastery map." I grimaced at the thought of what I had to do. "Varla and I... well, we'll try to talk to Commander Hegarty about the stones."

"Good luck with that," Merik murmured.

A voice sounded from outside the door. "What's going on up there?"

As there were only a few girls who became Dragon Riders, Varla and I shared separate quarters from the boys and were watched over by the ever-vigilant Matron in her black skirts and pulled-back hair. Her iron-shod boots clattered on the stairs. "I heard someone."

"Boys aren't allowed!" Varla hissed.

We'd all be put on cleaning duties for a month if Seb and Merik were found here.

I nodded to the window. Ivy ran up one side of the keep, so the boys would have to use it to climb down.

Seb went out first, then Merik. Matron rapped on the door with her cane. I heard a rustle and a garbled shout as the boys slipped out. The door burst open and Matron swept in. "What is going on in here? And why on earth do you have a collection of dirty old rocks on your table?"

I stood next to Varla. "Why, Matron, don't you know? It's part of our new strategic study of better flight tactics." Varla and I both pasted on stiff smiles.

⊗⊗⊗

The next day we didn't have a chance to carry out our plans. The blare of the Dragon Horns woke us at dawn, the clear sound echoing against the mountains and vibrating in my chest. I rolled from bed and gave a yelp when my feet hit the cold floor.

"What is it?" Varla asked, mumbling the words and poking her head out of her covers.

I put my head out of the window to see message flags already being hoisted. "Another practice. The commander wasn't joking when he said that he was going to push our training hard now."

Yawning, Varla got out of bed. "It's still evaluations. Let's hope Matron doesn't mention our rocks."

I tried not to think about that as we dressed and headed to the keep. I had the feeling that if someone knew we were trying to find the Armour Stone, it might be bad for us—they were supposed to be a secret. But I was starting to wonder if Lord Vincent already knew—or had—the Armour Stone.

68

In the keep, everyone was grabbing rolls and a fast bite of porridge.

"Plan's off for now," I whispered to Seb.

He nodded.

Instead of Commander Hegarty, Instructor Mordecai came into the keep, scowling like always and looking even more stooped today. "That's a slow start you've had. Just how will you respond to an attack if the enemy hits before dawn?"

"The enemy?" I jabbed an elbow into Seb's side and mouthed, "The Darkening."

Jensen stood, washed and dressed, his tunic, pants and boots perfect, just his hair a little too long. His bowl of porridge was steaming. "Which enemy, sir?"

"It doesn't matter which," Mordecai barked. "Just know they are out there and that one day you will have to fight them. Double-time to the practice fields. Breakfast is cancelled."

Beside me, Seb groaned. He grabbed a roll and stuffed it in his mouth. I copied him and jogged to the chilly practice yard, then I saw we had a special visitor on the battlements—Prince Justin.

Most thought him a handsome young man. He was just a few years older than I, with blond hair, high cheekbones, and I'd heard that every girl at court had a crush the size of a dragon on him. I remembered him as a boy who used to pull my hair and steal my sweets—the disadvantage of a noble house was that there were no illusions about royalty being perfect.

"Dragon Riders," Prince Justin called out to the assembled riders. "I have come to announce that the Crown will be asking your instructors to begin placing you in squadrons and asking you to take forward duties."

A ragged cheer swept up from across the riders in the yard. Finally, I thought. But it was also early for us to be assigned. Why was there a rush now?

Prince Justin nodded at us. "The king depends on you—on your courage, on your strength, but most of all on your skills. Because of this, new training will begin in the field. Nothing is wrong. The kingdom remains at peace and will continue to do so, thanks to your fine efforts in the skies!"

Another cheer went up and Commander Hegarty took to the front of the stage. "Today, all protectors will be assessed as to their combat effectiveness and the navigators assessed for their orienteering readiness. To the training yards." He clapped his hands. Cheers turned into groans and moans.

"See you on the other side, and good luck," Seb said, hitting me playfully on the shoulder. I heard a disapproving grunt from Beris—he still didn't approve of commoners fraternizing with those of the noble houses. I shot him a glare and collected my practice armour.

But I kept thinking—why had Prince Justin said nothing was wrong when he knew as well as the rest of us that the Darkening was coming again?

I kept thinking about the prince's words. Jensen took another swing at me with the wooden practice staff and I barely brought my own staff up in time to block it before he was returning with another blow. Ducking backwards, I lost my balance, tripped and fell. The instructor nearest me raised the flag to indicate my failure.

"Better luck next time, Thea," Jensen grinned and offered me his hand.

I slapped it away. "I can get myself up, thank you very much!"

Jensen's eyes narrowed. "It's unlike you to go down so easily and so quickly. If you want to make the Black Claws, you have to do better."

I knew he was only trying to look out for me, but I still felt like I was being judged and I didn't like it. "I'll be fine. But if I keep this up, we'll be lucky if we get to even deliver packages." Picking up my staff, I rolled my shoulders, and found myself looking into Beris's small, dark eyes.

"Ah, Flamma," Beris said. "You worrying too much about your pet peasant and how he's doing on his tests?" I swung my quarterstaff at him in a jab, letting that be my answer. "Whoa! Testy!" Beris dodged, grinned and started to circle around me. "Some of your navigator's rough habits are rubbing off on you. That's what you get for hanging around a smith's son."

I jabbed again, moving forward, but Beris had been expecting my attack. He sidestepped, sticking out his quarterstaff to bang me on the shins, hoping to bring me down. I took the blow and stepped forward to ram my shoulder into his chest. Surprise bloomed on his face and he went down with a heavy thump.

"Beris lost to Flamma!" The instructor held up his flag.

I stood over Beris. "Don't test me, Beris. Ever."

"Let's see you do that in the air then," he said, staggering to his feet.

The wooden quarterstaff in my hand felt heavy and very useable all of a sudden. I wanted to wipe that smirk off of his face.

"Thea!"

I knew the voice. I turned as Beris bowed. "Prince Justin?" My heart was still pounding from the fight and a tremor ran through me from the rage I had almost unleashed.

The prince looked at Beris, who'd gone red-faced. "Beris Veer, let us not keep you. And tell your father that Prince Justin is looking forward to seeing him at court."

"Certainly, your highness." Beris nodded again, before shooting me a poisonous glance as he strode away.

The prince turned to me, and I bowed low. "Oh, you don't have to do that, Thea, we've known each other long enough, haven't we?" He smiled.

I straightened. "What brings you to speak with me?"

"Just to see how you are getting on." His smile widened, and I had to admit it was hard to remember the little brat I had known. His smile made me want to smile back at him and I had to resist that tug. It wasn't that I couldn't like him, but someday he was going to have to marry—and I wasn't able to think of myself as ever being a princess. Or a queen.

Rubbing my sore ribs, I said, "I think you've caught me on a bad day."

He frowned for a second. "About that…did you have a preference for your eventual squadron placement?"

"Black Claws." I grinned. "Could you put in a good word for me?"

His face darkened with worry. It was suddenly clear the prince had some different notions for where I should end up. "I thought you said that your navigator—what was his name? Smith?"

"Sebastian Smith."

"Yes, the smith's boy. You once said he wasn't much of a fighter?" The prince began to walk.

I fell into step with him. "Seb is amazing with the dragons. To be fair to him, he is far better than he used to be. And he has already been of great service to the Crown."

Prince Justin nodded. "I must see what your brothers think, of course. It was just—I was hoping you might have a desire for the signals corps?"

"You mean never see combat? Fly around delivering goods?"

He winced, stopped and faced me. "To be blunt, it's your mother, Agathea. To have all three of her children on the front lines, it's…it's become clear to her that she might lose all of you. She has petitioned my father—"

"The king?" I felt dizzy. "For what? My dismissal?"

His face paled. "I've put my foot in it. Look, come on a ride with me tonight—not dragons, just a simple horse. We'll talk. Your mother doesn't want to take your position from you; she is just thinking to have you further back from any battle."

"I thought you said everything was fine?"

"Of course," he said just a little too quickly. "But come. Meet me by the back gate, bring a pony and we'll talk about old times."

That was the last thing I wanted to do—despite his charm and his smile. But this might be the only chance I had to convince him I could be a Black Claw. I smiled, agreed, and even added a curtsey. The prince turned away, leaving me worried and cold.

Something was very wrong.

⊙⅌⊙

By the time practice ended for the day, I was feeling sore, tired and wishing I had one more bout so I could pound someone. Senior riders had been coming and going, helping the staff to erect a large wooden board at one end of the training yard. The different squadrons were written at the top of large columns and names would be going up.

The King's Own—the smallest unit, was made up of body-guards to the King and Prince Justin. After that came the Black Claws, then the Storm Blues, who acted as a reserve troop, the Green Flag messenger core, and the Heavy Whites who carried goods, and the Far Flyers, who served as long-distance scouts. It had been hard to keep my eye on the battles as names were added to the boards—and the names kept changing as instructors and senior riders were working out the best fit in each squadron.

Jensen and Wil stayed securely in the Storm Blues with their dragon, Dellos. Beris and Syl were also put into that squadron. But at the very end, Jensen and Wil moved up to the Black Claws—Jensen had beaten two opponents at once in hand-to-hand. Varla and Merik were put into Storm Blues to start with, but were moved to the Green Flags.

"This board does not reflect your final position, but our current decision," Commander Hegarty had said.

I started to hope that Seb would somehow be really bad at navigating, meaning that we would make terrible messengers.

"The best of the best, of course, will join the King's Own, who are able to do anything, be anywhere, lead armies or protect their leaders," he announced, pointing to the blank space under the list behind him. "None of you have made it there yet."

That sounded like a challenge to me, and I hated that Seb and I were still set to join the Storm Blues.

Nothing but patrols, I thought in despair. We'd be stuck watching the roads and repelling the occasional wild dragon.

Heading over to where I stood in front of the board, Varla punched my elbow. "Hey, maybe you'll join Merik and me in the Green Flags. We get great tunics and we'll fly all the time. It's the Green Flags who keep the whole kingdom together, making sure the watchtowers are working and signaling the approach of any enemy."

I glanced at her. "Messenger service," I muttered.

Varla smile faded. "I'm sure you'll get where you need to be."

I wasn't so sure. Varla headed away, and I turned from the board. And as I turned from the board, Seb and Merik were just arriving to take a look. I wasn't sure I wanted to talk to them. Seb would probably be fine with being a Green Flag. He'd get to fly all day and hang out with other dragons. I could have howled in frustration.

Instead, I ducked away and headed for the stables, but I heard Seb and Merik talking and slowed my steps.

"Do you think it's true? What I heard about Deep Wood? One of the senior riders came back from there today—said it's gone, disappeared. Like King's Village did when the Darkening took hold."

"Must be why the commander is so touchy," Seb said.

I moved away, heading for the stables.

With Bill saddled, I threw on a warm cloak. Extras were kept on pegs near the stable doors. Bill, one of the tough mountain ponies used for carrying packs of supplies to the academy, followed me out of the stables and to the back gate.

Prince Justin waited for me, standing next to his grey gelding. "Lady Agathea," he said and bowed over my hand. My cheeks warmed. He wore simple riding leathers but his wool cloak glinted with gold embroidery at the edges. When he smiled at me, a little thrill chased over my skin.

"Shall we?" The prince mounted and I swung up on Bill. We headed up the narrow mountain trails. The prince's horse had the longer stride, but Bill had the advantage on the hillside and easily kept up.

The sun was starting to go down over Hammal Mountain, causing a wonderful display of red and orange clouds. I pointed at it, "Dragon's Breath."

Justin smiled. "I know. I went to the academy, even if it was dragon's years ago."

The ponies clipped their way upward. Oddly, the prince didn't even try to choose the trail, so I let Bill pick the way.

The orange clouds turned to a red, fiery haze as the sun finally started to set. We came to a halt at the top of the hill and I glanced back at the prince. "You never could beat me in a race, remember," I said and grinned. I let Bill nibble grass.

The prince frowned and shook his head. "No, I remember winning often."

Sure he was joking, I glanced at him. But his forehead was lined and his eyes vague as if he didn't seem to remember us racing and my winning. "You have the benefit of a selective memory."

"I have the benefit of being right. But I didn't come here to argue. I want to talk about the future. Your future," he said lightly.

Tension gathered inside me. "What of it? I'll be a Dragon Rider and guard your royal highness for the rest of my days." I smiled. I was going to avoid even thinking about the Darkening right now.

"I promised your mother I would talk to you about all of that," he said evenly. "You have to understand, Thea—what would it be like if she lost all of her children in some battle? House Flamma. How does the old saying go? 'Nothing as close as a Flamma and their dragon?' Your house has been standing beside the kings of Torvald for centuries. You are one of the backbones of our kingdom. If we lost all of you..." The prince shook his head. "Think of the good of the kingdom."

A breeze came up and I shivered, but I kept staring at the prince. "But apparently all is well. Isn't that what you said? Although, if you ask those from King's Village they might have a different view on the matter."

"King's Village?" Justin scratched his chin. "I am certain someone was talking to me about that just recently."

I frowned. How could he have forgotten King's Village and the battle for it? My throat tightened. "Prince Justin—the Darkening? There are new attacks?"

"It cannot be," Justin said in a weak voice. He shook his head. "There are raiders and Wildmen as always. That is why we increase our patrols." He smiled. "Which is why I want you to consider a request to be a Green Flag."

"I can't believe you would ask this of me. You know I am the best archer at present. I've beaten you enough times!" I pointed a finger at him. "When we were younger, it became embarrassing how often I would win against you."

"No." His face hardened into that of a stranger's. "I have always been the better archer. Why seek to annoy me?" He sounded haughty and nothing like the Justin I knew.

"Do you—do you remember the apple tart incident? Or the mud pies?" I asked.

"What on earth are you talking about? I would never have been allowed to play with mud pies. My father would have had a fit."

You're right, he never did allow you—but you did so anyway, because you knew you could bully everyone into letting you, for you were the heir to the throne.

I remembered those days—but he did not.

Worry grew into a nibbling monster. I could think of only one thing that would change him—someone had used the Memory Stone on the prince!

But if Commander Hegarty had the Memory Stone, had it been him? But why? Or had the commander lost the stone? Was that why he was sending out patrols. It had been a long transport to bring it home. Perhaps the stone had gone missing then?

I turned Bill for the academy. "I'm sorry Justin, I—I thank you for taking an interest in my career, but I must get back. There is something very important I have to look into." The prince was looking annoyed—but a few moments from now he wouldn't remember why. That was as sad as it was terrible. "Thank you for your advice." I turned and headed back at a fast trot. I needed to find Seb.

Then we needed to find out just who had the Memory Stone—and why was it being used on the prince.

CHAPTER 7
BURGLARY

"It's simple," Thea said, her voice breathless and her face flushed. She had just come back from what she'd said was supposed to be a moonlit ride with the prince. And why hadn't she told me about that before? I stared at her. Sunset was still glowing with a fading purple in the west—she hadn't even been out until the first star appeared. I didn't know what had gone wrong, I was just glad that it had. I didn't like how the prince had been looking at her all day.

But now Thea was saying crazy stuff.

"You distract him and I'll sneak into his study." Thea gave a sharp nod.

I shook my head. The Dragon Horns had sounded almost an hour ago. Around us, the keep echoed with riders talking about the squadron placements. I sat, along with Merik and Varla, where our little group always sat, at the back near one of the windows. Thea got here late, missed most of dinner, had barely even made an attempt of putting anything in her bowl then finally she starting talking about this crazy idea.

"But—tonight? This all seems a little last-minute."

"Scared I'll get caught?" Thea looked at me with a challenge lighting up her blue eyes.

"Yes. Which is only sensible. If you get caught—"

"I won't. Something is wrong. Commander Hegarty has been spectacularly close-lipped lately."

"Spectacularly bad-tempered lately," Merik said.

Thea nodded. "Prince Justin was even worse. *We* found the Memory Stone in the first place. What if it's bringing trouble, just like the commander said it would?"

I shook my head and dropped my voice. "Who would do that?"

Thea flicked a glance to the head table where the instructors sat. She leaned closer. "Who hates all Dragon Riders, and us in particular? Who doesn't look at all as if he ever rode a dragon? Who is a bitter old man who might laugh to see the academy brought down?"

I glanced at Instructor Mordecai who was scowling into his cup as if he really did hate everyone.

"She might have a point," Merik said, his voice soft. "He was really, really mean to you last year."

"That doesn't mean he's a servant of the enemy," I muttered.

Varla glanced from me to Thea and back again. "You could find out. If Commander Hegarty has the Healing Stone and the

Memory Stone, that means it's not being used, and the prince is just…well, being a prince, I guess."

Letting out a breath, I told Thea, "I'll go."

She shook her head. "I'll know if it's there."

"That's not going to work. We need a diversion. Do you really think I can manage one? What—should Merik and I fake a fight? That's going to be too obvious. Or should Varla and I start yelling at each other?"

Thea was frowning now. "Okay—I see your point." She glanced around us. "You'll have to search. I'll get everyone's eyes on me."

"Just what are you going to do?" I asked.

She grinned, stood and said, "Just get ready." Picking up her bowl of meat, she walked toward the main table in the center of the keep. I slipped away from our table and headed to the side door that led to the kitchen and the back stairs.

Thea didn't waste any time. Right next to Beris, Thea accidentally tripped, spilling her cold mutton stew onto his shoulder and head.

Jumping up, Beris yelled, "What did you do?"

The room erupted into howls of laughter.

Hands spread out, Thea smiled. "I'm sorry, Beris. Guess it's just been a very long day."

"You did that on purpose." Beris kicked at the bench where he'd been sitting and swiped at the stew clinging to his jerkin. A chunk of meat stuck to his hair. Riders started to slide out of the way, leaving space for a possible fight.

Thea widened her eyes. "It was an accident."

"If you're so prone to accidents, you'd better watch your step," Beris muttered, snatching a cloth that Syl offered.

A whisper rippled through the crowd—I knew bets were being made.

"Why don't you just go back to your blacksmith boy? That's your kind now, isn't it? You'd rather go slumming than be with your own kind."

Thea gritted her teeth and muttered, "One more word, Beris. Just one more."

Beris stuck his chin out. I shook my head. He was so stubborn he couldn't see a baited trap in front of him "What? Standing up for that peasant? Because he can't do it for himself."

"Oh, he can do more than you can. And he's not a mutton-head like you."

Beris's face reddened. He swung first. Thea ducked back and then struck out. Her fist hit Beris so hard that I was sure everyone in the room heard the crack.

"Stop this at once!" Commander Hegarty shouted.

Beris hit the table, clutching his bruised jaw. He pushed up and pounced on Thea. The two of them slammed into a table— metal plates, stew and goblets went flying and a shout went up. All backs were turned to me now. Everyone—riders and instructors—were concentrating on the fight.

I turned, slipped out, headed along the stone passageway and made for Commander Hegarty's study.

It wasn't hard to find or get into. I'd been here before and I knew the commander liked a clean, sparse room. He had a small library, a conference chamber and a room to sleep in. All of it kept nearby to the enclosure, so he might be on the ground or in the air right away.

Heart pounding, I stared at his room.

No one at the academy should be a traitor or a thief—any cadets caught in any crime were sent home at once. A Dragon Rider was supposed to think of nothing but dragons and helping others. Yet here I was sneaking into the commander's rooms.

Guilt wrapped around my throat. Was I betraying the commander's trust? What would happen if he found out I'd been here? I tried to think of this as just confirming what I knew—that the stones were safe. But some part of me was certain that the commander would know I'd been here.

I took a breath and started to search.

This part of the academy and the keep were a part of the old monastery that had once stood here. The stone walls and floors were old and worn smooth. There were few places to hide anything, and the commander had only a few bookcases and a desk or two.

The room was surprisingly small considering Hegarty was the commander and could have any rooms he wanted. One narrow window looked out onto the training grounds and a small lamp hung on one wall, giving light. Maps hung on the walls and scrolls stood stacked on the desk. A stand in the corner held the commander's armour which gleamed in the dull light.

Peeking into an open doorway, I saw a narrow bedchamber with a cot. I felt uncomfortable looking at his things. The bed held clean linens and a thick blanket. On the small side table another lamp glowed, showing a dagger and a length of harness that the commander must be fixing. A clothespress held a few of his jerkins, his boots and pants.

He had as little as I did, and I wondered if it was because we both came from rough parts of the city. Turning away, I headed into a smaller room that held weapons, spare dragon saddles and old clothes. All the things a Dragon Rider and soldier would need. I went back to the study.

Maps and scraps of parchment lay on the desk. I was a good map reader, but not as good as Merik, and some of these maps made no sense, showing weird shapes and blobs of different colours. Others clearly showed troop movements. I could see on one the curve of the Leviathan Mountains, the tiny red circles for the city of Torvald, and the nearby villages.

I wondered if Commander Hegarty was mapping the enemy's territory, or was he looking for something else?

Shifting the maps, I found another map with arrows pointing to the south and to the wide seas and islands. That had to be a rough outline of the Southern Realm. Some of the islands had only half of the coast marked. Another map showed deserts with the word *dragons* scribbled across it. Was the commander trying to map where all the dragons could be found?

The sound of heavy booted feet sounded outside the room in the hallway. My heart jumped. I ducked into the storeroom and hoped the shadows would hide me. The heavy steps moved away and I let out a breath. I needed to stop looking at maps and start looking for stones.

Heading back to the desk, I checked under the papers and opened the two drawers in the desk, but found nothing other than more papers and quills. Moving fast, I scanned the bookshelves, looking for anything out of place, or for a box, or something to hold the stones. Still nothing, and I was losing time.

I knew the commander at least had the Healing Stone. He'd used it on Thea, and he'd said he'd been tasked with protecting the Healing Stone. He'd also taken the Memory Stone from Thea—and it was supposed to be someplace safe. Desperation gnawing at me, I checked his armour and found nothing that shouldn't be there. I stomped on the floor but nothing appeared to be loose.

That left only two places—the bedroom and the storeroom. I headed into the storeroom, rushing now, my heart pounding and the sweat cold on my skin. If this took any longer, I'd end up swallowing my own tongue in a panic.

In the storeroom, I ran my hands over the top shelf and found spare candles and lamp oil, bottles of ink, sheaths of blank paper and old boots. One boot seemed a little too heavy even for a Dragon Rider's boot. Putting my hand into the boot, I touched something smooth. I tipped over the boot and the Healing Stone rolled out and into my hand with a comforting weight.

Light from the stone warmed the room. A cool, soothing sensation spread up my arm. My heart beat slowed and I took a deep breath. Was this what gave the commander so much vitality and strength? I felt its optimistic energies spreading through me.

Suddenly, a stick slapped my hand. I dropped the Healing Stone and staggered back. The feeling and the light winked out in a bright flash. Holding my stinging hand, I looked up to see Instructor Mordecai. He held his wooden cane out in front of him as if he was planning to beat me with it. Leaning down, he knocked the Healing Stone back into the boot, then turned to me. "What are you doing here?"

My mind was racing; the fog the stone had started to cast into me was wearing off.

Mordecai glared at me with narrowed, suspicious eyes. "Tell me why you are here. Tell me everything you know."

I shook my head, but I couldn't talk—I didn't know what to say.

Mordecai leaned closer. "You think you're special because you were chosen by a red. Because you ride with a Flamma. Because…because!" He cracked his cane on the floor.

Kalax's thoughts slid into mine. *Danger?* I knew she was alert now and could sense my fear. I felt her unfurl her wings as she got ready to leap into the air. I had a sudden image of Kalax tearing rocks and splintering windows as she strove to protect me.

Wait, I told her. I also gulped a breath and knew I had to think of something. If Mordecai suspected me of wanting to steal the

Healing Stone, I was done as a Dragon Rider. But I couldn't tell him I was searching for the Memory Stone. What if he was on the side of the Darkening? What if he was being controlled by the Memory Stone?

Gulping in another breath, I blurted out, "I know about the Healing Stone because Thea remembered it. She was injured… the battle for King's Village. And my father is sick. I just wanted…I thought it would…would make me be able to heal him"

"Your father?" Mordecai raised an eyebrow. "The smith of Monger's Lane?"

I nodded. It was true, and I was hoping that would help me. "Margaret the cook told me. My folks…they deserve more than just money from me. Dragon Riders are supposed to help the people of Torvald." My stomach tightened. I was sure the truth of that was on my face, but would Mordecai still suspect me? "I was…I wanted to ask the commander about it. I thought… well, he might even heal my father of his drinking, of his bad chest." My throat tightened and I felt my eyes start to burn.

Mordecai gave a snort. "The Healing Stone doesn't work like that. It just goes to show how little you know of it. It can't cure a man of thirst, or…there are some wounds that go too deep, that have been with a man too long."

Was that why Mordecai crippled leg hadn't been healed? It couldn't be healed? It was too old a wound? It had been too deep to repair? Or was it just that the commander wouldn't heal him? I didn't understand why the Healing Stone couldn't heal my father. Was Mordecai lying about that?

The instructor must have seen me looking at him with confusion. He shook his head. "The Healing Stone cannot be used for what ails your father—which is himself. One day you'll understand that boy, perhaps, although I doubt you will ever live that long. Sometimes wounds are meant to make a person." His gaze slipped to the commander's suit of Dragon Armour. Once upon a time Mordecai would have worn just such a suit. Did it sit in his rooms gathering dust?

I shivered. Mordecai was no longer a frightening instructor who could throw me out of the Academy, but he was a broken man capable of a great deal. Was the past that had twisted his body also bad enough to turn him to the Darkening? Did the bitterness of not being able to be healed, even when the commander had such a power, eat at him?

Mordecai turned back to me, his eyes small and narrow. "I can't suspend you like you were a cadet—but I give you leave to visit your ailing father. You'll not come back to the Academy for three days and two nights—I don't want to see your face here. And this...this will be recorded as a mark against you," Mordecai said, his mouth curving down. "I would be surprised if you are trusted with so much as guard duty of the supply ponies after this."

"But...but, sir?"

"But what? This is a light punishment." He waved his wooden cane. "Now out from here and come with me." He turned and left.

My feet heavy, I followed him along the stone hallways. After a few twists and turns and stairs, he threw open a wooden door and waved me in with his cane. I stepped into a study room, this one lined with bookshelves, lamps, large leather-covered chairs and thick rugs. A fire burned in the hearth, making the room almost too warm. I started to sweat and my stomach lurched. Mordecai headed to a table and opened a book labeled *Disciplinarium.*

He opened the book and under the last blank page wrote:

Sebastian Smith, Dragon Rider. Infraction. To spend three days and two nights solely with family, Monger's Lane, Torvald.

Stepping to a shelf, he picked up two small bottles. One looked to be filled with dried herbs and the other with a clear, almost golden liquid. He pushed the bottles across the table to me. "Give your father a tea of the herbs for his, ah…indulgences and the tincture on his chest for his lungs. Now get out of my sight."

I stared at the bottle and the mark against me, and finally got my words back. "Yes, sir." Taking the bottles, I fled. I couldn't quite work out if Mordecai had punished me or gifted me. Had he, another man with a chronic illness, taken pity on my father?

I had no idea, but I wasn't about to argue just in case he decided to give yet another mark against me.

CHAPTER 8
OF MAPS & MONASTERIES

S eb was gone.

I wanted to punch him and hug him. How could he have let himself get caught like that? He had managed to send me a note before he'd had to go. It was simple, but told me enough.

One, not two. Three days with family and a black mark.

That last had me ripping the note to shreds.

He'd gotten caught—which meant it was going to be even harder for us to prove we belonged in the Black Claw squadron. But at least he'd managed not to tell anyone why he was in the commander's rooms. And that first sentence meant the Memory Stone wasn't with Commander Hegarty.

Had he sent it somewhere? Or did Mordecai have the stone and he'd sent Seb away from the academy so he could continue with his plans? But if Mordecai really was working for the Darkening wouldn't he just have killed Seb? Maybe Mordecai worried too much about being found out—realizing that making Seb disappear might cause too much talk, unless Mordecai worked hard to erase Seb's memory. And I knew that it took a lot out of a person to use the Memory Stone.

We still had more questions than answers—and why were we being rushed through the squadron selection process?

The thought had crossed my mind when I started the fight with Beris that Mordecai knew something. It hadn't been Mordecai —who usually broke up any fight—but Hegarty who'd stopped Beris and me. Somehow, Mordecai had seen that Seb was missing and had followed him. And now both Seb and I were in trouble.

Just what we needed.

Letting out a sigh, I stared at the yard. I'd been up since dawn, raking the grounds, then I had to clean the equipment shed as a part of my own punishment for brawling. Beris had gotten stable-cleaning duties.

"You obviously have too much energy, the pair of you, if you can fight in the keep after hours," Commander Hegarty told us. But I was thinking this was a way of keeping us apart.

But it also gave me too much time to think.

Like about the evaluation scores. I groaned and glanced at the boards that stood on the far end of the yard. Was part of the reason I'd been put here so that I'd spend more time thinking about my eventual place in the Dragon Riders?

At the moment Seb, Kalax and I stood as Storm Blues, cursed with a lifetime of guard duty and highway patrol. It wouldn't be nearly enough action, I knew. And today's results weren't up yet, so Seb's mark against us and my punishment might push us into Green Flags. Well, at least Seb would be happy there. If he was happy, I guessed Kalax might be, so I'd have to put up with it.

Signals?

The thought swept over me, shocking me with its strength, knocking me on my butt. I stood, brushing the dust off my riding leathers. That had been Kalax. I'd heard her thoughts, even without Seb here! That was weird. Seb had always formed a bridge between Kalax and I—I'd gotten feelings from her, but I'd never heard her as clear as this.

Bridge? I could feel her amusement—it sat inside my chest almost like my own, but not quite the same. *You too busy to hear, and Kalax not want signals.*

Her scorn for flags and scrolls rose up in me. I knew now that she understood Seb was fascinated by them, and they were useful, but I could feel how silly she thought all these little markings on paper. *Hunt, nest...fight. Swim for fish. Dragons know best.*

She didn't want to be a messenger dragon, and I was glad of that. I don't know if she could sense that from me. The brief, intense connection slipped away as if it had never been there. Was she going to sleep? Talking to Seb? Talking with other dragons?

Why had Kalax decided to share her thoughts with me this morning? Maybe Seb's affinity was rubbing off on me somehow—or maybe it had something to do with my having been healed by one of the stones. I didn't have time to think about it. The Dragon Horns blared. Another day of evaluation was beginning. I dragged the heavy rake behind me and headed for the equipment shed.

Without Seb here, I had no navigator. So no flying for me. But I was a protector—I could always fight. And I would show everyone I was no messenger.

❧

"Well, that was all fairly disastrous," I admitted to Merik and Varla. I dragged myself up the stone steps to the map tower after the day's trials. My arms ached and I'd picked up a dozen new bruises.

"It wasn't that bad. Just wait and see." Varla at least tried to sound optimistic. By the end of the day, Merik and Varla had a solid place in the Green Flag, which Varla wanted. I hadn't managed to move Seb and myself up or down. I'd lost two bouts and won three. I'd also had to ride the dragon simulators.

I hated them. They were like barrels with saddles on and the instructors could move the barrels as if they were dragons. But it wasn't anything like real flight.

Without Seb, the points I could earn were nothing compared to the ones that a full team of riders could make. I was sure we were going to slip down. Seb was gone for another two days. We might even end up in the Heavy Whites, where we'd be stuck hauling tents and supplies for the real fighters.

I felt a shudder of anger from Kalax—she wasn't happy with that idea. I tried to think up some calming thoughts I could send toward her—something about how we'd do better when Seb came back. Or maybe I could tell the instructors that somehow I had managed to develop some of Seb's affinity with dragons—that might impress them.

But if I told them about that, maybe they'd think we were too odd to be riders. Or that we were lying about that just to get ahead. With a sigh, I pushed open the heavy door to the map room. It was better to keep this between Seb, Kalax and me.

Brood never alone.

The powerful thought rumbled through me, making me grip the wooden doorframe.

Varla gave me a nudge. "Thea, are you feeling well?"

"Just tired from a long day, I guess." I slid my gaze away, hoping she wouldn't catch the lie. Sometimes, there was just too much going on to explain everything.

Merik yawned, stretching out his arms. "You're telling me!" Stepping into the map room, he pulled forward one of the high-backed wooden chairs and slump into it. He and Varla had spent all day in the saddle. I just wished that my muscles were aching from flying—that was a good kind of tired.

Kicking the leg of the chair, Varla muttered, "No time for sleeping."

I nodded and sat down across from Merik at the map table. "Varla's right. We need to make new plans. The Memory Stone isn't in the commander's room...so where is it? Does Instructor Mordecai know something about it? And what about the monk?"

"Monk?" Merik frowned and sat up. "What monk?"

Varla sat down, too. "You really are tired. The wandering monk? The story about the Dragon Stone?"

Shaking my head, I looked at the table. All the maps we'd been using were under a layer of other maps. I started trying to sort them, pushing one set of maps aside to get to ours. Pulling out an older map, I recognized a curve of the Leviathan Mountains. Smaller maps were marked with odd symbols, and I didn't know if they were they monasteries or armouries. I wished Seb was here—he was much better at this navigation stuff. "Do you think the commander might have sent the Memory Stone to a monastery?" I glanced up.

Merik was staring at me, his forehead pulled into lines and his eyes big behind his optics. "What, by the First Dragon, are you talking about?"

I glanced at Varla and then back to Merik. Was this a joke? But Merik never could hold in his laughter. And he kept staring at me, his brown eyes tired and confused. "You really didn't know what we're talking about? The order of monks, the very same ones who set up a monastery here?"

Merik's frown deepened. "That was before even Torvald was founded. What's that got to do with the Darkening?"

I bit my lower lip and glanced at Varla. "This is like what had happened to Prince Justin." I looked at Merik again.

Leaning forward, Varla patiently told Merik the same things he had told us just a few days ago—about the stones, how they'd been hidden after the final battle against the Darkening a long time ago, and how Merik had said he'd found a map from the time of the old monasteries.

Nodding, Merik said nothing and Varla glanced at me, her eyes dark with worry. "Do you think…?" She let the words trail off and glanced over her shoulder as if she feared someone might be listening to us.

I nodded. "Everyone knows Merik's the best with maps. If someone took his memory, it was because of the stones."

"Instructor Mordecai knows Seb's friends with Merik," Varla said. "And he caught Seb looking around the commander's rooms."

Knowing we were in for a long night, I let out a breath. "Or maybe someone saw the maps we'd been using here. Let's try to find those old ones that showed the monasteries." I glanced at Merik again—he didn't even seem worried. It was like he didn't know he'd lost some of his memories. "Do you have any idea where the oldest maps are, Merik?"

He sat up. Turning, he pointed to a set of shelves. "They are usually—no, wait." He faced the other direction. "They were filed…I mean left…I mean I think they used to be on the top shelves?" Merik rubbed at his cheek.

It is going to be a very long night, I thought and let out a low growl. *Seb, now I really wish you were here.*

CHAPTER 9
HOME IS WHERE...

The streets of Torvald were wet, the cobbles slick from rain that had come and gone, leaving the air damp and cold. I hurried back to Monger's Lane, more from a desire to get inside to a warm fire rather than wanting to get back home again. I'd gone out to buy a few things for my family—some meat and bread from the market—but I'd gone to the better part of town to get the food. Monger's Lane usually offered stale food and there was only old mutton to be had.

I kept my cloak pulled tight around me, my basket under my arm where it wouldn't tempt any thieves, and my head down. Around me, shopkeepers and traders were shutting up their stalls or locking their doors and packing away the few goods they had to offer in the market just outside Monger's land. They all looked tired and worn. Another day for them was done —another day of not making enough to feed their families here in the poor quarter.

I'd never before noticed the looks of mistrust cast my way. Was I a stranger now—an outsider? Or had the mood here changed while I'd been gone?

Even though Beris and Syl and a few of the others could be mean, I knew I was lucky to be at the academy. I got to do something I was good at—ride a dragon—and I had regular meals, a bed and warm clothes.

It was a different story for those who lived in or near Monger's Lane.

The people here were looking not just at me but at each other with fear, as if they expected trouble. I wondered what Thea would think if she came here— the Flammas probably had no idea how the city-folk had to manage on so little.

Turning a corner, I ran into another man's elbow. The man shoved and I stumbled back, losing my grip on the basket. Margaret had given me some bread, fresh meat and a few pots of last summer's fruits that she had bottled. One of the pots smashed and the bread fell into a rain-soaked gutter. That food was meant to help my family.

Fury flashed through me. I was a Dragon Rider, not some kid to be bullied. The smell of fruit mixed with the smell of dirty and sodden streets left me even angrier.

Looking up, I saw the guild deacon who'd shoved me stop to pick up market taxes from the vendors. My training at the academy had made me bold, so I headed over to him, my mouth tight and my fists bunched.

"How dare you!" I shouted at him.

The guild deacon—a corpulent man wearing a velvet tunic under a heavy, brocade coat—turned to look at me. The man next to him stepped out from the crowd—a guard I realized. He reached to grab me but I slipped past and stood in front of the deacon. "I demand that you pay me reparations. And apologize," I snapped. I reached to my belt, but I wasn't wearing a sword. I'd left it at the academy.

The deacon sneered at me. "They're probably not even yours." He waved a fat hand with a number of gold rings on it. "Get out of my way, boy."

I'd worn my old cloak, but now I threw it back, revealing the tunic and pants of a Dragon Rider. The deacon's eyes widened slightly.

Seb? Hunt?

Kalax's thoughts roared through me. I could almost see her lifting her head and snorting a few wisps of smoke at the entrance to her nest, shifting as she got ready to come to my aid.

"It would teach you some manners if the largest crimson red since the old days flew over here to drag your fat carcass off to Hammal Mountain."

The man's face paled. I heard some muffled laughter and a scuffle behind me, and a man's curse.

Forgetting the deacon and Kalax, I turned and saw youngsters darting out to grab the food I'd spilled. A man in a grey cloak swung away from them. I headed back to grab a jar and meat wrapped in a cloth, and one loaf that hadn't been soaked. The youngsters and the man vanished. I swung around again and saw the guild deacon and his men also fleeing. I could only see their bright cloaks vanishing down the street.

I let out a long breath, and in my head, I felt Kalax relax too. *Seb not hunt?*

No, my friend. Not tonight. Shoulders slumping, I glanced around. What would be the point now in my calling Kalax to scare a few self-important people along with some of the poorest people in Torvald? *Just get some sleep, my beautiful dragon.*

I could tell she'd rather be hunting and flying. But she settled down and the tie to her winked out—she'd fallen asleep.

With a sigh, I headed back to my family. But I kept thinking about what had happened. The man in the grey cloak—the one who had cursed and drawn my attention away from the deacon —I was sure I'd seen him before. He'd had a beard—black but streaked with grey.

Stopping, I turning back, but now I could see only one drunken man and one woman, huddling under the eaves of the market and sharing a little of the soggy bread they'd pulled from the gutter. I shook my head. It couldn't be, but I also kept thinking back to the man who'd been in the Troll's Head—the one who'd seemed to take too great an interest in me. Was it the same fellow?

"Too late to find out now," I mumbled, heading over the narrow bridge that led to Monger's Lane. I strode past the old tavern. The sound of angry, harsh voices spilled out into the lane, making me shiver and remember darker days.

The lane still looked smaller to me than it once had, as did the house I'd once called home. It seemed cramped and small, and nothing like the wide, open air of being on a dragon's back. I was already missing the academy—and Kalax and Thea—so much. And I still had another day before I could go back.

Before I could knock on the door, my step-mother pulled it opened and smiled. "Sebastian, I thought you'd got lost, you were so long." She sighed, putting a hand to the small of her back as she walked ahead of me into the tiny, two-room house. Her hair seemed faded and wispy. She moved a little slower than she once had. But she sat down at her spinning wheel beside the kitchen table to start work again, one eye on a bubbling pot, the other on her work.

She'd taken up piece-work, fixing jackets and mending skirts and spinning yarn from wool. It had helped to pay the rent and make ends meet while Da had been ill and unable to work the smithy. My sister was out this night—she taken up work as a maid in a fine house and only came home on her day off. Now I wished I could somehow make life easier for them—but what could I do other than send them what money I could?

From the other end of the room, out of the light of the fire and a lantern, a shadow coughed and croaked. "Boy?"

"Go to your da, Seb, he's been asking for you," she whispered to me. I don't know why she spoke so softly because he was getting as deaf as a stone.

After putting the food on the table, I went to stand before my da. This gaunt man in the chair—all sinew and knots of muscle that had pounded iron into swords, and me a number of times, was not the man I remembered. He'd been more of a taskmaster to me, expecting me to work faster, harder and carry his work as well when he was too drunk or hung-over to manage. But he'd changed.

He seemed a quiet man now, and smaller. He still looked at me with displeasure in his eyes—but sometimes there seemed maybe just a touch of pride.

I guess that was enough.

"Where were you, boy?" he coughed. His eyes glittered as if he wanted to say more but hadn't the breath for it.

"I was buying some food." I nodded to where my step-mother stood to pull out the little I'd managed to save. Turning back to my da, I asked, "Did you take the medicine?"

My father coughed and winced. "A drop—but that's not what I need. Did you get a bottle, boy? Some of Old Dukes will chase this infernal fever away."

Old Dukes. Even the name of the sharp, bitter-smelling spirit that he'd once loved to guzzle made my stomach heave. "That's not what you need, or what you have." I turned to the table, preparing once again the tincture and potion that seemed to bring ease to the old man.

"Don't want it. I know what I need, boy!"

I ignored him. Once, I'd have flinched at such an outburst, but I'd been through far worse. I'd seen death and war—and I would never again be a boy who could be bullied by a weak, old man. "Here." I pushed the glass to his lips and held it as he swallowed. His face twisted with a look of disgust, but after a moment his features relaxed and he gave satisfied sigh.

From the kitchen table my step-mother called out, "Food will be ready soon."

Da nodded, his eyes closing. "You're a good boy. A good boy." He started to snore.

I returned to the kitchen table and my step-mother set out a bowl of stew. I traded bowls with her, giving her the one with more meat. "You need this more than me. I'll be back at the academy soon enough."

"You are a good boy, Seb." She sat down to the meal. "And remember to thank your instructor for the medicine. The apothecary stopped by while you were out. He said your father might even be able to work again."

I poked at my stew. "Have you and Da talked about—well, what'll happen to the smithy?"

"Oh, Temple's looking after it. You know Temple?"

I did. He was older than me by a few years, a big fellow with arms like tree-trunks. He was also a little simple. Da had once been fond of telling me that Temple was the son he should have had. I was glad enough Temple had the work I'd once hated.

"It's not a lot he makes for us, once we take out his wages, but it pays the rent."

I nodded. Perhaps this was right and how it should be. I'd been a poor blacksmith. My work had been weak and crooked—I'd never had my heart in it. But it still felt painful to realize I didn't belong here anymore. "I'm glad to hear that," I said.

She looked up at me, her eyes bright—almost as if she could sense how strange I felt just being back here. "Sebastian Smith, all I want is for you to do well up there in the academy. You've a good life for yourself. Keep it, and keep doing us proud."

Choked with tears, I stood and wrapped her in my arms.

Another day of helping my step-mother around the house, buying some supplies, such as flower and sugar, and tending to my da's moods, and I was more than ready to return to the academy. My da was getting better, but it seemed that he would never be the same man he'd been. The local apothecary—a thin bird of a man with his mouth pulled down—took me aside to tell me my father might not be long for this world. I thanked him for his time, paying him with my last golden piece.

"Make sure he takes the medicine," I called out as I left. It was a few hours before evening and I wanted to get back to my life. I wanted to know what Thea had been doing, and if Merik and Varla had made any more progress toward finding the Dragon Stone—if it existed. I had an itch at the back of my head, as if we might be running out of time. And I could do more to protect my family from the back of a dragon than I could from Monger's Lane.

Headed back up through the tiers of streets to the academy, I felt as if I was leaving one world for an entirely different one. The walk up had once left my legs shaking and left me gasping for breath. Now I easily strode up the wide, stone steps as if they were nothing, swinging my walking stick along with me. My training had been good for one thing—I was fit.

The light was starting to fade as I passed through the better parts of the city. Here, people glimpsed my leather tunic with its red embroidered symbol for a Dragon Rider, and would give a nod of respect and smiles, as if they couldn't believe someone so thin or so young could be a Dragon Rider. The houses on either side of the streets grew in size, with finely-decorated glass in the windows and iron gates. The streets widened and the stores had fine windows to display fine good. Some houses even flew the banners of a noble family, but I didn't see the Flamma banner.

Heading up the street, my walking staff thumping against the cobbles, I started to hear another echo—like a second staff. Many in the city used walking poles and staffs to help them go up and down the streets and stairs, but this thump seemed a little too regular—it was a steady rhythm behind me. I'd brought my staff because a Dragon Rider always carried a weapon of some kind. But who would be following me? Another rider?

The head of Hammal Mountain rose before me as I approached the last city gate—little more than a watch tower over an open bypass into the mountain path that led to the academy. That same, steady rhythm followed me.

I turned a corner and stopped. The lamplighters were out; setting alight the lanterns that lined this part of the city. The ruddy glow of sunset warmed the street where I'd stopped.

The sound from the other walking stick paused, too. I peered around the corner to see a large man in a tattered grey cloak with a salt and pepper beard, holding a walking staff in one hand.

I leaped from my hiding place to face him and pushed my staff at his chest. "Why are you following me? Who are you?" I took another step toward him, my staff now held ready for a fight.

He looked at me with dark eyes. From what I could see of his face under the hood of the cloak, his skin looked tanned and his teeth gleamed white as he growled at me. "Do you want to be thrown in jail for attacking a harmless, old man?"

"You've been following me. I saw you at The Troll's Head. It's not me who's going to be to be questioned—it's you! Now drop your staff and come with me."

"Hey, what's going on there?" one of the lamplighters called out. He pulled out his guardsman's whistle to alert the city guard.

The man in the grey cloak moved as fast as a dragon and lashed out with his staff, knocking the lamplighter's whistle from his hands. I stepped forward and struck the other man's staff down. He had confirmed what I knew—this was no drunk or tramp. It took training to use a staff like that.

I aimed a blow at him, which he easily knocked out of the way. He darted out of my reach. The man in the grey cloak spun on his heel, his staff whipping around. I raised my staff. He dropped his staff low, aiming for the back of my knees. The wood hit and I fell with a thud of pain. I heard the clatter of booted feet—the man in the grey cloak leaped over me and ran out of the city gates.

One of the lamplighters shouted, "Stop in the name of the king!" I could hear others calling for the guards but I didn't want to be held by them for anything. I'd already had one mark against me, and if word reached Commander Hegarty or Instructor Mordecai that I'd missed my return, things would be even worse.

Scrambling to my feet, I grabbed my staff and ran out of the city gates and up to Hammal Mountain. Heart hammering, I headed into the darkness. The man I'd meant to question had vanished, just like before. I was sure, however, that the city guards would be too lazy to follow me up a narrow path on a dark mountainside.

"Let the dragons eat him," I heard someone shout as I scrabbled up the path.

Eat? No, Seb too scrawny. And Kalax likes fish.

I grinned, hearing Kalax's thoughts. Despite everything, I was relieved to be heading back to her, to Thea, and to the academy.

CHAPTER 10
OF MONASTERIES & MAPS!

The commander was frowning as he stared at Seb. He had stopped right in front of us in the practice yard. My heart was in my throat. Was there going to be yet another mark put against us? What had we done now?

"I hope you've learned your lesson?" the commander said.

"Yes, of course, sir. It won't happen again," Seb said the last words with a little too much force. I wanted to roll my eyes, but I didn't. I could hear the lie in Seb's voice, but the commander didn't seem to.

We were in the practice yard at the crack of dawn, and my feet and hands itched with the desire to get going already. It had been three days since the fight, and since Seb had been caught in the commander's study, and I wanted to be back up in the sky. On the rankings board our names were now almost the lowest in the whole academy. We were Heavy Whites for sure if we didn't shape up.

We'll just have to do better. Seb—like me—at least had enough sense to get himself ready for morning practice early today. We had to show we meant to be great riders.

It was cold this morning, but the sun had only just peeked over the mountains. It felt like it would warm into a clear day with enough of a breeze to make for perfect flying. Seb got back last night when I was still pouring over old maps with Varla.

The commander eyed us both. I'd been the first up, just like always, which always earned me a lot of comments from Beris about how I was like every other Flamma. I could live with that —it was a compliment. Looking from Seb to me, the commander said, "Instructor Mordecai mentioned there was, well…a good reason, Smith, for your action. Your father—how does he?" The commander raised an eyebrow.

Cheeks reddening, Seb glanced down at the ground. "He seems to be on the mend, sir, thanks to Instructor Mordecai."

The commander smoothed his mustache. "Yes, well make sure that you thank him. He does a lot for the academy."

I stared at the commander. Was there a bit of drowsiness or blankness to his eyes as he'd said that? Or was he just tired? Had Mordecai been using the Memory Stone on him too, making the commander believe that Mordecai was loyal and well-meaning? Or did the commander really think Mordecai was a good instructor? I wanted to demand answers, but I couldn't let anyone know that we suspected Mordecai. That wouldn't be safe. Merik hadn't been any help with remembering if he'd seen the Memory Stone or had it used on him, or even who he'd seen of late. So we still didn't know who—or what—had the Memory Stone. It could well be that someone had been able to sneak into the academy—or had gotten to those here while they were in the city.

"Rider Flamma." The commander skewered me with a hard look, and I straightened and fixed my gaze on him. He gave a nod and smoothed his bristling mustache. "I happened to be meeting with your brothers and the king last night at a council meeting. Ryan said you will attend the Winter Ball, and I hope you will show that Dragon Riders have not only fighting skills, but other more refined talents."

My heart sank. I could sense my mother's hand in this. Varla's mother and father just wanted to convince her to come home and be a lady within their house. But I'd had letters from my mother lately where she was starting to hint that the Flamma line must be preserved and my brothers showed no signs of marrying. She wanted grandchildren, I knew, and she was starting to look to me to provide them.

I gave a nod and tried not to show any anger, but I was certain my hot face had paled a little bit. "Thank you, commander," I said.

"Good to have both of you back in the air. Today will be a free-flying day and I advise you both to try and get in as much as you can." The commander's stare once again slid to the side and his eyes blanked, as if his thoughts had somehow slipped away.

"Sir?" Seb asked. Was he going to ask the commander about the Darkening? Or the Memory Stone? I held my breath.

Instead, the commander turned from us and barked out, "Dragon Riders, assemble. Inspection now."

Others had been heading to the keep for breakfast, but now everyone ran over and fell into place, snapping to attention as the commander moved along the line. He once again looked the part of a stern taskmaster—the administrator of the entire academy. Any hint of the friendship we might have shared after the battle for King's Village seemed to be gone as he stalked up and down the line, inspecting boots, tugging at leather jerkins and slapping at sloppy bracers.

"Free flying today," he said. His voice sounded harsher now. "You have an entire day to practice your maneuvers, build up better stamina, and improve communication. The last practice session showed me you still look more like cadets than riders! You have to be able to fight in the saddle, to fly, to move, to talk, to look, to listen. I want you to be so comfortable in your saddles you could eat a twelve course meal up there and not spill a morsel."

"Yes, sir!" Everyone answered him, but I couldn't find the strength to bark my reply as strongly as the others. I slid a quick glance at Seb. His dark eyes looked worried, too. He had to be thinking the same things.

Why was the commander ramping up our practices? Were we preparing for war? Or was something else about to happen?

"Riders to your mounts," the commander shouted. The Dragon Horns blared, signaling the start to another glorious day.

It felt good to be back in the saddle again. In front of me, Seb glanced back over his shoulder—he was positively beaming.

He'd fallen into silence almost as soon as we'd mounted Kalax, not even shouting directions back to me. Usually, his telling me things was annoying, but today I missed it. And I could see that three days without flying and away from the academy had changed him a little bit.

He seemed a little more thoughtful and focused almost entirely on Kalax.

Yes. Good. Kalax, Seb, Thea hunt together! Kalax sent her thoughts to me. In her mind, this was what we should be—one unit, hurling across the skies.

I'd been right about this being a perfect flying day. A chill wind from the Leviathan Mountains made me glad of my flying leathers, but only a few clouds dotted the blue sky and the sun warmed my back. Kalax flapped her wings, huffing breaths of enjoyment. Far below, the land turned a darker brown—harvests had been brought in. The green leaves of the forest trees were starting to turn orange. I wondered how long it would be before frost and snow arrived.

Kalax likes snow cold! I chuckled at her thought.

"You heard that?" Seb glanced over his shoulder at me.

I nodded. Before I could tell him anything about my ever-increasing closeness with Kalax, she decided to take us through our paces. With a trill like a bird, Kalax fell out of the sky, turning in a spin as she did so, heading toward the ground at a frightening speed. She roared her delight, and pulled up, skimming over the treetops. Seb gave a shout and I found myself joining in, his enthusiasm and mine mixed with Kalax's.

After another couple of hours of barrel rolls and sharp turns, sudden drops, dives, and steep climbs, we'd flow far from the academy. Hammal Mountain seemed only a small, dark hump in the horizon. We had also left the other dragons behind. I tapped Seb on the shoulder. Now was the time.

Fumbling inside my small travel pack, I pulled out the scroll I had been working on with Varla last night as we tried to piece together Merik's shattered memory of the monastery locations.

"What's this?" Seb called out.

Kalax glided while I told Seb about Merik's memory loss and about us trying to map out the old monasteries. I waved a hand for us to head southwest. "First one is that way."

I pulled my cloak a little tighter and kept one hand on my bow. I didn't say anything, but it must have been obvious to Seb that with all of these strange losses of memory happening, it didn't seem likely that we were the only ones looking for the Armour Stone.

We found the first set of ruins easily. The old towers stood much taller even than those of the academy. We soared over the foothills near the end of the Leviathan Mountains. The air here seemed cooler with a touch of ice on the ground—winter was on its way. The old monastery looked as if it had once had a large, square tower and walls, but only two of the walls still stood. I could just make out carvings of dragons on the stone.

Seb brought Kalax down to a landing near the tower. She began to sniff for rangy hill-sheep for a snack as I followed Seb into the ruins. Most of the stones had long since tumbled down from the tower, leaving just the foundation. To judge by the cart track, some of the stones had been taken away to be used in building cottages or field walls.

I wondered if some shepherd had found the Armour Stone and took it away. Maybe it was sitting on some rough mantel over a fireplace? My stomach lurched at the idea. Something as powerful as the Armour Stone wouldn't stay long in a peasant hut. Anyone who touched it would have to feel something special about it. I was certain of that.

Dragon eggs grow in those they touch. The sudden thought from Kalax made me stumble. I put a hand out to steady myself on the nearest stone wall.

Seb glanced back at me. "What is it? Did you see something?" He stared at me, his head tipped to the side, and I realized he hadn't heard Kalax's thought.

Kalax, can you shield your thoughts as you wish?

She didn't answer me, but I had a feeling of concentration and focus on the scent of a rabbit. Glancing at Seb, I shook my head. "Fine. Just…well, thirsty and hungry. Want lunch?"

What did Kalax mean? That the stones are like dragon eggs? That they change whoever touches them? Is that me? When Hegarty saved me with the Healing Stone, had that changed me somehow? A wave of darkness rose up in front of me, like night rising up from the ground to swallow me. A sharp, agonizing pain lifted in my side. Had I almost given way to that darkness? Had I been about to give up when the commander healed me?

"Thea!"

Blinking, I looked at Seb. He stood in front of me, one hand on my shoulder. He was staring at me, his brown eyes worried.

Annoyance flashed through me and I shoved his arm away. "I'm fine. I don't need help!"

Seb gave me that same puppy-dog, measured look I'd seen a lot on him over these past few months.

"Come on," I said. "Let's just get this over with so we can get back to the academy."

Pushing past him, I stepped inside the ruined tower. What little of the walls still stood gave a sense of what this tower must have once been like. I could see where a large hearth had been, similar to that of the keep at the academy, and a stone floor. It looked like something was nesting here—maybe foxes—but mostly it was just weathered stones of all shapes and sizes and carvings that had almost disappeared.

Seb stooped to pick up a few odd-shaped stones from the floor. Some were darker than others, a few even looked egg-shaped, but none of them *felt* to me like the Healing Stone had. When I told Seb that, he shrugged and put them in the bags I was carrying.

By the time Kalax finished her lunch, we were all ready to leave. The ruined tower seemed a sad place to me—a place forgotten. I wondered who had lived here and what dreams they had once had. And if the Darkening had destroyed this place.

My thoughts also kept circling around one worrying thought
—*am I different?*

Coming over to me, Seb pulled a meat pie from the bag he'd
brought with him. He handed it to me and said, "You know, I
think someone knows that we're after the Armour Stone."

I nodded and took a bite of the pie. It tasted dry and dusty in
my mouth. "But why not come after us directly? Why Merik
and the prince? Why just a few of their memories?"

Seb leaned his shoulder against the stone wall. "Maybe to help
push us to find it—so they can take the Armour Stone from us?
Or maybe to steal those memories—so someone else has
them."

I shivered and suddenly wasn't hungry. "Come on. There's
another set of ruins not far from here."

We mounted up on Kalax, I fed her the last of my meat pie, and
we flew to ruins that were little more than a circle of tumbled
rocks on a barren hillside. I found a bit of old statuary that
might once have been a foreleg of a dragon or a horse. I picked
up a few rounded bits of stone to add to the collection, my
shoulders sagging and wishing we were done with this search
so we could be working on our skills.

Leaving those ruins, we flew west and found ruins with an
almost intact hall that someone was using to store hay. I
sneezed and found more egg-shaped stones, but none of them
felt special. Turning to Seb, I asked him, "What if we never
find the Armour Stone?"

He shook his head. "Wait till we get these back. We'll clean them up and have a proper look. You know, any one of these might be it."

I spread my hands wide. "How much further could this wandering monk have gone? Miles? What about sailing? For all we know, the stone could be at the bottom of the ocean or in a lake or river." Heat warmed my face. "If we spent more time training instead of running around like this, we might be in a better position to defeat the Darkening when it comes."

Seb opened his mouth, closed it, and said, "What if we have to have all of the Dragon Stones? All of them. You know the stories better than I do. It was only with all the stones that the Dragon Riders were able to fight back the Darkening."

"Stories." I stomped my boots and rubbed my arms. It was getting cold. I turning back to where Kalax was sniffing the air. "We don't even know if they're true." Pushing out a breath, I told him, "We've only a few hours left. And we have one more ruin on the coast."

I heard the crunch of Seb's boots on the ground, and then he muttered, "I've never been to the coast."

I could hear excitement in his voice and wished I could feel some of that too.

With a grunt, I mounted Kalax. Seb climbed into his saddle and she jumped into the sky, flying west toward a hazy glimmer of grey and blue.

Kalax gave a roar as we skimmed over the ocean. Kalax was pretty much flying herself, as Seb looked like he was locked into open-mouthed wonder at the sight of that much water. He hadn't been kidding when he said that he had never seen the coast. I had been here, but never seen the water from this high up—it was like looking at it for the first time.

The Middle Kingdom only had a small patch of access to the shore. North of here, the shore became wilder, broken and mired in the tribal lands. But we had one port and I could see the bay and the bright gold and red banners of the town. Further south and east from here, I knew the shore grew rangier and wild again—as well as hotter, and there the Southern Realm ruled that coast.

Seb pointed to the south and shouted, "The Southern Realm— that's the map I saw on the commander's desk. I think he was looking for dragons!"

I shook my head. Of course there were dragons down there. There were dragons everywhere. I was about to make that point when Seb waved at the far side of the bay, opposite the port. I could see the faint white stones of more ruins. "That must be it!" Seb shouted.

I looked up at the sky. It was well past mid-day. We'd have to make this last stop fast so we could get back and not earn any more marks against us.

Kalax chose a water landing, raising her wings behind us. She settled into the water as smooth as any swan might and soon we stepped up on a rocky beach. The waves soaked my trousers, but I didn't mind. Both the air and the water were warm.

The stones here seemed to be much smaller in size, nowhere near as large as the others we'd seen, but still with dragon carvings cut into the stone. Like all the other sites, this one had egg-shaped stones littered around the ruins, but none of them seemed to be anything but an ordinary stone.

Seb kicked aside dead wood and grit from the inside of the open-roofed chapel, and said, "I was followed again the other night."

I glanced at him. "Followed? Like that night in the Troll's Head? Why didn't you mention this before?" I said sharply.

He shrugged. "I thought he was a drunk at first—but he fought like he knew what he was doing."

I stared at him. "A fight? I can't believe it. You tried to fight him? Do you realize just how much trouble we'd be in if you'd been taken up for brawling?" Seb wasn't the best fighter at the academy, but I had led him through enough drills to know he was no slouch. "Who do you think he was?" I asked.

Seb kicked at another egg-shaped stone. "An agent of Lord Vincent? I don't know. And you're right—we should finish up and get back."

I nodded.

This site was just the same as all of the others—more ruins. If Merik hadn't lost his memory, or if we had more time, I would have liked to have spent the night here. But a cold lump settled in my stomach. This wasn't going to help us. We needed to become better fighters if we were ever going to defeat Lord Vincent and the Darkening.

Seb told me he wanted one last look around the ruins for any hiding places. I shrugged and left him to it. Wandering out of the ruins, I headed down to the small beach, idly picking up stones, rolling them in my hand and skipping them across the incoming tide.

Kalax was splashing in the bay, upending and disappearing with a splash, only to spring up with a pleased trill and a large fish she'd gulp down. I stood up and headed over to what looked like the remains of a carved dragon—it was worn by time and the water. Stones seemed to have been put into the carving. I put a hand on the stone dragon.

My stomach lurched as I thought of everything that was wrong right now. I wasn't going to prove myself as a fighter. The Darkening was rising—and no one seemed to want to think about that. And my family wanted to pretend everything was normal. It seemed like there was nothing that I could do about anything.

My head throbbed with a sharp headache. I put a hand over one of the stones on the carved dragon. This one was worn smooth —it was as round as any egg. Maybe rounder. It left me feeling a little calmer to have something solid under my hand. When I tugged, the stone easily came out of the carved dragon, leaving a hole where it had been used like a scale in the carving. I put the stone with the others in my carry-sack and turned to see Seb heading out of the ruins, his sack rattling with even more stones.

"Any joy?" I asked.

Seb shook his head. He lifted a hand as if he didn't know what to say.

I remembered how the Healing Stone had been blindingly bright as it unleashed waves of power. *Isn't that what we are looking for?* I dusting the sand from my trousers which had dried. Kalax swept from the sea and landed near us.

Pulling open his bag, Seb nodded to the stones he'd found. "I found these three tucked into what looked like a hiding place behind the door. We'll take a look at them later." He headed to Kalax, but she lifted her head and seemed to be looking at me expectantly.

I didn't say anything, but Kalax barked out a small, sharp sound. *What?* I thought back at her. *So I found a rock—just like all of the other useless ones. It'll only get him even more depressed to show him that it's another nothing-stone.* Catching up with Seb, I punched his arm. "Let's get in some maneuvers on the way back, so we can at least honestly report we've done drills."

Kalax trilled a much more excited call. She liked flying and thought most of our talk was boring and useless. I was starting to agree with her as I snapped on my harness, the heavy weight of the stones on my hip.

◐◈◑

"Thea!" Seb's voice pulled me out of staring at the ground. A note of panic in his voice snapped me alert.

We were heading back to the academy and the bulk of Hammal Mountain and the terraced city of Torvald were clearly visible. "What is it?" I scanned the horizon for the dark, sinuous shapes of attacking raider-dragons. Had Seb seen the wild, black dragons of the Darkening?

He pointed ahead of us and shouted, "Look at the flags."

I was no navigator, but that splash of orange, yellow and gold meant watchful readiness. "Those are the same colours they use for patrols," I said.

"And for important visits. Announcements. Something's happening," Seb called back. Leaning forward, he urged Kalax into ever greater speed.

I clenched my back teeth in frustration. Something important was happening and we might have missed it. "What is it? Is it Erufon? A royal visit?" I asked with my voice tight.

"I don't think so," Seb called out. "No Dragon Horns. But there is something odd going on."

Kalax's thought bust into my mind. *Dragons gone.* I could tell she'd thought the words at both of us, sharing with us the fact that the air smelled of much less dragon scent than usual, as if half of them had vanished.

"Kalax, you clever girl, you're right. Look, Thea—we're the only dragons in the sky," Seb shouted.

For Torvald and Hammal Mountain, the home of the dragons and the Dragon Riders, it was unheard of to only have one team of riders in the sky. There was no storm coming in, no strong winds or hail or snow. Just—no dragons.

At least we have the best choice of landing platforms, I thought, trying to not think about why dragons wouldn't be here. Had they been called to war?

Kalax trilled a high, shrieking call. A few calls came back from the academy and then more from the enclosure. Seb's shoulders visibly relaxed ahead of me. And I let out a breath. There were still some dragons around, then.

"It's just the squadrons," I said.

Kalax bellowed again, flapping her huge wings as she chose the largest platform for landing. I was the first to unhitch myself and hit the wooden boards of the platform. Seb dismounted and started to unharness Kalax.

I saw Commander Hegarty, so I ran down from the landing platform and asked, "Sir, where is everyone?"

He looked distracted, as if he had half a dozen other things on his mind. He waited for Seb to join us before he nodded and said, "We've had orders from Prince Justin to mobilize for a special training mission." The commander's stare slid away, and it felt to me as if he was holding something back.

Why don't you trust us? I almost blurted out the words, but a gentle nudge on the side of my boot stopped me. I glanced at Seb and he frowned and lifted his eyebrows high. I sucked in a breath, held my words and looked back at the commander.

He shook his head quickly, briefly, before staring at nothing again. Was that the Memory Stone working on him? His words even seemed a little vague. "Didn't want to leave the academy entirely defenseless. You two, Jensen and Will, Varla and Merik and the support staff will keep an eye on things."

"But, sir, you know we're some of the best riders. If you run into any trouble out there, you're going to need us."

"Flamma," the commander's tone sharpened. "We will not 'run into any trouble' as you so eloquently put it. This is training. The fact that you are good riders—despite your current rankings—means the academy is in good hands, understood?" He looked at me with one eyebrow arched.

I could only nod. I still felt stupid and useless. How were we supposed to prove our worth by staring at an empty building?

Seb straightened as if he'd been put in charge of the whole city. "The academy will be safe in our hands, Commander, you can be sure of that."

"Never doubted it, Smith. Now—there is one other thing. There's a little cabin out in Tabbit's Hollow, you know the place?" the commander asked.

"Is that the wood on the far side of Hammal Mountain?" Seb asked.

"A little bit beyond, but yes. From the sky, it's shaped like a leaping hare. I also want you to keep an eye on that place at night while I'm away." He smoothed his mustache.

Seb glanced at me. I could see he was as confused by this order as I was. Why would the commander want a cabin watched? And why not assign soldiers to this? The guards could do better at this than we could. "Uh, do you mean we—?"

"You have your orders. I'm already late to meet with the prince. Just see who comes and goes and what happens. Don't get too close, and report back only to me, understood?" He nodded our dismissal.

Before we could answer, Commander Hegarty was already striding away from us. I turned to Seb. "What do you think that was all about?" I watched the ramrod-straight back of the commander disappear into the armoury.

"I think that was the commander telling us that he can't tell us what's going on, so he gave us a clue." Seb faced me and dropped his voice. "This cabin—and who or what goes in and out, I bet it has something to do with Lord Vincent or the Darkening."

Or maybe the Memory Stone.

I nodded and followed Seb to the equipment shed to put away our saddles. It would be a small group in the keep tonight for dinner, I knew. I thought about how—with almost everyone gone—we might be able to sneak into the commander's rooms again. But if one search hadn't turned up the Memory Stone, a second one seemed even less likely to give us any answers. And Instructor Mordecai wouldn't be flying out with the others —he would still be here, watching us.

The Dragon Horns blew to announce the end of day—and the evening meal in the keep. Before we headed there, I glanced at the ranking board—our names were at the bottom of the Green Flags list.

Shoulders slumping, now I knew why the commander had told us to stay here.

But were the others really going off on a training mission—or something far more dangerous?

CHAPTER 11
THE CABIN IN THE WOODS

T*hea sick.*

Kalax thought the words at me and I nodded and yawned.

It was just before nightfall on the following day and it was my job to check the outer gates. The last day had been spent like this, with those of us left at the academy trying to cover all the tasks. I turned and waved to Jensen that the gates were locked. His lantern bobbed that he received the message. I walked on, my boots crunching on gravel, and headed to the next gate.

Kalax was right. There was something wrong with Thea. I'd come to believe that dragons had a sophisticated interior language—different means came from slight variations in emphasis in the feelings sent out and the images that could be sent. Kalax had used the idea of sick, but to me it felt more like Kalax meant somewhere between sad, unwell and pre-occupied. For a dragon, anything that left them feeling even a little worried was the same being unwell.

Do you think it was the Healing Stone? I asked Kalax, not sure if she could even make that sort of complex judgment.

Dragon eggs hatch in those that are near them.

The thought seemed to me like she was quoting from something. Did dragons even have literature? Did they mind-talk epic poems to each other?

No. Kalax coughed a spurt of heat and smoke. I wasn't sure if she meant the idea of dragon poetry, but then she thought, *Thea sick because Thea died.*

She didn't, I thought quickly, fear clutching at my heart. I could still see Thea's pale face, her bluing lips and her open but unseeing eyes. However, I knew now that the Healing Stone could not bring someone back from the dead—the person had to be alive and the injury had to be recent.

Kalax huffed a scornful thought that annoyed me.

They're not even real dragon eggs, Kalax! They're crystals or something that just look like a dragon egg.

All of a sudden, the full force of her mind pressed against mine —for a brief moment I knew what it felt like to be on the receiving end of Kalax's humour. Her mind sparkled with savage mirth. *What does a boy know about eggs?*

The connection vanished, leaving me wondering just what Kalax knew that she wasn't—or couldn't—tell me. And how could that help Thea—could I even do that?

I'd been wanting to talk to Thea, but with all the extra work we had at the academy, there hadn't been much time. But we were supposed to head over to the cabin tonight on our first spying mission.

It was already well past dinnertime and almost everyone had gone to bed. It had seemed to me the day had been spent working and waiting for a messenger and trying to keep up with all the tasks that needed doing—stacking and checking equipment, feeding dragons in the enclosure, making sure the flag systems were all working, sweeping, cleaning, and caring for the ponies and even helping unload supplies from the ponies.

At the back of the academy I waited for Thea beside the last unlocked door, which was the one that opened out to a path that led into the mountains beyond. I heard the jingle of a dragon saddle and harness before I saw her. She appeared out of the gloom and pushed back the hood of her cloak to grin. "Feels good to be doing something that isn't sweeping," she said, and I agreed.

I nodded and left the lantern hanging beside the door. We headed out to where I knew Kalax was waiting for us. "Why do you think it's so important to the commander that we watch a cabin, of all things? Do you think the Memory Stone could be there?" she asked.

"Why would anyone put the Memory Stone in a cabin? When Lord Vincent had it before, he kept it with him."

Thea nodded. "On a silver chain," she muttered. I could tell she was remembering how she'd cut that chain.

Glancing at her, I asked, "What's wrong, Thea?"

"I just—Seb, what if this is just a way for the commander to keep us out of the way and not even give us time to look for the Armour Stone? I'm…I'm scared, Seb, that…that we're just useless. That we can't help anyone."

In the darkness, I couldn't see her face, but I knew how much it cost her to admit to this. "You think they'll send you back to court?" I asked. She didn't answer. We kept heading up the hill to the meadow where Kalax waited. I had to say something to cheer her up. "The commander wouldn't have asked us to do anything that wasn't important."

"We'll see," Thea said, sounding glum.

A shadow loomed up in front of us, blocking the stars. Kalax snuffed out a warm greeting breath. I could tell she wanted us to hurry, so we threw on our saddles, and Kalax launched us into the cold, night air.

Tabbit's Hollow was little more than an oddly-shaped curve of woods in the far foothills of Hammal Mountain. There weren't many settlements, but a few deer and sheep tracks crossed the meadows. This was a little too close to the dragon enclosure for many herders to feel comfortable with leaving their sheep on the hillside. Only a few hunters lived up here, and those who didn't mind the company of dragons every now and again.

The cabin was set almost in the center of Tabbit's Hollow. The land was wooded with a fast-flowing mountain stream that splashed nearby. Kalax landed at the edge of the wood and I left her eyeing river fish with strict instructions only to make noise if she sensed any danger approaching. Ahead of me, Thea crept into the woods. We used only the light of the moon to guide us. I stepped on a twig—it broke with a loud crunch.

"They're sure to hear us if you keep that up," Thea hissed at me. She waved for me to follow her tracks, but it seemed like all I could hear was my boots on the crisp ground and my loud breathing.

At last, Thea ducked behind a fallen log and waved for me to do the same. Whispering, she said, "There's a light." She pointed to where one of the shuttered windows of the tiny cabin had a gleam of orange around the edges. "Candles. Not lanterns," Thea said. "They're trying to go unnoticed."

We waited, watching the cabin. The night chilled. The screech owls woke and gave a few hoots. The sound of scurrying animals in the forest answered—smaller creatures getting out of the way of the owls. My feet and legs started to feel like blocks of ice. The light remained the same, and no one came or went. I could tell Kalax was still alert, happily enjoying the night air.

"Well?" Thea hissed. "Is anything going to happen?" She shifted and started to stand.

Grabbing the edge of her cloak, I pulled her down. "The commander told us to keep our distance."

"He told us to keep an eye on things…that means investigate. It means knowing, at least, what we're supposed to be looking for."

"Thea, we're supposed to watch." For now, at least, she sat back down.

Two hours later, she said, "I can't stand this. What is the point of just sitting around?" She turned to me. "You have to let me get closer so maybe I can hear something."

"No—Thea." My throat tightened. "No, if anyone is going to go, it should be me."

"What?" She turned to look at me.

"Well, I'm...I'm bigger." I was glad it was dark and Thea couldn't see how red my face had to be.

She gave a muffled snort. "Seb, I'm the better fighter. What— do you think I can't handle myself in a stupid cabin?" I could hear she was starting to be annoyed, and knew that I would have to tell her something or her own sense of pride would force her to break into that cabin.

"It's because I don't want to see you hurt!" I pushed out the words with a fast breath.

"Hurt?" Thea sounded like she couldn't understand anything I said. "But Seb, we're Dragon Riders. We go into danger. It's what we do."

"I...I saw you wounded, Thea. I don't want to go through that again."

"Oh, Seb." Reaching out, she put her hand on my arm.

For a long moment, we just sat there, not saying anything. In the end, it was Thea who broke the silence, and she sounded as embarrassed as I felt. "If it makes any difference, I...I didn't know." She let out a sigh. "I've found it...difficult, too."

"It's okay. You don't have to say anything."

"Well, you still have to let me do the things that I have to do." She gave a dry snort of laughter. "You sound more like my mother now. She wants me to go to this Winter Ball, and I know she's going to try and make a match for me—thinking that'll be better than me wanting to be a Dragon Rider."

A mix of happy, hot and angry emotions bubbled inside me, churning like molten metal. I was happy that Thea was still so fiercely herself—but I hated knowing she'd be dancing with a bunch of other nobles and back in a world where I didn't belong.

I didn't like the idea, but I didn't want to think about it.

We took turns sleeping and watching, and at dawn we headed back to find Kalax lightly dozing and waiting for us. But I had the feeling not much of anything had been settled.

The next day was long and I was barely managing to get through it without wanting to burn down the academy. That night I headed back to the cabin with Thea. She insisted we creep just a little closer, and since we didn't see anyone there, we did. But we didn't hear anything, either. We took turns sleeping and watching, and this time I'd come ready with thick blankets. It also seemed as though something had changed between us, and in a good way. Thea complained about the waiting, but she seemed more relaxed—as if telling me what she was worried about had helped her face it. I felt like that, too—it was good that she knew how I felt.

By the third day, I was exhausted. I wanted the commander back just so I could stay in bed at night. Over porridge in the morning, I asked Merik, "Any news?"

I hadn't seen much of Merik. He'd been re-cataloguing the maps, and he blinked at me like his brain was still whirling with all of the map symbols and signals. "News?" he asked and blinked again.

Hoping that it was from long day like the rest of us had been putting in and not any more exposure to the Memory Stone, I told him, "From the commander? The prince?"

"Oh, I thought you meant the signals news," he said.

I kicked myself. Up in the map tower, he'd be able to see all the message flags and banners across Torvald.

Merik pushed his porridge around in the bowl. "No, no flags or messenger dragons from the squadrons. But the signals show we've doubled guards on Southgate—some travelers were attacked by bandits."

"Bandits? This close to the citadel?" I stared at Merik, my face cold and my hands icy.

"Yeah, up from the south. It doesn't seem like good news down there."

I thought back to the fierce men we had fought just a short time ago. They had been from the south. And that was where the commander was trying to map. "What do you think is going on?"

Merik pushed away his bowl and picked up a hunk of bread. "To be honest, the south was always more than a little lawless —sometimes they keep up diplomatic and trade ties with us, other times, they're more like a bunch of bandits. I think it's due to them having a lot of different dukedoms—they mostly keep busy warring with each other. But now we're seeing more pirate attacks and bandits across the border."

"You think rule and law has broken down?"

Merik shrugged. "Or…someone has them all organized and looking to us. Everyone knows the Southern Realm has a lot of dragons, but not as big as the ones we have." He leaned closer. "If I was the Darkening, I'd look there to gather new soldiers and strength."

Letting out a breath, I clenched a fist. Then another thought hit me. "Is that where the prince and the commander went? A stealth attack on the Southern Realm?"

Merik pulled back and shook his head. "Don't even think about it. Do you know what would happen to you if you and Thea took Kalax, unauthorized, and just flew off south? And what if you're wrong and you start a war?"

"What? It's not like we're not riders and can't fly when we want or need to."

"Yeah, but you can't leave me and Varla here with just Jensen and Wil to run the whole academy. What if Erufon decides to pick a fight with Gorgax again in the enclosure?"

I winced. He had a point. The older dragon wasn't settling in and kept picking battles with Gorgax, one of the largest blues.

"No one else has your gift with dragons," Merik said. "Just wait until the commander gets back, and then you'll know exactly what he did."

I groaned, but I couldn't let my friends down or get them into trouble. We had to work together if we were going to have a chance of succeeding. Besides, I needed to think about keeping an eye on the cabin tonight. I really was too busy to be able to fly anywhere. I stood and patted his shoulder. "Okay, Merik. Not yet. I'll just hit my bunk for a bit."

"Ugh, I wish I could do the same. But too much to do." Merik stood and we both walked out of the keep, each heading our different ways.

The bell that woke me wasn't the heavy, sonorous call of the Dragon Horns. It seemed a shrill clanking. I rolled off of my bunk and headed to the window. The practice grounds below looked deserted and the gathering purple in the sky told me it was nearing dark. I could hear distant groans of dragons, and that bell.

I'd tumbled into bed fully dressed, so I grabbed the large, iron ring filled with the master keys for the academy and followed the noise through the corridors, across the practice yard and up the stairs to one of the watchtowers. Opening the door, I pulled it back and walked into a complicated array of strings, bells and pulleys. Staring at them I wondered if I should go get Merik. But only one bell was ringing. I found a tiny brass plaque underneath the bell that had the words: *Northern Slopes 2.*

Where had I seen that designation before?

Then I remembered the maps of Hammal Mountain.

Most of the largest features were named, such as Tabbit's Hollow or the Ridgeway, but there were still areas which were just given codes like northern slope or southwestern reach. But what did the bell mean? We were being attacked?

From the enclosure, Kalax snuffed the air and I could tell she had picked up on my rising worry.

I didn't know if I should sound the Dragon Horns. But what if it was just a wild dragon that had somehow tripped the wires out there to ring the bell? I didn't know, but a dragon could find out. As everyone knew, dragons had an excellent sense of smell. They knew different people from different dragons and other animals, and even could tell what the person was wearing and where they had been. I glanced out the window to the enclosure and thought, *Can you fly out to—*

Yes! Kalax hunt! I glimpsed her red scales as she sprang into the air over the enclosure. She circled once and then headed to the north.

I waited nervously by the bell, wondering what was about to happen, what I was going to hear. The bell had stopped ringing.

Kalax kept the connection between us open as she soared into the dark sky. I caught some of her feelings—a ripple of enthusiasm, joy for the flight, the feel of wind on her face and under her wings. Her size seemed to become mine. I stretched out my arms like they were wings.

On the far northern side of the mountain, the smell of snow carried to me on the breeze. It seemed as if I could smell everything—the cooling earth, the smell of the animals below. And I could hear them too. Hearts pounding, little feet skittering as they saw my shadow blot out the stars and moon. I could have gasped. The experience was so much fuller than anything I could have imagined. I'd never known dragons were so sensitive. I could feel the tiniest breeze, and could sense when it was shifting. My leathery wings caught the smallest vibration from the land and sky. Even the clouds smelled differently—most were clean and wet, but some carried a hint of forest leaves or the salt of the ocean.

The smell of a thousand fires from the city wound into the sky and I could smell cobbles and meals and unwashed clothes. It almost made me gag, until another, fainter scent caught at my mind—a hint of sand and incense.

The south—you can smell the Southern Realm?

When the wind blows right. Kalax was proud and almost purring in my mind. *Now you know what flying is really like, little one.*

Yes, now I knew, and I was amazed.

Kalax turned her attention to the ground below, scanning it for movement, picking out the wet-lanolin smell of huddled sheep, then the scent of a small herd of deer, their hearts pounding as they hid under some trees, and the disgruntled, annoyed yap of a dog-fox who didn't like his prey being scared off. Kalax swept lower. She was showing off, I knew, showing me what she was really capable of.

I am tired of practice. I can fight better than any other.

I didn't doubt it, but I thought back at her that the training wasn't just for her—it was for me and Thea. Kalax gave a snort of laughter, and then I caught something, through our link—the scent of a human. The person carried dirt on him as if he'd spent a long time tramping through the woods, and something else—a collection of strange scents like herbs and flowers. Where had I smelled those before?

Kalax circled over the spot where the figure was—she could see far better than I could in the dark. *He's going to the place where we go at night. Want me to stop him?*

He's going to the cabin? No...don't stop him, I added quickly.

Clearly frustrated, Kalax thought back at me how easily she could capture people with her claws. She sent me an image that was more like a memory—one of her picking up Thea and then me.

I gasped with the thought of being able to share not just the senses and thoughts of a dragon, but a dragon's memories! Was this what the affinity with dragons really could do?

Kalax told me she was flying away from the man who smelled of forests and herbs so he wouldn't see her. But she also sent me an image of the man's face—one I recognized. It was the bearded man whom I'd confronted in Torvald.

You want me to hunt this man? Kalax wheeled in the air.

No, just see that he does go to the cabin. Then we'll go there together.

Yes. You, me and Thea hunt together! Kalax broke the connection and I slumped against the stone wall, feeling small and clumsy now. If I closed my eyes, I could almost remember the feel of wings growing out of my shoulders and the hint of the hot, southern trade winds to the sky.

Kalax sent a quick thought at me as sharp as a dart. *He goes to cabin. They smell the same.*

I straightened. To be honest I was almost grateful not to share more with Kalax right now. The dragon's senses had left me a little confused, as if I wasn't Sebastian at all, but Kalax. I shook my head and rubbed my cheeks. Then I hurried out. Thea was going to be waiting for me at the back gate and I still needed to get my gear.

CHAPTER 12
THEA STORMS IN

S eb was late. I stood in the darkness by the rear gate, my kit already on my shoulder. Tonight I was going to bring some snacks as well as another blanket. I still wondered if Commander Hegarty had used this assignment to keep us busy —but maybe it was better than hunting up rocks that weren't the Armour Stone. I was also angry that neither of my brothers had trusted me enough to tell me where they were going. Ryan and Reynalt were about as important as anyone could be, and they still acted like I was their kid sister who tagged after them.

I shuffled my feet and wished I had put on my thicker breeches. There was a frost to the air tonight, and this afternoon I'd even seen a flurry of snow. But it was clear now and I had no intention of missing out on anything that might happen tonight. I also had no intention of opening the large box my mother sent me.

I knew what it held. I had opened the note from her and read that she was sending me a selection of gowns for the ball. I was to choose two—one for the formal meal and one for dancing. She'd written that it was only two nights until the Winter Ball—much that I cared—and had underlined that part several times.

I was tempted to write back a note that I would wear the academy dress uniform. But I knew that wouldn't work. Once she saw me dressed as a Dragon Rider, she'd just nag me until I changed.

"May the First Dragon strike me down if I ever, ever wear anything flouncy," I whispered to the skies. I also wasn't sure if I even remembered how to dance. I knew a two-blade fighting stance, and how to move with a staff, but the Jokozan or the Twimble Three-Step were only distant memories for me. I'd learned them when I was six, and that seemed almost another lifetime ago. Visions of me falling over in ridiculous, high-heeled shoes encrusted with diamonds left me shuddering. I didn't like that Mother seemed to be putting so much effort into one ball—as if my future hung on this one event. Was she like everyone else—worried about me? That I'd die again?

A voice from behind startled me and I turned fast.

"Hey," Seb said, stepping from the darkness, his saddle slung over his shoulder. He grinned at me. "You would not believe what just happened. It was amazing! Although a little bit uncomfortable. But amazing!"

"Do I want to hear this? Was it a spectacularly good apple pie tonight?" I asked. We headed out, latching the gate behind us. Seb, I knew, would have a key that would get us back in again.

Seb ignored my attitude and rushed to tell me how Kalax had shared not just thoughts, but all her sensations of flying and even memories with him. I nodded, but I couldn't help but feel a little left out, as if Kalax liked Seb better than she liked me. I pushed the idea away and asked, "So you think this is the same man who has been following you?" We climbed up the mountain path to where Kalax sat waiting for us, her eyes bright even in the dim starlight.

Seb started to harness Kalax. "He has to be. But he doesn't know that we're watching him. He just thinks that he's watching us. And then there was the smell on him. Well, the smell that Kalax picked up and then I smelled it, but I didn't realize what it had reminded me at the time."

"What?" I asked. I had my saddle in place and mounted Kalax. She leaped from the ground with a powerful thrust. The cold air hit my face.

Seb turned to me. "Instructor Mordecai's laboratory," he said. "When he made me that medicine."

I gave another shiver, and not just for the cold.

We quickly reached Tabbit's Hollow and I could feel Kalax's desire to hunt up this man and have battle. My heart answered with a fast jump and I smiled.

But Seb coaxed Kalax into a landing and told her, "No. We have to wait and watch, like last time."

Kalax cocked her head sideways to look at me, I nodded. I knew she could sense what I was thinking about doing and she approved. I turned to find our path back through the overgrown and crowded woods between us and the answers we were seeking.

"Hey, Thea, wait." Seb followed behind me, crashing through the brambles. "We're supposed to be quiet. Slow down."

In just a few more minutes, I saw the dark shape of the log cabin ahead. One window was framed with a faint, orange glow. I glanced at Seb and then settled my kit behind the fallen log where we'd kept watch on the other nights.

"Thea?" Seb said his voice soft, but also thick with worry.

I faced him. "Seb, this guy attacked you. He's been following you. And while you might be content to keep waiting, I'm not." I hopped over the log and reached for my sword.

"Thea, the commander said—"

"The commander's been saying a lot of things that don't always make sense. I'm not going to wait for this man to catch you alone again." Turning, I headed for the cabin at a fast, soft run.

I didn't tell Seb what else I was thinking—that if we managed to get some answers out of this man, we might also earn our way into the Black Claws.

Bounding up onto the wooden steps outside, I kicked open the door. I could hear Seb behind me, his sword hissing as he pulled it out, and Kalax took flight, heading to the cabin to help us.

The door sprang backwards with a crash to reveal a long, narrow room crowded with shelves. A small candle lay on a worktable, and in a chair sat a large man with a pepper-and-black beard and a graying cloak, a book open in front of him.

"Stop where you are, old man," I shouted, leveling my sword at him. He put one hand in the air, and his face twisted. I thought I'd frightened him, but then I realized he was making an 'I have been frozen' face like a travelling actor might do at one of the summer festivals. "Stop that."

Kalax's roar rattled the cabin's shutters.

"No, Kalax, pull back," Seb shouted.

The old man straightened and smoothed his cloak. "Make up your mind. Stop? Go? No? What?" He stood, moved to one of the wooden barrels at the back of the cabin and started to uncork it.

I stepped closer. "Leave that alone."

The man glanced at me. "Your dragon is hungry, isn't she? Of course she is. Dragons are always hungry." He popped open the barrel and the smell of salted lake fish wafted up, making my stomach growl even though I'd had dinner. That seemed a long time ago now, and I loved salted lake fish.

Fish? I heard Kalax's thoughts. She landed nearby, branches cracking and breaking under her. Seb stepped up to my side, holding his sword out to match mine. "I feed my dragon, not you. Now…don't you recognize me?"

The man laughed as if we were children he'd known for years. "A dragon will feed itself, with or without its rider's consent!" He pulled out a large fish, took a chunk and popped it into his mouth. "See, it is fine. I wouldn't poison myself, would I?"

I'll judge if food is bad. Kalax's nose pushed into the doorway and she huffed out a long, hot breath.

"There's a well-spirited one!" The man laughed. "I bet she's a beautiful flier, too."

Seb's eyes narrowed, but I could see the blush of pride on his cheeks. "The best."

"I'm sure she is." He threw the salted fish to Kalax. Even within the narrow doorway, she managed to catch the fish and gulp it down.

She pulled back and announced, *Fish good.*

"And yes, young Sebastian, the smith's son, I know you. Just as I know you, Lady Agathea Flamma." The man wiped his hands on a cloth and smoothed his beard, before nodding at Seb and bowing deeply to me. "My brother told me to expect you two."

I glanced at Seb and back to the man. Seb's sword tip dropped, but I kept mine up. "What do you mean your brother?"

The man smoothed his beard. "I am very sorry for any harm I may have caused you the other night Sebastian, but I couldn't afford to be caught by the city watch. Those dullards would have kept me from important work. The whole game would be ruined!"

"Game? You think this is a game?" I waved my sword in front of him. "We came for answers."

"And you shall have some." He sat down again at the work-table and waved to an unlit fireplace where a group of rickety stools sat. "My name is Jodreth and Commander Hegarty is my younger brother."

Staring at him, I could see some resemblance. Both men had clear, grey eyes, and both shared a similar muscular build. But this man seemed taller. I also knew it was easy enough to claim blood ties. "Why hasn't he told anyone about you?"

Jodreth laughed. "Well, we had different fathers, which is why he is so short. But we shared the same mother." He looked at Seb. "We grew up in similar circumstances to you, young man, as it happens. But take a seat and we'll get down to business. We must be done before dawn touches the horizon."

"Done with what?" I kept my sword up. I still didn't feel we should trust this man.

He nodded and smiled. "My brother told me to expect you—he knew the academy was being watched, and he did not trust talking to you directly. We do not want to put you in danger of the Memory Stone being used against you—and that will happen if someone on the other side finds out I am here."

His words sent a chill through me, and my sword wavered.

Seb put a hand on my shoulder. "Thea, I think he's telling the truth—Kalax at least seems to believe that he is. She just told me this man smells like the commander."

I lowered my sword, but I told Jodreth, "Someone already used the Memory Stone. On a friend of ours—and we suspect on the prince as well."

Jodreth's shoulders slumped. "It's worse than we knew then. For not only has the Memory Stone been stolen, it's in the hands of our enemies again."

CHAPTER 13
THE THREE KINGDOMS

It took a lot more persuasion from me and from Jodreth before Thea would sit down and listen to the rest of what Jodreth had to tell us. She didn't trust him, but I was going to go with Kalax who'd told me she liked the smell of the man. And his fish.

We sat by the cold hearth. Jodreth offered us wine, but Thea refused any food or drink, so I copied her and just sat and listened.

"My brother is, as you must know, a stickler for the rules. Once he had the Memory Stone, he knew he could not keep it. He was charged already with care of the Healing Stone, and as he must have told you, it is dangerous to keep the stones too together, for it is such a temptation to use their power. But the king demanded the Memory Stone to be brought to the palace," Jodreth said.

"And the commander agreed?" I grimaced.

Thea shrugged. "Well, they'd have guards and vaults."

"That is not what protects any Dragon Egg Stone—it takes courage and a man who will die for what is right to offer real protection." Jodreth stroked his grey-streaked beard, and the gesture reminded me of Commander Hegarty. Shaking his head, Jodreth said, "The only safe place for any Dragon Egg Stone is near dragons, and with people who know what is at stake."

Eyes narrowing, Thea straightening her back on the small stool. She didn't appear to be about to attack the man, but she still had her naked blade sitting across her knees which added tension to the room. "Are you trying to tell us the king himself stole the Memory Stone? I would remind you, that the Dragon Riders serve the king."

Jodreth shook his head. "Spoken like a true, loyal Flamma. No, what I am saying is that the Memory Stone is missing from the king's vaults." He stopped to pierce Thea with a sharp stare. "Did you not say you have seen evidence of its use?"

Thea frowned, but she nodded and rested her hands on her sword blade.

"And that is not all," Jodreth said. "Have you not been feeling it? You've been touched by the Healing Stone. It's said that those who have been touched will feel them, like a pain or a sickness that can't be explained."

Thea nodded.

I swore under my breath. "Why didn't you tell me that?" I asked her. "Is that what's been wrong all this time? The Healing Stone did something to you, and now—"

"I used to feel queasy around the commander at the academy, and then it stopped. I thought...I don't know what I thought. Yes, maybe it was something to do with being healed, but I thought it was something that went away." Thea gave me back my stare.

Jodreth whistled through his teeth. "The stones are very, very powerful. Not even the ancients understood them. The Draconis Order was set up in order to try and understand the stones and the dragons and how they all fit together."

"The Draconis Order?" I asked, looking at Jodreth. "We've never come across any mention of that."

He smiled, showing that one of his back teeth was missing, and pulled a leather cord from under his cloak. Next to me, Thea gasped. I could only stare. A golden circle, a little smaller than the palm of my hand, hung from the leather cord. On it, a stylized serpent curved around the edges, looking smoothed by decades of use that rubbed it down to little more than a golden zigzag on a hoop. For all its simple craftsmanship, there was something about the lines and curves of the wings, body and neck that perfectly captured the idea of a dragon.

And I had seen such a carved dragon before—at the monastery ruins.

"I am the last monk of the Draconis Order and I was initiated by my mother when I was barely older than you are now," Jodreth said.

Looking up at him, I met the steady stare of his grey eyes. "That's the same order of monks that built the academy and who started to catch and tame dragons centuries ago."

Who can catch what doesn't want to be caught? Kalax's loud voice resounded in my mind and I blushed. Thea hid a smile. I thought I saw an answering shadow of a smile from Jodreth, too. Could he also hear dragons?

"Not capture. Study. Get to know. Placate, more often than not." Jodreth's smile widened. "To be honest, much of what the Draconis Order did is a mystery even to me. We fell from grace a long time ago, after the first rise of the Darkening."

Wetting my lips, I nodded. "We…we've heard some of the old stories."

He let out a breath and leaned forward. "But not all the old stories. Ignorance can be a shield sometimes, but you two have special gifts that may be our salvation in these dark times."

I leaned forward too, and braced my elbows on my thighs. "Is that why the commander has kept us at arm's length and not let us into what's going on? To keep us from becoming targets?"

Thea shook her head. "But what about Prince Justin? And why have all the squadrons been taken out? Is that really just a training exercise?"

Jodreth's eyes glittered. He shook his head. "That troubles me as well. Neither I nor my brother knows the truth there. The prince seems to be affected by the Memory Stone—but who is using it on him and why?"

I nodded. "You think someone is controlling him with the Memory Stone—stealing some of his memories and giving him new ones?"

Thea straightened. "No."

"We can only hope not, for all of our sakes," Jodreth said. "But…a few months back, the Deep Wood vanished—just like with King's Village. No one even remembers where it was or what happened to it."

I nodded. "That's exactly like the Darkening. We know Lord Vincent is still free. And he knows how to use the Memory Stone."

Jodreth sat back and his chair creaked. "That is why you are here, and why my brother knew you wouldn't be able to resist storming in. We needed a way to arrange a meeting without arranging anything. I am here to tell you what I know of the Darkening from what I know of my order. To forewarn you and forearm you."

Thea shook her head. "We know this already."

"And do you know that before the dawn of recorded history but after the birth of the known world, there lived a powerful king and queen. In those days, the lands would have seemed strange to us, and the king of that time did many great things. He tamed the frost giants of the Leviathan Mountains…he even created the many islands to the far south and raised the land and broke it where it had to be broken."

Thea swapped a glance with me. My stomach growled. Jodreth smiled and stood to fetch us all fish—Kalax included. As we sat eating our salted fish, Jodreth began to talk again, his voice low and melodic.

"The people of the known world looked up to this ancient king and his queen. They loved and feared them in equal measure, as it should be with mighty rulers. The king had the best of advisers—monks who befriended the dragons of the mountains and forged an alliance with the great beasts. It was said that the people even grew a little more dragon-like, and dragons grew more like humans. Dragons took to speaking with humans, sharing with them their thoughts and their lives, and that the people became a little wilder."

Thea shifted on her chair, but I held still, almost able to see these old times.

"In time, the king and queen had children. Three strong boys. The eldest was a tall man with fair hair. The youngest had brown hair and a quick way about him. The middle had hair black as night and skin pale as moonlight. As the princes grew, the middle child was ever stuck between the other two. He was never able to ride out to battle or to treat with the frost giants like his older brother, but he was also never allowed to be care-free and without responsibilities like the youngest. And that caused problems."

Jodreth paused to clear his throat. The candle was nearly guttered. It flickered and Jodreth pulled it closer to him. "The middle child grew bitter. His words and deeds took on a sharp edge. It was later said that some evil star must have been rising when he'd been born and some of its pale, chill light must have tainted him. In time, when the brothers were old enough to think of becoming rulers, they started to quarrel. The king, now old, feared for his kingdom. To keep the world at peace, the king decided to split his realm into three kingdoms."

"The three realms," I said the words softly.

Without looking at me or nodding, Jodreth kept talking. "One to the north where the snows and deep forests hid rich mines.

The south reaches of hot sands, beaches and islands held food and treasures from the sea. But the Middle Kingdom—made of lush meadows, lakes and streams and pleasant woods—went to the eldest brother. The middle brother took the north and the youngest the southern lands with trade winds and adventure. And the king took his queen with him to live the rest of their days in an unknown, but finely-built palace, a place kept secret by magic. Their reign had come to an end, and now it was up to their three sons to govern the known lands."

Nudging me with her elbow, Thea rolled her eyes. I straightened and sat back. She might have heard some of these stories growing up, but I never had. Truth was, Jodreth's voice held me still where I sat.

"Peace should have held forever if not for one thing. The queen, in truth, came from the old line. She had magic strong in her blood. Some say she was descended from the first dragon and that was why she created the Draconis Order. It was her magic that allowed her husband to grow so powerful and it was her magic that she passed to one of her sons. But not to all of them. The eldest son and the youngest had nothing of the old ways in them, but the middle son had the greed that sometimes takes hold of a dragon."

Sucking in a breath, I thought to Kalax and asked her if she had ever heard of such a thing. She gave huffed a smoky breath and said, *Erufon has such.* I remembered then how Erufon kept picking fights—the old dragon was too used to having everything and wanted everything to be that way again. A dragon's greed could be awful.

Jodreth's voice pulled me back to his story. "The queen tried to school her favorite son in the ways of magic and the ways of dragons, but she could not see past a mother's love to the darkness growing within him. He learned spells and how to talk to dragons. He also learned how to bend others to his will."

"The Memory Stone," Thea whispered.

Jodreth went on as if he hadn't heard her. "The years rolled by and the middle son grew jealous of his eldest brother's richer lands. The lands of the north had rich mines, but also deep snows and cold mountains. He had to trade for food and treat with giants, goblins and storm-wolves—but his brother didn't have such trouble. He began to think that since he was the one who took after their powerful mother, he should also rule the Middle Kingdom." Jodreth pushed out a breath. "You can imagine what decision the older brother arrived at. And if he had decided to wage a war of soldiers and knights, stallions and chariots and even dragons, our fate today might be different. The battles would have been terrible, but they would have ended. However, the queen had gifted to each of her sons something that changed the fate of the world. She had given each brother one of her most prized possessions—the Dragon Egg Stones."

I sucked in a breath. *Is this true? Are the stones this old?*

As if Jodreth could read my mind, he said, "Who knows if she found them or made them with her magic. Or if they did indeed come from a dragon's power, perhaps from the first dragon itself. These three stones had been the secret to her husband's long and successful reign. To the oldest brother, she gave the Armour Stone, jet black and making its wielder impervious to harm. To the middle brother, she gifted the Memory Stone so he would forever remember his love for her and hers for him. To the youngest, the one who was always trying to keep the other brothers from fighting, she gave the Healing Stone, for he had a natural gift as well. But when the queen finally died, the middle brother never got over her loss. He used his Memory Stone to try and peel back the veils of the world, to try to snatch his mother from the chains of death. It was there in those dark places that he found—or perhaps it found him—the Darkening."

Thea and I swapped a look. We'd never heard this part of the story, I wondered how much of it was true. But it sounded…it almost sounded as if Jodreth had been there, even though that was impossible.

He went on, his voice dropping even lower. "That brother used one of the Dragon Egg Stones for dark purposes, crossing boundaries that should never be crossed. He perverted his own magic to do this and came back changed. When he went to war, he did so not just with his mortal armies—with lords who had joined his strength—but with the blackness of the Darkening. He used the Memory Stone to convince generals and whole armies to change sides or to forget who they were fighting. He became stronger and stronger. The youngest brother of the south cared not who ruled, and so he gave up and left his brothers to fight. The middle brother drove his older brother and his dwindling army with only a few dragons back into the mountains. But the monks who had once advised the king came to the older brother and told him the secret they had kept. There was a counter-magic that could be used—the old king had kept the one Dragon King Stone, the one that could unify all of the powers of all of the stones—and it had been buried with him."

I sat up, my heart racing. This was what we'd needed—well, almost. But at least it was true that the Dragon Stone really existed. Unless…unless this was just a story. I glanced at Thea, but she was leaning forward, her eyes glazed as if she couldn't look away from Jodreth.

He started to talk again and I looked back at him, too. "The elder brother found his father's hidden palace and the hidden location of his father's tomb. He found the Dragon King Stone. With it, and the Healing Stone and the Armour Stone from his brother of the south, the eldest was able to defeat and take the Memory Stone from his middle brother. But he could not bring himself to kill his brother, and so he banished him forever from the lands. Or so he thought. The north was left to become a lawless place of wild dragons and wild men. The Southern Realm no longer had a strong king, and so the lords divided the land between themselves. But the eldest brother allowed the monks who had helped him to found the academy and then city of Torvald grew strong. But over the years, the eldest brother became afraid—both of what had happened and of the Dragon Egg Stones. He feared the stones had too much power. He also feared the monks knew this and might one day take him from the throne. And so he banned the Draconis Order and the monasteries became ruins. He hid the Dragon Egg Stones, and soon even the stories were forgotten. The old magic weakened in the veins of the people, and now the only thing that has survived is the friendship between dragons and humans here at Hammal Mountain."

Sitting back, Jodreth blew out a breath as if he had run a very long way and was tired. He shook his head. "But the Darkening, our old foe, is patient. And was never really defeated. The middle brother, in exile, twisted himself with long years of darkness and with whatever he had called into the world. He and the Darkening became one and the same, a hideous mix of magic and man, undead and undying. It took a great power to banish him, but it will take even more to bring about his ultimate defeat."

Jodreth fixed his stare on Thea. "It used to be said the Dragon Egg Stones changed people—those that felt their use, and those that lived near them, became attuned to the old magic. It was even said the Dragon Affinity—the special connection that some have—is a touch of the old magic that links dragons, humans and stones. Whoever has been touched by the stones, they are now the only ones who can rise to the challenge and use their gifts to defeat the Darkening. Fate has decreed that the tale of the three brothers must be told once again." He looked from me to Thea. "But this time, it will be told through the lives of Sebastian Smith, Lady Agathea and Kalax."

I yawned and blinked as if I'd just woken from a deep sleep. Images were still swirling in my mind—the clash of swords, the flights of dragons overhead, the sulking features of the pale, middle brother with the black hair and heart. Sitting up, I rubbed my eyes. I was still in the cabin. The candle had died and the room was so dark I could barely see.

"Seb?" I heard Thea's voice and her sword glinted as she stood and held it in front of her. She pointed her sword at the empty chair.

Jodreth was gone.

Kalax? I reached out with my mind and felt her warm presence. She lay curled around the cabin. *Kalax, where did Jodreth go?*

No one left.

I got more than a hint of defiance. She was annoyed that I'd question her ability to stand watch. I told Thea that Kalax hadn't seen him go. She frowned and shook her head. "Come on, dawn can't be far off. And I don't like this one bit. I hope that really was a story we needed to hear, and not a crazy old guy spinning some tale that won't help us one bit."

CHAPTER 14
THE WINTER BALL

At the rear gate to the academy I told Seb, "We have to see the king."

He let out a breath, and I couldn't blame him.

To be honest, I didn't really know what to make of the story Jodreth told us. How could it be real? Did that mean Lord Vincent was the Darkening—and he was the middle prince? Had he been alive for thousands of years? Was that even possible? It would certainly explain why he knew how to use the Memory Stone better than anyone—and how it was he had survived our last encounter. But...but how did you defeat someone who is magical? One way or another, the king needed to know his son had had the Memory Stone used on him, and that the stone was no longer safe and under guard.

I couldn't help but think that if Commander Hegarty had used so much planning and secrecy to arrange for us to meet his brother, that meant he suspected spies of the Darkening were at the academy. Or was it all lies? But Jodreth sounded sincere—and I could feel that Kalax had accepted him. That had to count for something.

My thoughts spun like clouds under a hard wind as we flew back through the dawn to land on the slopes behind the enclosure. The sky was already grey and some of the owls who'd been hunting were joined by the first blackbirds to be awake this morning. Hammal Mountain was waking up with bright, wintry light, the heather and gorse flowers turning the rocky hillside colourful as the day dawned.

But I was worried, and not just about Lord Vincent, or that ancient prince, or whoever he was and Jodreth.

The Dragon Stones change you.

Why should I—who'd had the fortune and misfortune to be healed—be changed forever by that stupid Healing Stone? Already it seemed I had a much better connection with Kalax —nowhere near as good as Seb, but I shouldn't have the Dragon Affinity at all. I'd never had it before. *Is this what the stone did to me? Would it do more?* Maybe it would even turn me to the Darkening the way Lord Vincent had been turned. It could be a connection that left me bitter and angry, too. Maybe that was why they used to gather those touched by the stone together—because they were a danger.

I glanced at Seb as he rubbed between Kalax's horns. She butted her nose into me, as if to tell me not to worry. But the story we'd heard had only made the whole situation seem a lot worse than I already thought it was.

Heading into the academy and carrying our saddles and harnesses, I told Seb, "We not only have to find the other Dragon Egg Stones, we have to defeat an ancient evil that wasn't defeated before. Is that even possible?"

He nodded and let out a breath. "At least we know where the Healing Stone is."

I shook my head. "It's the Memory Stone we have to worry about. I'm supposed to go to the Winter Ball. It's in two nights. I can at least warn the king."

Seb shook his head. "I should go with you. If all this is true, the palace isn't a safe place for anyone."

"Neither is the academy," I said.

Stepping into the equipment shed, I threw my saddle on a rack and then stepped out again. The sky behind us had turned yellow with the warming day and the clouds were streaked pink. "You're a Dragon Rider, Seb, but you're not a noble. I'm sorry, but I don't see any way of getting you into the ball." His face hardened. I felt like I'd just hit him with a staff. I punched his arm lightly, trying to show him we were still friends no matter what. "Besides, if the commander gets back, you need to be here and see if he's okay. And find some way to let him know we met with his brother without letting anyone else know."

He nodded, but he still had that hard look in his eyes and his mouth pulled down tight. He lifted one shoulder. "I guess you're right. Too much to do here."

"Quite right, you have too much to do, Smith." We both turned to see Instructor Mordecai step from the shadows on the far side of the equipment shed. How much had he overheard? I straightened and so did Seb. Mordecai looked from me to Seb. "So you two thought you would sneak off, is that it?" he snapped. He jabbed one bony finger at the air in front of us. He wore a mixture of riding leathers, a jerkin and a dirty woolen cloak. His boots were still spattered with mud and his face look pale. I was surprised to see that it looked like he'd been travelling since it didn't seem as if he ever went anywhere.

"We were speaking of the Winter Ball." I waved a hand. "My mother sent me dresses and I can't decide what to wear. I was asking Seb if he thought if the commander would mind if I wore my Dragon Rider uniform."

He shook his head and squinted at me and then at Seb. "A likely story." He jabbed a finger at Seb. "Dresses is it, Smith?"

Seb nodded his face blank. "I like blue."

Mordecai gave a snort. "And where were you last night?"

Seb swallowed hard, but he straightened and answered right away. "Checking the—uh—northern slope. An alarm went off yesterday, but there was just an old drunk wandering the woods."

Mordecai glanced at me and back to Seb. "As I say—lucky. No sense in punishing just one of you if I can't do both, and Flamma here has a ball to attend. And not in a Dragon Rider's uniform."

Anger flashed—hot and itching. "We weren't breaking any rules," I said coldly.

Mordecai took a step back and sighed. "Let me be the judge of that. But enough for now. Go see about your morning meal."

I turned, but Seb didn't move and he said, "Sir, can I ask, do you know where the commander and the squadrons are? Are they on their way back?"

Mordecai rubbed a hand over his eyes, and I would swear he almost looked worried. Was he that good an actor? Or was he, too, under the influence of the Memory Stone. I realized we wouldn't be able to trust anyone. Putting down his hand, he frowned at Seb. "Can't you see I'm tired, boy? And that's none of your business! Now, I'm certain you have duties—or do I need to give you additional work?"

He turned, one hand on his staff, and headed back toward his rooms. I let out a breath. We'd gotten off lightly—but I wouldn't have minded being told I didn't have to go to the ball. It wasn't going to be fun, trying to speak to the king and trying to deal with my mother at the same time. However, if Mordecai did have the Memory Stone and he was working for the Darkening, why hadn't he tried to use it on us to find out where we'd been?

꧁꧂

"Ow!" I flinched and glared at Varla. She'd poked for the second time with one of her pins.

She looked up at me. "You get what you pay for, and I'm not the best seamstress."

We were standing in our room and Varla was fitting one of the dresses my mother sent me. It was a deep blue that changed to a darker colour where the hem met the floor. I kept telling myself I hadn't picked it because Seb had said he liked blue but because it made my eyes seem even bluer. It wasn't—thankfully—flouncy. For a second dress, Varla picked out a shorter blue gown with glimmering sparkles that fell to just above my knees. The dress seemed too big on me now—I was a fit Dragon Rider, not the girl who'd come here as a cadet—which was why Varla was trying to pin it so it fit.

I yawned and pulled at the dress. I'd managed a short nap after Seb and I ate in the keep, but it wasn't enough to make up for staying awake last night. Rubbing my eyes, I stared at my reflection.

Am I different? Changed? It looked like it right now. I'd pulled my hair up and it seemed more gold than red these days. My face looked older—narrower, I thought. And in this dress... well, I didn't know who I was in this dress. I wanted my leathers on again and my boots and...and not to have to go to this ball. But I had to think of my duty to the king. I had no intention of batting my eyelashes at anyone, but I did need to be at this ball. It was the best way of seeing the king without letting anyone know why I must talk with him.

Smoothing the front of the dress, I said, "You're doing great, Varla. It doesn't have to be perfect."

The dress was designed for grand entrances. We'd already lost a handful of pearlescent sequins from the other dress and I knew I'd have to sweep them up later or get an earful from Matron for that.

"Who's going to be there?" Varla asked. "And breathe in." She pulled the lacing at the back a fraction tighter as I sucked in my stomach. At least the dress now felt more like a tight-fitted battle harness. I started to wonder if I could wear my sword strapped to my thigh under the dress—or a knife at least. I asked Varla about that.

She sat up and raising a questioning eyebrow. "Excuse me? You want a weapon to fight off anyone who wants a dance?"

I shrugged—the dress didn't really let me do that since the sleeves and straps seemed designed to hold me at attention. "I expect the king will be there with his mistress of the moment."

"Thea!" Varla stood and put her hands on her hips. "That's no way to speak of His Majesty."

"But it's true. Since his queen died, he's been flirting with one lady and then another—all of them widows. I think Lady Milice is the favorite at the moment or maybe Lady Regina. I forget who it was my mother mentioned in her last letter. I think she's jealous because she still has a husband to hold her back and they don't."

Varla tried to not snigger too much.

Heading over to my riding clothes, I pulled my knife and sheath from the belt. My stockings were tied up with garters above my knee and that would have to do to hold a knife. Or I could slip it up my sleeve—they were tight enough to hold anything.

I slipped the knife into place in my left sleeve. Turning to look at myself in the mirror, I decided the dress was good enough. And the knife was well hidden. "There won't be any Dragon Riders there, but Lord Westerforth will no doubt attend with his sons, Tomas and Terence."

Wrinkling her nose, Varla shook her head. "Mother had the Westerforths over once. He was a horrible goat of a man, and his sons are going the same way. You'll notice no dragon would have them. Do you think Lord Franbury will attend?"

Giving up on shrugging, I waved a hand. "Who keeps track of them all?"

"My mother," Varla said. She sounded glum. "She knows all the guild families, the nobles, the lesser nobles, even the clock master. But she thinks balls like this are a waste of money."

"She's not wrong."

"Well, you're still a lady," Varla said. "Go and have a night of fun."

I turned and parted my lips. I wanted to tell Varla some of the story, but I kept thinking how the Memory Stone had already been used on Merik. If I told Varla anything, I might be putting her in danger and I couldn't do that.

A knock on the door interrupted us and Varla stepped back, rolling her eyes and muttering, "Matron."

Matron swept in, thin and dressed like always in a severe black gown. She glanced at me. "In the name of all, Flamma!" Matron shook her head. "You look a candied sweet. What an insult to the flag of the academy, running off to dance and sip wine, no doubt!"

"Matron, it is at the king's request that I attend." I smoothed the front of the dress. I felt more like a noble Flamma than a rider right now.

"Yes, well," Matron muttered. "I have never seen the like in all my days. I came to tell you there is a fancy carriage outside the gates with a footman dressed up like a fool asking for you."

"I'm on my way now." I grabbed a velvet cloak and swept past her. "Please don't wait up."

"Well, of all the cheek." I heard her say. Next to me, and holding my second dress, Varla giggled. We clattered down the stairs, her boots making a reassuring thudding noise next to the dancing slippers I had to wear. *What I wouldn't give to be wearing flying boots right now.*

It was almost dark as we crossed the practice yard to the front gate. Jensen lounged by the gate, his arms crossed and grinning. Somehow, he had managed to duck out of attending the ball, probably by convincing his parents that he was needed here more than he was at the palace. Either that or they had other sons and so they didn't mind what he did.

That made me think of the three prince brothers, and I shivered.

Jensen straightened and bowed. "You look a delight, Agathea."

I shoved an elbow into his stomach. "Shut it, Jensen. I could still beat you in any bout with staffs, even wearing this ridiculous dress."

He laughed. "At least I would see you coming. And hear you, the way that thing rustles. Give my regards to Lord Westerforth and his sons, will you." He winked. He knew—as did everyone at court—that no one really liked Lord Westerforth or his sniveling sons.

Varla pushed my second dress into my arms and asked, "No Seb to see you off?"

I turned, half-expecting to see him racing over, late as usual. But I didn't see any sign of him. I wondered if I'd hurt his feelings by being so blunt that he couldn't attend the ball. *It's not like I had a choice.* I wanted to kick the ground, but that would hurt in these slippers, so I just slapped Varla's arm. "I'll tell you all about it when I get back," I promised.

She gave me a wave and headed for the keep with Jensen. I turned to stare at the carriage my mother had sent to take me to the palace. It was pulled by two white horses. Ribbons fluttered in their manes and tails. The carriage itself was small, shaped like an egg, with doors on the side and glass windows and gilt.

I groaned and my face heated. The thing looked designed to show off wealth, and the Flamma banner fluttered from the top. Everyone was going to go back to thinking I was nothing but another noble, spoilt Flamma.

A man wearing a white wig with delicate ringlets, a deep red jacket with golden buttons and a pair of tight, black leggings— the sort that mother always preferred on men, thinking it showed style—stepped down from the carriage.

Matron was right—he looked a fancy fool.

"Francis," I said, recognizing our footman. He looked little older around the eyes with a few more wrinkles, but he had served our household all my life. I had never seen him express more emotion than a twitch of a corner of a mouth or a slightly raised eyebrow. He opened the door for me and offered a hand to help me up. I didn't need the help and jumped inside.

As I was settling my other dress on the seat opposite me, Francis gave a nod and with a fraction of a smile said, "Glad to have you back in the fold, my lady." He shut the door with a click.

To me, it sounded like the clang of a prison gate.

I'll say this for my mother—she gave everything of herself to the causes she believed in, even if the cause was just keeping up appearances. My carriage joined a small line of other carriages heading toward the palace which had been built a little above Torvald.

The city was built on concentric, raised terraces and layers, but the palace sat enclosed within its own pale, stone walls and gardens. Beyond it, fine orchards and then woods led up to Hammal Mountain. It was a landscape I knew well, but it had been a long time since I'd been to the many-spired palace. Even I felt a little awed by its size and elegance.

The palace was actually made up of a lot of outer walls and several buildings, each one fitting a different purpose. I'd been in the coop-like round building that was the Royal Library and the cathedral-like spire of the Royal Astronomer's tower, but I had no idea what the other ten buildings were. Thin bridges connected one tower and building to another. Along the walls, the palace guards lived in smaller houses. But the main structure was an older castle of blocky stone, with buttresses jutting out, towers soaring high and pennants flapping.

Tonight flaming torches lit the road to the palace and huge braziers burned beside the entrance. I knew the main hall led to stairs that went up to a ballroom in the center of the castle. My brothers and I had once played on those stairs, running up and down and hiding behind the tapestries in the ballroom.

The carriage wheels crunched on the fine gravel between outer gate and the inner castle and then stopped. I stepped out without waiting for Francis and I saw my mother sweeping down the white, stone steps toward me.

She wore a deep red dress, our house colour, beaded with obsidian and malachite so that it almost seemed as if she wore dragon scales. Around the neck, gold wire glittered in the light of the flames. Her sleeves were long and exploded into tongues of orange and yellow.

Ignoring the other lords, ladies and guests as they disembarked their own carriages, she called out, "My child, Agathea."

Face hot, I accepted her clasping my hands. "Mother, it's not as if I've been held captive in a dungeon for months."

Her mouth pulled down. She looked as she always had—beautiful and perfect. Her blue eyes pale and flashing, and her skin even more pale. She wore her hair up in an arrangement of curls that must have taken hours. Either that or it was a wig. She touched a finger to my cheek. "You didn't wait for Francis to help you down. Do you want others to think you an ill-mannered Wildman?"

"Mother," I managed to say from between clenched teeth. "It's obvious I'm no man, and I am a Dragon Rider."

She waved away that idea. "The long dress looks perfect on you. Just what I wished you to choose. What about the short one? When you dance, we want to show off your legs."

I decided right there I wasn't changing dresses. I tried to cross my arms, but the dress wouldn't let me. "Who has time to change?" I asked.

"Oh my child, the king will think we've become penniless. I'll send Francis for it."

Linking my arm through hers, I started to pull her up the steps with me. "No, mother, you won't. No one at the academy has time for this and I have to get back to help, too. So let us enjoy the evening that we have, and you can tell everyone I'm setting a new fashion."

Her eyes brightened. "Yes...yes. Now that you are a Dragon Rider, the Flamma household has a new-found minimalism and courageous attitude toward money and dresses. Just one dress for us. I won't change either," she whispered. She nodded to the servants at the main doors and gave them our names, then turned to me. "Now, Agathea, I have some news."

"From Ryan and Reynalt?" I asked, my pulse quickening.

"What? Why would I need to know about any events in the provinces? No, the last news was quite dreadful about King's Village and I wish to hear no more. This is about Lord Wester-forth. He wishes you to dance with his eldest, Terence. There's no match there for you, but I will ask you to at least show some manners."

I sighed. "You want me to flirt and smile like I haven't a brain?"

My mother waved her hand. "Don't be dim, Agathea. It doesn't suit you."

The doormen nodded to the crier, who blew a small silver horn and announced, "Lady Flamma and Lady Agathea."

My mother, with a grip as strong as a dragon's claw, pulled me into the stiff faces of Torvald society. I could hear music from stringed instruments—something staid and polite being played, nothing you'd ever hear in any inn. People bowed or nodded at Mother and me, we bowed or nodded back. Leaning closer, she told me, "King Durance himself may request a dance with you and I will not have you disgrace our house with poor manners." She managed to talk without disturbing the beaming smile on her face.

"And?" I asked, as my mother led me deeper into the ballroom. Vivid colours swirled around me and the room seemed hot with the candles burning overhead in heavy chandeliers.

Her smile widened. "The wishes of a king and a prince trump those of a mere lord. Do your best to charm the king, then perhaps you can give Westerforth no more than a smile and your regrets."

My stomach seemed to hollow. I put my hand over it. "Are you matchmaking with me and the prince?"

She patted my hand and turned to a lord with very short black hair and a fine, black brocade jacket. "Lord Franbury, what a pleasant surprise. Did you bring your darling daughter, Yolanda? Oh yes, there she is. I quite mistook her for someone else. Such a little thing." She smiled and swept past the startled Lord Franbury. I glanced back to see Yolanda burst into tears.

"Mother," I whispered. "There was no need for that."

"Yes, dear, there was. You'll understand one day when you have your own daughter. Now let us go and meet some of the better people."

Letting her drag me around the ballroom, I started to look for the king. He was the only person I wanted to speak with tonight. Looking for the king, I wondered if any of the lords or ladies here really were working for the Darkening. When I'd been a girl, the palace had seemed almost magical to me, a world of gold and silver and jewels. Now I kept seeing shadowed corners and what looked like a lot of silly people who didn't want to know about the dangers outside these walls. And maybe even inside. The windows along one wall of the ballroom gleamed with the reflected glow of the chandeliers and the people moving about. *Is everyone here loyal? Or have some decided the Darkening will win and so sided with Lord Vincent? Or are some even under the control of the Memory Stone?* Lord Vincent had been able to control entire villages—managing a few lords and ladies would be easy.

Uneasy, I kept looking around. The floor was marble and tiled and a circular higher level, larger than the practice yard at the academy, stood empty. The king and his choice of lady would dance there. Everyone else would dance on the next level down.

A thought from Kalax suddenly intruded. *Mates want to see how you fly.*

I choked back a laugh that had my mother glancing back at me with a frown. But I had to agree with Kalax—I'd want to see any potential mate up in the air on the back of dragon. Kalax had no use for fancy clothes, but she liked the gold and jewels she picked up from my mind.

"Are you quite well?" my mother said.

I smiled and nodded. "I'm fine. Just a little tired—and hungry." I headed toward one of the small tables set out on the side of the ballroom with food and goblets of wine.

"One glass, Agathea. Remember a lady has a bird-like appetite and the grace of a swan. And bring me a goblet while I bid Lady Gertrude good evening." She turned to a large woman in a blue gown and a heavy white wig.

Breathing out a breath—my ribs were aching from this dress—I headed to the table and loaded a plate with meat and pastries. I downed a goblet of wine and picked up one for my mother. Turning, I found a large a man with a thin, yellowing beard and errant tufts of grey hair behind his ears. His coat was decorated with medals.

He smiled at me. "Ah, Agathea Flamma."

I stiffened. I was about to ask just who he thought he was to address me as if I was one of his family when I noticed the two young men lurking behind him, both of them skinny and looking like the sneaks they were.

"Lord Westerforth," I said and managed a nod.

My mother bustled between us, took the plate from my fingers and made it disappear somehow, whisked away the goblet and gave everyone a cool, disapproving smile. "Westerforth. Please. No woman likes to be accosted on her return to court."

He put a hand on his chest, but he also took a step back. "My sons and I were only eager to welcome her." Westerforth bowed more deeply to my mother, and then waved his sons forward. "Terence and Tomas, make your bows."

They did so, the oldest, Terence, was a year younger than I, five inches shorter with wispy blond hair and sharp, sulky features. He looked as if he hated being here, but he swept into a perfect bow and extending his hand to me. I glanced at my mother and she was already staring at me, willing me to behave.

Trapped, I briefly touched his hand with mine and turned to his brother.

Tomas looked round as a ball—round face, round body, and he had to be at least three years younger than his brother. He kept peering over my shoulder at the food and I almost wanted to grab his hand and pull him with me so we could both eat. The food smelled wonderful and I hadn't had time to stop at the keep for even a crust of bread, the plate I was holding was almost too much to resist and I almost laughed out loud when I saw Tomas finally notice what I was holding.

"Tomas," Lord Westerforth said with a low growl.

Ducking his head as if he expected a swat, Tomas bowed. He looked thoroughly miserable and I started to feel sorry for him. It couldn't be easy living with his father, or that weasel brother of his, and it'd be even worse since everyone pretty much knew to avoid the whole family.

"Lovely to see you and now we really must attend to the king." My mother began to sweep me away.

"Ah, but he's not yet—" The blare of a horn cut off his words and stopped the music and all other talk. The wide doors at the far end of the ballroom swung open and the crystal-clear tones of the crier called, "Lords and ladies, King Durance."

Everyone turned, Mother swept us away from the Westerforths, propelling us both into the king's path where we made our bows.

King Durance looked so much like his son—with high cheekbones and piercing blue eyes—that there could be no mistaking them as anything but father and son. I remembered him from years ago when he'd been lean and graceful—very much like Prince Justin. His figure had thickened and he moved with just a slight hesitation, as if he had to be careful of not jarring old injuries. He wore a short cloak of midnight blue over a high-collared jacket of deep gold, with black leggings and soft, black boots.

As he saw me, his eyes seemed to brighten. "Ah, Lady Agathea. You've grown into a fine, young woman," he said, his voice low and hoarse, and just a touch vague.

"Your Majesty." I bowed again.

King Durance turned to my mother. "Esmerelda, would it be possible for me to steal your daughter away from you for just a moment. On behalf of my son, I wish to claim the first dance with her." He smiled at her and then at me.

Even though I was certain this was exactly what my mother wanted, the reality of the king wishing to stand in for his son here still seemed to overwhelm her.

She gasped and managed to say, "I am certain Agathea would be delighted."

What I was, was someone who suddenly felt stupid and clumsy. With all the eyes of the court now on me—and most everyone scowling—I wished I had an excuse to leave. But I'd come here to talk to the king and I wouldn't have a better chance than in a dance. Besides, I'd had dancing lessons. A very long time ago.

King Durance raised a white-gloved hand and took my fingers in the gentlest of grips. The musicians struck up the chords of a new dance, and the king led me across the dance floor and helped me up the step to the reserved, royal circle.

My heart was pounding harder than it had when Kalax had chosen me as her rider. Oh, I'd met the king any number of times, but somehow I needed to tell him his kingdom was in grave danger, the Memory Stone had been stolen from him, and there might be a traitor right here in the palace. Somehow I had to get him to believe all that.

He took my other hand and said, "Do not worry, my dear. I am not so bad a dancer as they say!"

I realized I must look pale and shaken, but it wasn't because I was worried I'd forgotten all of the steps. I was worried about bigger things.

With a flourish of his hand, he guided me into the steps. He moved stiffly, but he was a skilled dancer. I followed the steps, starting to remember the lessons that had been the fate of every Flamma child—Ryan and Reynalt had hated dancing. We turned once around the circle, and I kept wondering how I could bring up the subject of the Memory Stone. Should I just blurt it out?

We had to turn again, and the king took my hand and said, "I only regret it is I and not my son here to be dancing with you."

Well, that was an opening. "Yes, I understand Prince Justin is...out on a special training mission. The last time I saw him...well, he seemed to have forgotten a few things."

The movements of the dance made us turn and step apart. I started to chew on the inside of my lower lip. I was sweating now and I wondered if this really was the best place to talk to the king. What if he didn't believe me?

King Durance stepped back and took my hands again, his face smiling and bland. I glanced around—I couldn't ask the king to leave the dance floor without everyone seeing us. I could see everyone was watching, even if they were pretending to dance.

I saw my mother beaming proudly, Lady Gertrude next to Mother with her face set in stern, judging lines. For a wild moment, I wondered if I was going to be pushed into marrying Prince Justin. The prince was...well, he was handsome and he seemed nice, but I wasn't sure anyone would let a princess or a queen remain a Dragon Rider. Of course, in the past, princesses had been Dragon Riders.

Turning back to face the king, I pulled in a breath. "Your Majesty, there are things wrong in the kingdom you must know about."

He gave a vague nod. "Yes, but not at this very instant."

The faces whirled around me as King Durance spun me around. Was something wrong here? My stomach lurched and my head started to pound. I could see the king was smiling—probably enjoying the proof that he wasn't so old yet. I glanced around us, trying to find a way to be private with the king. My head was pounding even harder now, and then I saw him.

For the briefest of moments he stood out from the others, a tall, thin man with pale skin, long dark hair held back with a strand of silver such as the kings of old might wear, a thin beard and dressed in black. I'd never forget that narrow face, or those eyes, which seemed to be more like a dragon's eyes than a human's.

Lord Vincent—the man who'd almost killed me.

I stumbled. The king caught me and I heard a ripple of whispers rush through the room.

"I'm…sorry, Your Majesty," I said, looking at my shoes on the floor. I had embarrassed him, and my mother would be furious. The king stopped dancing so the music stopped as well.

The king bowed to me. "The fault was all mine. I led too fast." I wondered if he meant it, and when I looked into his eyes I saw only kindness. "However, I am sure my son is a much better, and safer, dancer than I."

The smile I gave him back felt stiff and false. My headache faded, but my stomach was knotted and I could feel the sweat cooling on my skin.

How do I tell him I've just seen his sworn enemy here?

I opened my mouth, but I glanced around and now I couldn't see the man in black. Had I really seen him? Was the Memory Stone in use and making me remember things—perhaps even making me see someone who wasn't here? I shivered, suddenly cold. What if the man Seb and I had met last night wasn't really Commander Hegarty's brother—what if he'd done something to all of us, Kalax included?

Not knowing what to do, I let the king lead me back to my mother. But instead of disappointment, she stared at me, tears of pride and joy glittering unshed in her eyes.

The king bowed to her and said, "Esmerelda, please forgive me for overtiring your daughter. The prince will be furious with me." With a smile, he turned away.

I started to go after him, but my mother grabbed me in a hug. I could smell her perfume of roses and I tried not to struggle. "Oh my child," she said and held me back at arm's length. "It was perfect. I couldn't have planned it better. The way you stumbled, the way he held you up—he acted the perfect father-in-law, gentleman and protector. The match has to go ahead—anyone can see it."

Blinking, I stared at her. "Match? What match? And did you see a man in black watching us? With a narrow face and black hair and—"

"Forget such nonsense. You and Prince Justin! Think of it—the House Flamma allied to the throne at last. You've made your family proud." She hugged me again.

I started to protest that I was not about to make a match of anyone, but a flash of silver and black hair caught my eye.

Pulling away, I called out, "Sorry, Mother. I...I must use the...the ladies retiring room." Pushing past the other dancers, I strained to see over the heads of those crowded around me. I also touched a hand to the knife hidden in my sleeve.

If it was Lord Vincent, I was going to find him. This time, I'd kill him.

Dancers kept whirling across my path, so I headed to the side of the room and glimpsed a tall man in a black, brocade coat. From the back, his hair was the right shade of black and the right length—long and dark.

A twinge pinched my side, just under my rib cage—the spot where Lord Vincent's blade had struck. Cold spread through my body. I gasped as I remembered the wave of darkness that pulled me down.

From the enclosure, I sensed Kalax raising her head and snuffling the air. *Thea hurt?*

I'm fine, really, I'm fine, I thought back, but I knew she could sense the lie. My heart was pounding, sweat dampened my upper lip and forehead. My breath was coming in short gasps.

An exuberant young man bumped into me, almost spilling his wine over me. I stepped back, annoyed at the distraction. I also pulled the knife from my sleeve. But I kept thinking, *why would Lord Vincent be here?*

If he had the Memory Stone, he had no need to attend a ball. What could he want?

The man in black now stood only a short distance from me. He was about the right height—and he had that narrow build that had been burned into my memory. I eased closer.

The man in black was talking to another man, this one a stocky fellow who dressed in the red and gold of the palace guards. That had to be captain of the watch. My stomach knotted and I stepped even closer.

I heard a voice as smooth as velvet, fine and cultured with the slightest hint of an accent that I couldn't quite place. Slapping my left hand down on the man's arm, I spun him around, my knife ready in my other hand.

The cold and clear eyes of a stranger looked down at me with surprise and disdain. It wasn't him. This man didn't look anything like Lord Vincent. Yes, he had a narrow face, but his features were…well, blurred. As if roughened by drink or age.

A wave of pain swept up my back. I swayed. My head was pounding and I felt sick.

"Good heavens, Lady Agathea?" The man in uniform offered me his hand and so did the man in black. Something—an unwillingness to touch him—stopped me. I couldn't think why I couldn't bear his touch, but I just couldn't. I was having trouble thinking—or even breathing. It was like being under water—everything seemed so far away right now. I turned away and the room seemed to spin around me.

"Perhaps you should sit down," the stranger said, his voice a soft purr. A buzzing, like a swarm of insects started in my ears.

Stumbling away, I mumbled, "Sorry…sorry." I made it to a wall and leaning against the heavy tapestry there that covered the stone walls. Fumbling with my knife, I tucked it back into its sheath in my sleeve. How could I have been so wrong? And yet…was I? Wasn't I feeling how I always did when one of the stones was near? *Why can't I think?*

Mother loomed up in front of me. "Agathea Flamma, just what do you think you are doing, rushing off like that, saying first you need the facilities and then…then speaking with an utter stranger. I wonder if he is one of the southern lords."

"Mother, I must sit down," I said. I rubbed at my temples. My head felt like it was in a vice. "I really must."

She pushed a goblet into my hands. "Drink that, child—and please do not have the poor taste to faint. Now I promised the Van-Stoutgartens we'd join them in the group dance. You'll only have to pick up your feet for a couple of turns and then you can sit down all you like."

I groaned. Group dances were always exuberant movements, with long lines of people crisscrossing, exchanging elbow-holds and forming circles. It was almost a game with some to stay dancing as long as they—or the musicians—could stand it. I groped along the wall for a chair and started to sink into it.

But Mother grabbed my elbow and pushed the goblet into my hands. "Agathea, drink, please. And do recall that you cannot dance with King Durance and no one else. Think of the scandal. It will be whispered that you've become his new flirt, and that is not something even the House of Flamma can overcome. Come—one more dance and we shall leave."

I threw back the wine. The strong, sweet liquid helped clear my head—the buzzing in my ears eased. So did the pounding in my head. And I knew Mother was right. The group dance didn't involve any partner dancing. It was the perfect dance for declaring no particular romantic interest to anyone.

It would also give me another moment to look around the ballroom for a man in black with longhair held back with silver, a narrow face and empty eyes.

Mother shuffled me to the others as if I were ten again. The bandy-legged, balding, but intensely cheery Baron Van-Stoutgarten and his wife welcomed us to the group. I glanced around, but could see no one in black.

The music started and I had to mind the steps.

Three steps to the left, curtsey and sway forward.

This was one of the most well-loved dances in Torvald, almost every child, noble or peasant, learned it from a young age. The baron smiled cheerily, clapping his hands before we locked elbows and spun. That gave me another chance to scan the room, and still no man in black—not even the stranger who had been talking with the watch captain.

I almost missed a step and a young gentleman who had been about to lock elbows with me had to grab my hand instead. I spun him a little too hard, and he staggered, then suddenly I was looking at the Baroness Van-Stoutgarten.

She grinned at me. "It seems we've missed a step somewhere. Oh, well, the men will have to dance together too."

Another bob and two steps misplaced saw me collide with the Count of Rhiasa who laughed good-naturedly, but I could tell he was annoyed, and once he turned away, I heard him say,

"Clearly her feet are more used to military marches now, and not dance steps."

Well, they were.

The dance ended with a scattering of polite applause, whispers and stifled sniggers. I swung around, hands on my hips, just about daring anyone to offer me pity or scorn. I didn't care what they thought. I'd been chosen by a dragon—not just a dragon, but a red. I was a Flamma. I had danced tonight with a king.

And I was going to find out if Lord Vincent was here if I had to attack every man in black. Pushing through the crowd, I started my search again. I made it to one of the side refreshment tables when someone hissed at me.

I turned and saw a servant dressed in a white shirt and brown leggings. He looked up and I recognized the brown eyes at once. "Seb?" How could a shirt and leggings make such a difference? He looked…well, broader than he often did in his riding clothes. And…and cleaner and…well, he looked almost handsome with his face scrubbed and his long, lean arms and legs so clearly defined. "What are you doing here?" I asked.

"Thea, something's not right."

I rolled my eyes. "Tell me something I don't know. Now you'd better go before you get caught." I started to move away, but Seb reached out to grab my elbow.

A shadow fell over us both and I looked up to see Lord Westerforth scowling at us. "Lady Agathea, is this…this wretch bothering you?"

He had his boys in tow, the older one looking on eagerly, the younger one looking even more miserable.

"No, Lord Westerforth, it's fine, really. We were just..." Pushing out a breath, I gave up on being polite. I was done with lies and I didn't even know why. "You know, Lord Westerforth, you shouldn't be so hard on your sons. If you were nicer to them, they'd not only be better sons, but actually might turn into someone you could like. A dragon might even pick one as a rider."

"What...what did you just say?"

"It seems obvious to me." I blinked. But I couldn't remember why I'd just said that. Looking past him, I saw I wasn't the only one having problems.

The dancing in the ballroom had dissolved into a confusing tangle of people, some beginning to argue with each other and others just staring at the floor as if they couldn't remember how to move their feet. The musicians were playing at least three different tunes in all—not all of them on key, and people were starting to spill and drop their refreshments.

"The Winter Ball never used to be this exciting," I muttered.

And couldn't remember why I was here.

'Ware, Thea. Remember.

The world suddenly seemed to shake and rocked on its side. I was falling to the floor, my mind empty, but then a voice rose up and seized my thoughts. *Kalax. Remember!* Blinking, I put a hand to my head.

Whatever Kalax had done, she had shaken the fog that had been settling around my mind and rising up through my bones.

Smell magic, Kalax growled at me with her mind.

"The Memory Stone," I gasped. My head was pounding, but not so hard I couldn't think. Turning to where Seb stood, I reaching out a hand and put it on his arm. It felt even better to touch him—to have a connection that made this world real.

Seb looked pale and shaken too so I knew Kalax had been mentally yelling at him also. Pulling me away from Lord Westerforth and his boys who were now blankly staring at nothing, Seb said, "Kalax warned me. She told me you were hurt."

I remembered feeling the pain again of a blow meant to kill me. With Kalax helping me now, I could remember again. "Lord Vincent. It *was* him! I saw him—he was here."

"Where?" Seb glanced around us, his face going dark and tight.

"Jodreth said the Memory Stone was commandeered by the king. Lord Vincent must have tricked him out of it—or used magic. He has it again. Did someone take it for him? Doesn't matter, he's been using it—he's been here amusing himself. Playing with our minds."

Seb shook his head. "But why?"

Kalax was huffing and growling. I could hear her and other dragons now, starting to raise an alarm. The dragons sensed something. We didn't have to wait long before we, too, knew what it was.

An almighty thump shook the room, breaking glass windows, shattering the crystals in the chandeliers. Flaming candles fell.

Women screamed, the music stopped at once as did all talk. A sound like nails across a tutor's slate raked the roof above us. The ceiling rippled and cracked, lines spreading out over the plasterwork as dust fell.

"Take cover," Seb shouted.

He and I ducked under a serving table.

The next thump hit and the ceiling burst apart. A dragon's tail, black and studded with spikes, crashed into the room. Deadly shards of glass, entire chandeliers and splintered wooden beams fell on screaming nobles. And I knew we were under attack.

Lord Vincent had come here not to dance or to amuse himself by playing with our minds, but to deliver a death blow to Torvald.

CHAPTER 15
FLAMES IN THE NIGHT

Holding Thea close, I stayed under what little protection the table offered us.

The roar of the black dragon above almost drowned out the screams as the nobles here woke from whatever mists the Memory Stone had woven around them. Pieces of masonry as large as my head struck and shattered on the floor. Terrified shrieks filled the night. I heard Kalax call to us as she rose into the sky and flew to our aid. I could almost feel the wind across her face as she raced toward the palace.

"Thea, we have to get the people out of here!" Holding onto her hand, I ducked out from where we'd been hiding and pulled her with me toward the doors.

"Mother!" Thea yelled. She pulled free of my grip, ripping the sleeve of her dress and jumped over a cowering man.

I shouted her name and followed into the press of people trying to escape.

Above us, the black tail of the wild dragon flashed again. The wicked spines along its curving edge slashed through the room. Dragons had to attack in waves if they wanted to remain airborne, and I knew this one couldn't sit on the roof—that wouldn't hold the dragon's weight. We'd have a few moments before it could sweep down and attack again.

Cupping my hands around my mouth, I yelled, "Everyone! To the walls!" I pushed ladies and lords in now dusty and bloodied finery toward safety. Some of them managed to hear me—the brain fog created by the Memory Stone had been released. But Lord Vincent's plan had been almost perfect.

I was certain he'd used the Memory Stone to convince the prince to send the dragon squadrons away so this attack could be made at the exact moment that most of the important people in Torvald would be in one place. He'd used the Memory Stone here to confuse the guards—perhaps to do more. And then he'd let go of his control so that everyone would panic —and die.

"Seb!" Thea shouted. I looked up and saw a pane of glass shatter. Jumping, I launched myself away from it, hit and rolled across the floor. The glass shattered in the spot where I'd been standing. The black dragon roared and rose up into the night to ready for another attack. I could sense the wild dragon's anger. Something, Lord Vincent probably, was making it think the palace was an enemy to kill. The copper smell of blood, of burning wood and candles, and the stink of fear filled the room. I could hear moans now—those trapped by wooden beams.

Arms and feet stuck up out of stone rubble. There would be many deaths this night.

I told Kalax, *The academy. We have to rouse all the dragons and any riders we have.*

Thea stumbled to my side and pulled me to my feet. Her mother stood next to Thea, her face pale, her hair tipped to one side. "Take her," Thea said, pushing me toward her mother. "I have to help the king."

I nodded even as Thea pushed past me and headed to where she must have last seen the king.

"Agathea?" Lady Flamma looked up, confusion in her eyes. Her gown had been torn on one side and her hand shook as she put it to her head.

"This way, my lady." I seized Lady Flamma's elbow, trying to shelter her as much as I could as we made our way over the rubble and toward the doors.

"But—but who would attack?" She sounded confused, and I wondered if the Memory Stone had left almost everyone like this. The palace guards wouldn't even be able to mount a defense if that was so.

"The Darkening, my lady," I told her.

Above us, the black dragon roared as it made another attacking dive. I could hear the howls and shrieks of Wildmen, the mountain tribes that Lord Vincent had previously forced to serve him, and the rougher shouts of bandits—men from the south.

Waving my arm, I yelled, "Get to the walls, away from the glass and ceiling!"

Seb! Kalax shouted in my head. *Many dragons come!*

"Thea?" Looking around, I spotted Thea pushing at a knot of men. They all looked to be elderly lords—all of them dusty from the debris. I caught a glimpse of King Durance, his gold crown glinting, as they pushed him out one of the side doors.

"Out of my way!" Thea yelled. "I'm a Dragon Rider. The dragons can protect the king."

I had no time to decide, but had to act. Pulling Lady Flamma with me, I crossed the dance floor. The large black dragon overhead was approaching at speed and I was sure that Kalax wouldn't make it in time.

"This isn't the job for a girl," one of the men told her.

"Oh, stuff this!" Thea growled. Leaning down, she pulled something from her sleeve. I saw the flash of a knife blade and she ripped off the bottom of her skirt, freeing her legs. Moving fast, she darting in, seizing one of the older lords by the wrist and twisting. He squealed in pain and moved out of her way.

"Hands off the duke!" A man shouted the words. Thea let go of the man she had and thumped the man who'd shouted in the center of the chest, propelling him out of the way. By the time I reached Thea with Lady Flamma, Thea had cleared the door.

Thea waved the lords away. "Go save who you can. Get everyone out—get them to the dragon enclosure or to the woods." She turned to me. "Come on. The king was taken this way and we must be certain he was not taken by the wrong hands." She gave her mother a quick glance. "If it is any consolation, Mother, I'm a much better fighter than I am a dancer."

Lady Flamma didn't have a response, but managed to keep pace with us as we ran through the palace. Kalax could get King Durance to safety, but first we had to get to the king.

Near a turning that opened into three more passageways, I stopped to catch a breath and braced my hands on my knees. Thea wasn't even winded. She still held her knife in one hand, and looked behind us to make sure no one was after us.

Straightening her back and her hair, Lady Flamma said, "The Eastern Gate. The old kings kept it as an escape route in times of danger."

She pointed the way and we pounded across marble floors and deep carpets, bursting through rich studies and running up grand stairwells. I was glad Lady Flamma knew where to go, for I lost track of all the turns and the doors we threw open. Terrified servants darted out of our way and the palace guards seemed to not know what to do as they ran past. The sounds of the black dragon's attack had faded behind us, and I hoped that meant it was over, but it had been replaced by the whoops of Wildmen warriors and so I worried that another part of the battle had begun. We needed to see the king safe so we could come back to fight.

"How much more of this?" I asked, my breath ragged and my lungs burning.

"Not much—not much!" Lady Flamma pointed to a long gallery, one side edged with statues, at the end of which was a grand set of double doors. Two men stood in front of the doors, and one of them was King Durance.

"That's the watch captain with the king," Thea gasped, as we ran down the corridor toward them.

The captain swung around and pulled his sword from his sheath.

Lady Flamma stopped before him and said, "My daughter and her navigator—they have a dragon overhead."

The king nodded. He looked older now, and smaller than he had in the ballroom. His hands shook. He had lost his crown and he glanced around us as if he wasn't certain what was happening around him. "But—but…the ball?"

"Don't you worry about that, Your Majesty." The watch captain turned to the doors. Taking out the keys from his belt, he unlocked a smaller door set into the bigger ones. He eased open the door and cold air flowed into the room. The captain glanced back at us. "Wait until I make certain it's safe."

He ducked out into the night, and we heard a gargled cry. The captain fell back in through the open doorway, an arrow lodged in his throat. From outside came the hoots and calls of Wildmen.

"Thea, his sword!" I shouted.

She gave a nod, knelt and drew the dead captain's saber. Spinning around, she held the blade up, her eyes glittering. I knew just how dangerous she could be when she was in a fighting mood like this. The only other blade we had was a thin one that the king wore—it looked more for show to me, but it was better than nothing. "Sire, may I?" I asked. He didn't answer.

The first Wildman burst through the door, his long hair braided and flapping, his upper body crossed with leather straps, studded with foul-looking barbs. Thea's blade cut true and the Wildman fell with a strangled cry.

The king shook his head as if he couldn't quite remember why he was here. I seized his blade, sliding it from the scabbard with a hiss. Turning to Thea's mother, I said, "Lady Flamma, please stay with the king." I stepped up next to Thea.

Three more Wildmen were heading for the open doorway. I wanted to shut it and lock it, but we needed to be outside to get to Kalax.

Above us, I heard a dragon's roar and then Kalax thought to me, *Seb...danger!*

Take care of yourself, I thought back at her, worried the wild black dragon would attack Kalax. Around us, we could hear screams and the war cries of the battle—the palace guards were doing what they could.

There was no time to stop and think. We just had to fight.

Thea stepped outside the doorway, becoming a deadly whirlwind. I held back, doing what I could to protect her from any attack she couldn't see.

In her ruined blue dress, she spun and slashed, her blade cutting the night. The Wildmen darted in, trying to get at her with their short blades.

In a few savage moments, we had four dead Wildmen at our feet and three more coming out of the dark. I struck at the knee of one on the left. Thea darted left, then ran through the one on the right. The Wildman I'd injured threw his axe at me. I ducked and Thea finished him.

I heard a shout and turned to see a Wildman running at the king with a knife raised.

"No, you don't!" Lady Flamma seized one of the marble urns that stood in the gallery behind and smashed it over the Wildman's head. He staggered and fell, bleeding from the head.

Thea grinned at me. "Not bad for a navigator." She stepped to her mother's side. "Like I said—I'm a much better fighter."

Lady Flamma swallowed and offered a tight, nervous smile. "I can see that, dear. I always said you could succeed at anything you put your mind to."

The night was growing warm from fires. Ash floated in the air and I could smell acrid burning. A shadow cut in front of the flames and smoke—a smaller black dragon that was rocketing into the night air. We helped the king step into the night. Two towers had been set ablaze and I could hear the ringing clash of steel on steel.

I pointed to where stairs ran up to the high outer wall at the back of the palace. "Kalax can land there, we can get the king to the academy."

"What good will that do?" Lady Flamma muttered.

I glanced at her. "The dragons can protect the king."

We hurried across the courtyard to the stairs, keeping King Durance between Thea and myself, trying our best to shield his body with ours as we clattered up the steps.

"We need help," I told Thea.

Before I could say more, sparks landed on the outer wall next to our heads. Below us dark shapes raced from the palace, heading toward us, firing black arrows from short, wicked bows.

"Wildmen," Thea yelled. Arrows fell on us, the heads sparking off the stone walls. "Protect the king."

Thea and Lady Flamma pressed closer to the king, but we kept on running. The curve of the stairs helped us, giving us some shelter. We crawled up the steps, trying to stay as low as we could. At the top, I peeked over the wall and saw the terraces of Torvald stretching out. It was burning.

The city of Torvald was burning.

My throat tightened and my eyes burned too, and not just from the smoke thickening the air. I had no idea if my folks were safe or not, but I could do nothing to help them. Small fires had sprouted all along the outer tier of the city—Monger's Lane and other poorer parts of the city were bright spots of orange. I could see small rivers of light which must be from bandits from the south or Wildmen who were closing on Torvald. We were being attacked by land and—judging from the roars above —by air.

Looking up, I searched for Kalax. I could feel her anger as she chased off the wild black she had been fighting. Turning, she spread her wings and headed toward us.

And then I realized something. "Thea?" I called out. "There are four of us." Thea frowned for a moment, then nodded. A dragon had four legs—two in back and two in front. And we needed to catch a ride.

Starting to run down the top of the wall, I yelled, "Run!"

Arrows flitted past us—deadly and sharp.

Next to me Thea was shouting at her mother and the king to move faster. More arrows rained down, randomly shot at us by the Wildmen who were chasing up the stairs after us. Ahead, a shadow detached itself from the sky, racing toward us like a dart. I ran faster. Dragon wings glinted in the reflection of the fires below, more light shone on teeth, talons and claws.

Kalax—ready? I threw all of my mental energy at her, letting her know what had to be done. She swept low, straight over my head and Thea's.

The king screamed, but Kalax had him. Kalax grabbed Lady Flamma in the other front claw. Kalax flashed over us. We had run out of wall. Thea jumped. I saw Kalax catch Thea, and then suddenly, my body was squeezed by dragon claws.

Kalax had caught us all, one in each claw, front and back. It was almost like when Kalax had chosen us as riders, picking us out of all the others in Torvald.

Like catching fish, Kalax crowed. But I knew we were far from safe. We'd flown up out of the reach of the Wildmen's arrows, but now we had black dragons swooping past Kalax. She roared at each one, warning them to keep a distance.

Reaching up, I hauled myself up onto Kalax's back. She relaxed her grip enough on me for me to get back to where my saddle usually sat. Kalax tucked her front legs close to her chest, holding her human cargo next to dragon scales that were better than any armour.

The wind snatched at my shirt and leggings. I saw Thea's hand come up from below—she was climbing up on Kalax's neck, too—and I reached out to help her into her place right behind me. This time we were flying without saddles or harnesses. I'd done this before, but Thea hadn't. And we didn't even have bows or any other weapons.

Fly, Kalax, fly!

She responded with a powerful beat of her wings, tearing up into the night sky above the broken palace. Wrapping her arms around my middle, Thea rested her head on my shoulder. Her warmth felt comforting against my back, and I could have almost forgotten the danger we were in were it not for black dragons whirling around us.

"How many?" Thea shouted.

I knew just how many—I could feel their wild fury. Wild dragons usually never left the north, but the Memory Stone could be used on them too, to make them think they had to fight to defend themselves.

"Ten," I called back. I had to cling to Kalax's horns as she dove and turned—Thea and I weren't gripped tightly in her claws.

The wild, black dragons were generally smaller than Kalax, but they were fast, able to turn like a bird with short, powerful wings that made them look like crows. In the dark night, their black colour gave them an advantage—they seemed to come out of nowhere, whirling past us. Glancing back, I saw one black dragon topple a tower at the palace with a strike of its tail. I feared with so many wild dragons loose, Torvald was doomed.

"Watch out!" Thea shouted, squeezing the breath out of me. A black dragon with the spikes on its head jutting out, roared as it fell from the night sky, its fore-claws stretched out to rake Kalax's hide.

She turned and lashed out with her thicker tail—and with her own spikes raised. The impact as Kalax hit the smaller dragon vibrated in my chest. Kalax roared at the other dragon as the black fell below us, catching and righting itself only at the last moment before it hit the ground.

There are too many, I thought, throwing the thought to Kalax.

Kalax didn't care about the numbers—she wanted to fight. I tried to show her the situation as I saw it—we had the king to think of *first*. He must be safe—and we needed better weapons. With a frustrated war cry, Kalax beat her powerful wings rising up into the air. I could hear the beat of other dragon wings around us.

"Are we going to be able to outrun them?" Thea yelled. I felt her shift and knew she must be looking back at the flames behind us. The burning palace—and the flames from Torvald— lit the night sky now like dawn had come early. The wind smelled of smoke and destruction. I could hear the black dragons making screech-like, eerie calls to each other, and their wild fury beat at my mind, leaving me wanting to join Kalax in deciding to turn and fight back.

But I had taken an oath as a Dragon Rider—we had to protect the king.

And then I wanted to see to my family.

Pressing a hand on Kalax's warm scales, I called out, "Kalax is the best flier in the skies." It felt good to say that, and even better when Kalax sent me back approval for believing in her.

She puffed out a smoky breath, but suddenly pulled her wings tight. She started to plummet toward the ground. My heart banged against my ribs and wind tore tears from my eyes.

Were you hit? I asked her.

She didn't answer, but fell like a stone. The cries of two wild, black dragons followed us downward. At the last moment, Kalax twisted and turned, opening her wings, lifting her head and thumping the ground with her tail. She launched back up at the blacks. They tried to turn, but Kalax knocked into them, sending them twisting and tumbling. Their wings tangled and they fell.

An almighty crash rose up behind us as the two black dragons smashed into the trees. I doubted that would be enough to kill any dragon—and I could already feel their groggy thoughts— but it might be enough to shake them out of their killing frenzy. They'd leave for the wilds again. Two down—how many more to go?

Kalax crowed at us as she skimmed over the treetops and headed for Hammal Mountain, and she thought at me, *Dragons defend now.*

She was right.

Thea released one hand from my waist to point ahead at the walls and landing platforms of the academy. Signal flags were up—but I could also see that the top of one tower had been tumbled, and the map tower seemed nothing but a pillar of flames. My throat tightened. I hoped Merik hadn't been up there like he usually was—and I thought of the loss of our maps. Merik would hate that.

"That's why help hasn't come to the palace," Thea yelled.

With the squadrons gone, the only real defense for Torvald was the handful of riders and their dragons—but this second attack had kept them busy just trying to stay alive.

There weren't just Wildmen at the front gates of the academy, but mercenaries from the Southern Realm like those we'd arrested as bandits. A dozen or more were pounding at the thick wood with axes. Thankfully, the gates held strong. But another group of twenty or more were dragging a log they'd cut down to use as a battering ram. Overhead, more black dragons screeched, their wings fanning the flames as they circled overhead.

Why aren't the blacks attacking? I thought, watching the wild dragons blot out the stars.

The Dragon Horns blew a deep, growling call and the clatter of a huge ratchet answered.

"The trebuchets," Thea said. She breathed out the word, her mouth close to my ear. I had never seen these massive war machines in use—not even for practice. They sat between the landing platforms, carved logs and metal that seemed more like decorations than weapons. I remembered Commander Hegarty saying the trebuchets would only ever be used as a last resort against an aerial defense. And that was now – the time of last resort had come.

Someone had manned the machines, which cranked so loudly they could be heard over all other battle sounds. The trebuchets looked almost like vast angular mousetraps with an extending arm that swung out and up, flinging the contents of a sling on the far end. The first one made an odd whistling noise as it flew forward. A collection of stone blocks from the ruined towers flew into the air, out of the sling and fell onto the mercenaries at the front gates. The wild, black dragons rose up, ducking out of the way of the flying blocks—now I knew why they didn't want to attack the academy.

As the first trebuchet started to be drawn back, the second launched, throwing more debris into the air and over the walls. The mercenaries—those still on their feet—pulled back, but there were still far too many enemies all about us.

"Seb—it's Instructor Mordecai!"

I looked to where Thea was pointing and saw Instructor Mordecai limping between the trebuchets and the landing platforms. The firelight from the burning towers lit his bent form. I glimpsed Varla and Wil with him, their uniforms a flash of colour in the smoky night. I had no idea where Merik, Jensen or the others were. With his cane, Mordecai batted away stray arrows shot up at him from below as if they were an annoying insect. For an instant, I feared he was trying to disable the trebuchets—that he had turned traitor. But no, he bent to help Varla ready the next trebuchet for launch.

"We were wrong about him," Thea said, her voice soft in my ear.

"It doesn't matter now," I shouted. I urged Kalax to fly high, and then dive down to land in the practice yard. We couldn't risk the king up on the landing platforms.

Merik, wearing a battered helmet, his metal armour, riding boots and leather pants, headed toward us. "Seb? Thea!" He sounded relieved, angry and scared at all once. "We thought you were trapped at the palace. They came at us before we could call the dragons."

I slid from Kalax and put a hand on the side of her head. *Just a little longer, and then we fight.*

She approved that idea.

Sitting up a little, Kalax opened her front claws and gently settled the king and Lady Flamma onto the ground. Merik's eyes budged. The king lay still and I wondered if he had fainted, but Lady Flamma gasped, stood and immediately stumbled over to the king. "No…no, it cannot be. The king is wounded."

I shook my head. "Kalax would never let that happen."

Thea knelt next to the king's side. She glanced up at me, her face pale. Smoke streaked her legs under her tattered dress. She looked a lot more like a peasant than a noble right now.

Kalax sent me a thought. *Hurt before caught.*

I stepped closer. For a moment, I could see nothing, but then I notice the blood on the king's upper thigh. Thea pulled back his robes. The broken stub of one of the Wildmen's arrows jutted out from King Durance's upper thigh.

"Just before Kalax caught the king he screamed. One of the Wildmen must have shot him," I said.

"What do we do?" Merik asked.

Ripping off her sleeves, Lady Flamma used them to tie the arrow in place. "He'll bleed to death if we pull this out."

"Instructor Mordecai," I muttered. Turning to Merik, I said, "Get Mordecai and do it now." Turning to Thea, I told her, "We need to take the king to Mordecai's study. He knows how to heal—and let's just hope the Healing Stone is still here."

Thea nodded. She took the king's legs, and I lifted his shoulders. The short cape the king had on kept getting in the way, so I yanked it off and tried again. With Lady Flamma's help, we got the king up and into the keep.

We moved as fast as we dared. The king groaned with every step and every shift of weight, but he didn't seem aware of what was happening around him. Inside the keep, the noise of battle lessened, but the air was thick with the smoke. I started to cough. At last, we reached Mordecai's study. The door stood open and the smell of spices seemed a relief from everything else.

Lady Flamma at once cleared a low couch and we eased the king onto it. Blood had soaked his leggings and part of his shirt. His face seemed far too pale, but his eyelids were fluttering as if he wanted to open his eyes, and he wet his lips with his tongue and asked for water.

Lady Flamma at once moved to seek out a flagon for the king.

I edged closer to Thea. "Go. Change. You're going to need battle-dress."

"And you're not?" she said. But she gave a last glance at her mother's pale face and left. She came back faster than I would have thought she could, looking ready to ride in leathers and armour. She also had an armful of my gear and swords for both of us. "Dress," she said.

I nodded and stepped back into the shadows to pull on my leathers over the serving clothes I'd borrowed from the palace kitchens. In a party, no one minds two extra hands. Now I wished we had a dozen more hands here to help us.

As I buckled my sword belt on, Thea and her mother were left to deal with the king, who seemed to be restless now and wanting to sit up. Thea pushed her hair back from her face— she looked a Dragon Rider again. I had nothing better to do than fold my arms and wish that Merik and Mordecai would hurry.

Kalax thought at me that we needed to be in the air. I asked her to wait for just a few more moments.

Mordecai —smelling of smoke and sweat—burst into the room, a staff in one hand and a sword in the other. He seemed changed. His eyes glittered bright as the fires from the map tower, but he moved like a young man now, hardly limping and his back straighter than ever I'd seen.

"Give me room," he barked at us.

I glanced behind him, but didn't see Merik, so Mordecai must have left Merik to help with the trebuchets.

Hearing those harsh tones typical of instructors was almost a relief—if Mordecai could order us about, at least a few things were still right in this world.

Putting down his sword and staff, Mordecai glanced around the room once then pushed up his sleeves. "Clean bandages—third shelf on the right, Flamma. No, your mother, not you. And hot water from down the hall, Smith. You, Flamma—no, now I want the younger one—find the valerian, woundwort, turmeric, comfrey and sage. Roots of the hellebore, tincture of poppy. Move!"

No one argued. Lady Flamma hurried from where she had been soothing the king's face with a perfumed handkerchief to fetch the bandages. Thea turned to the racks of spices and herbs and began to pile them in her arms. I grabbed a bucket and went for water—if the kitchens still stood.

It was a relief to run out of a room that had begun to smell of blood—I feared for the king. My hands were shaking and so was my stomach as I hurried to the kitchens. A copper pot was always left on the first—it was no different today. But the rest of the kitchen looked a shambles, and I hoped Margaret had fled to safety. Worry for her tightened my chest, but I had to get back to the king.

Water sloshing in the buckets, I stepped back into the room.

Mordecai had cut away the king's leggings, revealing the ugly wound. The arrow shaft stuck out, a terrible red and purple blotching spread out around it.

Shaking his head, Mordecai leaned down and sniffed. I didn't think he needed to—even from the doorway I could smell the foul smell that was rising, as if uncooked meat had sat too long in the sun. "Poisoned. The smallest nick would have killed the king—this…there is nothing to be done."

Face going pale, Lady Flamma looked from Mordecai to the king. Her legs seemed to give out for she sank to the floor.

"But there must be something!" Thea hit the table with the flat of her hand. "What of the Healing Stone?"

"Give me the poppy milk and valerian, child. We can ease the agony." Mordecai waved me over and soaked a wad of bandages in the steaming hot water. "We might slow the spread." He took fresh bandages, wrapping them tight above the wound. The ugly colour still seemed to spread—as did the smell—but it seemed to me it was moving slower.

Mordecai mixed his herbs into a thin paste that he dribbled into the king's mouth. King Durance spluttered and licked his lips.

Putting a hand on his arm, Lady Flamma sat up. "Be at ease, Your Majesty."

A boom shook the keep and dust drifted down on us from the ceiling.

Straightening, Lady Flamma looked up at Mordecai. "His will needs to be heard. He must give us his last command."

I knew then the king would die.

I had never seen Mordecai anything but angry, or so it seemed to me. Now…Now his shoulders slumped and his face paled. He aged again to an old man, but one who looked broken. I glanced at the king.

King Durance had been king all of my life. I'd known someday he must die—but it wasn't the same as seeing him die now before us. The poison was spreading. I could hear his lungs thicken with liquid—his breathing became heavy. I shivered. A king dying—in front of me. I was a smith's boy and now I was seeing the death of a king.

"Prince Justin?" Thea said her voice unsteady. "He should be here."

I nodded. This was a place for princes. Then I frowned and stepped up to Mordecai. Why was he delaying? My voice came out harsh as I asked him, "Where is the Healing Stone?"

For once, I wasn't afraid of Mordecai. I was a Dragon Rider— I'd sworn to defend the king and if I must, I'd go ransack the commander's rooms for the stone. But if Mordecai had hidden it, I needed to know.

Mordecai let out a breath and rubbed a hand over his face. "Do you not think that was not my very first thought? It's with Commander Hegarty. He thought that the one sensible thing he could do if that fool prince had ordered the squadrons away. He thought…he thought the prince was bound for danger."

I glanced at Thea. Her stare had gone vague, and I knew she must be trying to sense if the Healing Stone was near. If all she —and Jodreth—had said was true, she'd know. She seemed to sense I was watching her. Her stare sharpened again and she glanced at me and shook her head.

The Healing Stone wasn't near.

Mordecai straightened. "We thought…we didn't think the Darkening would dare an attack on Torvald. We were so…so very wrong." Rubbing his leg, Mordecai looked at me, "Sometimes we are asked to bear burdens that are not ours. But the fault here lies with me and the commander—we have been guilty of pride. Of thinking Torvald too strong to be taken. I guess it is time we all learned it is possible to make mistakes." His mouth twisted down and a shadow of his usual annoyance surfaced.

I no longer feared it.

Next to us, the king stirred and murmured, "Justin."

Lady Flamma shifted so she could again sooth the king's forehead. "It is your servant, Esmerelda Flamma. What is your bidding?"

Another boom echoed from outside—the battle was coming closer. I eased toward the door—we needed to be ready to fight.

"My boy…Justin," the king breathed out the words with pink bubbles of blood on his lips.

My throat tightened and for an instant I wondered if my father, too, had died this night. I clenched my fists at my side—the Darkening and Lord Vincent would pay for their terrible deeds.

"Yes, Your Highness?" Lady Flamma asked, wiping the blood from the king's lips. "You wish him to succeed you? To take the throne?"

King Durance coughed. His eyes opened, but the look in them seemed distant and empty. "It is my will that the throne of Torvald be held next by Lord Vincent."

"No!" Thea stepped forward, slashing the air with one hand. "It cannot be."

"It is the Memory Stone," I said. "Thea, you said you felt it at court—that you saw Lord Vincent there. That's why he attended the ball."

Mordecai's cold voice lashed out. "Silence."

King Durance let out a last shuddering breath. His eyes—so blank before—seemed to film over with grey. Lady Flamma sat back, her lower lip trembling.

Instructor Mordecai pulled off his own cloak and settled it over the king's body. "May the First Dragon carry your soul, King Durance." He bowed his head.

We all repeated the words, but I mumbled them. I was numb. I couldn't believe this was happening. Lord Vincent had come just to try and steal the throne—by force and by cunning. My city was in ruins—burning now. Would anything be left?

I could hear ragged battle cries outside. With the king dead, I wanted to be in the air—I needed to see if my family was safe. But duty still pulled at me. I glanced around the room. "No one is to ever mention this to anyone. Not ever. As far as we're all concerned, Prince…I mean King Justin is the rightful ruler. My sworn task as a Dragon Rider will be to make sure he takes his rightful place on the throne."

"If he's not had his memories changed, too, to give the crown to Lord Vincent," Thea muttered.

My hands chilled at that idea. I knew then we'd have to make certain the new king was not also under the control of the Memory Stone and Lord Vincent.

Mordecai straightened and glanced from me to Thea and back again. "Let's worry about what's in front of us. We've a sky full of dragons and an army of Wildmen and bandits pounding on the gates."

I scrubbed a hand over the back of my neck. I knew had soot on my face and it itched. "To be honest, I'm not sure we can save Torvald without the squadrons, but…well, all the dragons know there's danger. Right now—other than Kalax—the dragons are more worried about protecting the enclosure and their own. I think…well, I can pull them out and into battle. Not just Ferdinania and Dellos, but the older brood dragons and the young hatchlings. Erufon and Gorgax will have to work together tonight. We're going to need them all to have a hope of surviving until morning."

Mordecai nodded. He headed back out into the corridor. "Whatever it is, do it, Smith! At least buy time to evacuate the city as best we can." Mordecai paused and raised an eyebrow at Lady Flamma. "You, too, my lady. Everyone else should already be gathered near the rear gate—we have a tunnel that leads from the academy into the mountains. The ponies are there too, to carry food and water. Those from the city will head into the mountains as well and we'll have to help them get there."

Lady Flamma had been staring at the king's body, her head bowed. Now she stood, and Thea moved to her side. Glancing at Mordecai, Thea said, "Instructor, nothing will stop a Flamma on a mission."

For a moment, my chest tightened. I thought of Monger's Lane. Had my family managed to get out? I didn't know. I rubbed the back of my hand across my face. When Thea turned to look at me, I told her, "Come on. We've got dragons to call to battle."

CHAPTER 16
THE FALL OF TORVALD

I ran with Seb to the equipment shed to get our saddles. Seb was already shouting up at Merik and Varla, as well as Jensen and Wil, to get their harness ready. Kalax gave a roar and I knew Seb was talking to her—and to the other dragons. As I saddled Kalax, Seb stared up at the enclosure. I could feel him pushing at the dragons—the old ones were reluctant to leave their nests undefended, but the young ones wanted to fight.

Ferdinania and Dellos burst into the air, swiping at black dragons as they flew here to get their riders. A dragon roar shook the ground, and then Erufon erupted into the air, shooting out flames in a long stream.

Gorgax took to the air as well, and I wondered if Seb really would be able to control all the dragons—or if they go wild on us.

My mouth seemed filled with smoke. It burned my eyes—but still I kept thinking of King Durance. Sorrow for him clutched at my throat. He'd been so kind to me tonight. "Vincent," I muttered and climbed up on Kalax's back. Like her, I wanted battle now.

Heart pounding, I looked up at the top of the walls.

The trebuchets had given us time enough. I saw Wil and Jensen already up on Dellos, ready to take to the air. Varla was checking the last hitch of her saddle.

"Ready?" Seb called out.

I nodded and unslung my dragon bow. Two full quivers of long arrows hung from my saddle, along with my spears. Seb swung up on Kalax. "Riders to the sky!"

Kalax launched with a roar. Ferdinania followed her, then Dellos.

Dragons know how to fight, Kalax reminded us.

My stomach lurched as we soared up into the sky. Flames lit the night. Below us I saw the bandits at the gates pause and look up. Now they'd have to deal with Dragon Riders.

The fury of the dragons—Kalax's desire for battle—bled into me. I wanted to fight.

I thought to Erufon how King Durance was now dead—but Erufon knew already. And the old dragon wanted revenge. I looked over to see Erufon battling wild dragons, scattering them with harsh blows and fire. Turning, I leaned into the rush of wind as Kalax and two young, red dragons joined her in diving at the bandits near the main gates.

The bandits threw down their weapons and ran. Pulling my bow, I took aim, targeting those few who stood to face us. Two arrows flew and hit their marks. Kalax swept up two of the bandits and then dropped them on those who were fleeing.

Seb urged Kalax to turn and head to the city. He called back to me, "We have to make sure the people get out."

I nodded—and I thought of my mother and my father. Father had stayed home tonight—but he'd been a Dragon Rider in his time. He would have his armour and his weapon.

And then there was no time to think of anything but targets—of ducking, aiming, firing.

Several times I picked up a sense of panic from Seb—as if trying to keep all the dragons focused was slipping out of his control.

Around us, the screeches of the wild, black dragons shook the sky. They seemed to appear out of the night, barbed tails whipping, their wings just patches of inky darkness. All I could see was a flash of eyes and the bone-like white of long fangs.

"Brace," Seb shouted as he had Kalax flip and turn, dodging the blacks. Kalax would come around then, ready to engage with the wild dragon, but Seb kept urging her back to guard the city.

Let her fight! Let her fight!

I kept willing Seb to let Kalax loose.

And then I saw what Seb was trying to do.

He had seen that, as soon as we'd get into a fight with one dragon, three more would drop down from above. It was a good tactic.

They're trying to do this with Jensen and Wil and Dellos!

Kalax broke away from the black dragons crowding her and raced to where our friends were being mobbed.

I felt rather than saw Seb do something. A wave of sickness spread up from my belly, and Kalax shuddered too.

Seb flung out his hands—ahead of us, the wild, black dragons convulsed as if they'd been struck ill. They scattered, heading low for the trees, revealing Jensen and Wil still safe on Dellos. Jensen extended his protector harness. He gave us a wave and he and Wil turned toward the city.

"West gate," Seb shouted.

Wil waved a hand as if he'd heard.

"Seb, was that you?" I shouted. "What did you do?"

"I…I think so." Seb's voice sounded shaky. I could see sweat gleaming on his face as he glanced back at me.

Seb turned Kalax and we headed for the city.

Arrows spun up from the ground but they kept missing us. I glanced down, searching for a target. One of the arrows sparked off Kalax. *You hurt?* I asked her.

She gave me a shiver of annoyance and I realized the arrow must have hit a buckle or some part of the dragon harness.

"Now, Kalax!" Seb was urging her onward. I found my targets —a small group of Wildmen shooting at us from the edge of the city. I took aim and launched my own arrows down on them. That stopped any more arrows flying at us.

Glancing down, I saw that most of the streets were empty— people had been fleeing the city for some time, it seemed. Kalax swept down and we headed for the city walls, clearing the path for those who had not yet gotten out of the city. Small groups of bandits or Wildmen waited, but the dragons easily scattered them.

I glanced up at the sky.

Dawn was coming—and we didn't have an army, we had a mess.

Dragons careened across the night sky, the undersides of their wings and their bellies gleaming with the reflections of a hundred fires, their jaws dripping with blood. It was mayhem, and every minute I thought would be our last.

Battle and blood in the air, Kalax thought at me. She was right. The battle was making all the dragons return to their wild state. Some dragons were just circling overhead. Others were screaming out cries. Others were randomly diving at anything that moved—including the people of Torvald.

We have to get organized, I thought to Kalax.

She gave a deep, purring rattle in her ribcage that turned into a sonorous call like the sound of the Dragon Horns.

"She's trying to call the dragons to rally to her," Seb shouted back at me. But there was a glittering excitement in his eyes that made me nervous. I could tell he was straining to try to talk to all these dragons. How could he control that much energy?

"Seb," I said trying to warn him. He wasn't listening.

Neither of us knew the full dangers of using the Dragon Affinity. Varla had found only a few scant references in the old books—but the gift seemed to come at a terrible price. So much so that Varla had once confided in me that it had been viewed as more of a curse than a talent.

"Come on, come on," Seb called out, his voice hoarse. "Battle formations!"

A massive, scarred and ancient head swung into view and Erufon sailed past us. I had the feeling Erufon had come to Kalax's call, but now Erufon seemed to be trying to take charge. And then I felt an echo of Erufon's sorrow. Sadness. Incredible, terrible sadness and it was emanating from the older dragon itself.

Erufon mourns, Kalax thought at me.

No time for that. Time to take revenge, I thought back.

I felt Kalax agree, and she gave Erufon a high-pitched, shrill call.

Erufon soared higher.

I felt a sudden wave of vertigo and dizziness spreading out. I glanced at Seb and I knew he was doing that. I had a strange doubling of vision—I was seeing Seb, but I was also seeing Seb as Kalax saw. For an instant, it seemed as if every dragon's mind was mine.

I heard a low, dragon voice in my ears—it sounded like Kalax, but somehow her voice had become mingled with Seb's. It was as if he was using her voice—or she was using his—to talk to all our other dragons. Or they had melded into one being.

Wind's-teeth!

Fierce-stalker!

Flame-children—defend your home!

For a moment after I heard only the wind. The wave of power ebbed, leaving my stomach churning. Underneath me Kalax was fairly thrumming with joy.

Erufon gave a hissing roar and the other dragons began to circle around him, starting to form the battle formations I knew from training. But these were dragons without riders—with only Seb talking to all of them.

The youngest of the enclosure dragons joined up with Erufon. They soared around him, wings spread wide and claws glinting. The brood mothers—mostly blues and greens—fell in next. They weren't fast—they were more like flying fortresses. Behind them, the long and sinuous green dragons began to rally.

Even some of the wild blacks began to follow Erufon, as if they couldn't resist his summons.

The last to follow—larger and longer even than Erufon—was Gorgax. He soared past us, his long tail snapping the air above our heads, warning Seb, me, Kalax and all the others that he was really still in charge.

Mouth open, I stared, my pulse quick and my breaths shallow.

I had never seen such a sight before—riderless dragons, choosing of their own will—with a bit of help from Seb—to fight for humans. This was like seeing childhood tales come to life with the dragons of old.

We might…just might be able to save the academy, but we'd have to do it while we helped everyone escaped the burning city.

Turning Kalax, Seb urged her to fall in next to Erufon.

The black dragons circled over the academy—now that the trebuchets weren't firing they were attacking. Our dragons smashed into the hovering, circling crowd, scattering the wild dragons.

"They're too fast," I shouted and saw Seb nod. Then we were under attack.

Seb leaned, we scraped past the right wing of an approaching wild dragon. It flashed out its barbed tail and claws, but Kalax folded her wings and ducked.

Drawing my bow, I tracked the wild dragon who'd almost hit us. I fired. The arrow flew true, but at the last minute the black dragon twisted and caught the arrow—I'd never seen a dragon do that before. I wondered if that was the downside of the affinity—if the dragon had sensed my shot and my intent. If so, I was going to have to get better at shielding my thoughts the way Kalax could.

"Eyes front," Seb called. Another wild black dragon fell out of the dawn, its claws aimed at us.

Seb ducked, Kalax twisted, I was thrown to one side. I almost lost my grip on my bow. I felt a blast of hot breath on my neck, and narrowly missed becoming dragon food.

I caught a fraction of a message from Seb to Ferdinania, urging her to take Merik and Varla over the city and keep protecting the citizens who were fleeing. We were also heading toward Torvald. The fires were now smoky columns in the dawn and they made flying tricky—Kalax had to swoop around the worst of the flames and smoke and even so, I was left coughing. Trying to swing around to watch the sky, I searched for more black dragons.

Glancing back, I saw that Erufon had landed squarely in front of the battered academy gate. A flock of young dragons was helping him scatter the last of the Wildmen and bandits. More dragons circled over the academy, and I saw Gorgax break off with a group of blues to head to the palace—they were picking up and dropping Wildmen as if they were sticks to play with. Others of the enclosure dragons looked to be engaged in battles, driving off the wild dragons, and Jensen, Wil and Dellos soared over the skies above the academy.

Looking down I saw that while we were holding our own in the sky, on the ground the people fleeing Torvald were being picked off by the black dragons and attacked by bandits and Wildmen. I slapped Seb's shoulder. "We need to draw their attention away from those on the ground."

He nodded.

It was going to be risky, but I urged Seb, "Call the wild dragons —get them chasing us!"

He frowned and I wondered if he could do it.

Hunching over his saddle, he grew still. Through Kalax, I felt Seb's thoughts. His shoulders were shaking with the effort, but the words came out clear.

Fight me. Fight!

Looking around, I didn't see any wild dragons heading for us.

Seb called out, "They're too wild and Lord Vincent has too much of a hold on them."

Kalax skimmed the rooftops of the city and I heard a screech behind us. Looking back, I saw the obsidian eyes of the wild, black dragon on our tail. My heart lurched and I looked forward again. "You quite sure about that?" I yelled at Seb.

Silly thing to do, Kalax thought.

Looking up, I could see a half dozen black dragons flying toward us in a disorganized mob. I slapped Seb's shoulder. "Good work. We need to go. And fast."

Seb hunched over Kalax and we started to lead the dragons away from the city. The wild dragons focused on us and nothing else, making it easier for our dragons to come after them, pouncing on the black dragons from the air, knocking them from the sky.

Seb kept up a constant stream of whispers as we were chased. Kalax was fast, I knew, but just how fast was she? Seb didn't seem scared or panicked, but my heart was pounding hard and I clung to the saddle. I thought it must be taking all of his concentration just to stay ahead of the black dragons—and that worried me.

225

It'd be much less scary if he was yelling or howling.

Kalax kept her neck straight and only used her tail to shift the flow of air over her body. I knew that she, too, was concentrating with all of her might. She couldn't miss a single beat of her wings as she ducked, spun, swirled and soared.

Dipping lower, Kalax flew down a narrow street. The gables of roofs exploded behind us as black dragons smashed into the buildings, trying to keep pace with Kalax. Lifting up, Kalax barrel-rolled in a turn and took us under one of the river bridges.

I spared a look over my shoulder.

It was working—our dragons were protecting the escaping people, driving back the Wildmen and the bandits. Gorgax and the dragons with him were keeping the walls beyond the city safe. Torvald might be burning, but the people would be safe in the woods. For now.

The black dragons were also tiring. Knocked to the ground by our dragons, they'd rise and most would turn and head north. Kalax turned and flew straight at five more wild dragons—they scattered in front of her and other dragons took up chasing after them.

Wheeling, Kalax headed up into the dawn clouds. She, too, was starting to tire. She needed rest, food and water. Seb glanced back at me shouting, "We need to find the squadrons and bring them back here."

I nodded. A desperate knot clenched in my stomach. I didn't want to leave Torvald—my home. I wanted to know my parents were safe, that my friends were still alive, but I knew

Seb had the same worries. And without help, the black dragons might return and we could lose the small advantage we'd gained.

"Signal Jensen and Merik—let them know we're going for help. They're going to have to hold out here as long as they can and protect the people. We can't save the city, but we have to protect those who've fled. Tell the dragons," I said.

Seb turned and began to wave signal flags to the two other Dragon Riders—two dragons, two teams of riders. It was so little to hold the slender thread of hope we'd created.

Reaching down, Seb touched Kalax's neck. I thought I saw the air shimmer as he connected with her, asking her to transmit the call to our other dragons.

We go to find the Dragon Riders. Be safe—keep the people and yourselves safe.

Dragons began to peel away to head back to the enclosure—some would guard it. Others—under Gorgax—followed the people who were fleeing the city. Below us, Torvald was burning. Kalax swooped over the city once more and then Seb turned her away to the east.

Can you smell the squadrons? Seb asked Kalax.

She snorted and thought back, *too much smoke yet.*

I knocked another arrow to my bow—I was down to only a few arrows.

A loud roar echoed and a black dragon dove at us, claws out. The dragon knocked into Kalax and sent us spinning. Everything whirled about for a moment. I heard Kalax's grunt and her claws scrabbled on roof tiles and chimneys seeking a grip. She grabbed a building and stopped her fall. I looked up to see Erufon bellowing. He slammed into the wild, black dragon, tangling with it.

Erufon and the black slammed into the woods. I wondered if Erufon had survived—or if he and the wild dragon were both dead now. I had never heard of a dragon doing that for someone who wasn't its rider or mate.

In the pale dawn light, Kalax and the other dragons bellowed a call and the remaining black dragons seemed to scatter at the sound. And we flew away unpursued from the fall of Torvald.

CHAPTER 17
RESCUE

I don't think I'd ever been so tired in all my life. My head thumped as though giants had taken up living there and were trying to break out of my skull with hammers. I don't remember how we ended up in the cave in the mountains by the ruins of an old monastery. The sun was high, but hidden behind grey clouds. I could smell smoke on us and it seemed like the cries of those wounded or killed in the battle for Torvald still rang in my head.

Thea had been looking at me strangely for the past hour, I knew. By the time I'd slid off Kalax, I feared my legs would buckle. Leaning against Kalax so I wouldn't fall, I eased off my helmet. Thea sucked in a hard breath and her eyes narrowed as she stared at me.

Do I really look that terrible? I lifted a hand to wipe the sweat from my face. It came back tacky with blood—my own, I guessed.

"Was I hit by something?" I asked. Fear lanced through me. Would I go the way of the old king—struck down by a poisoned arrow? I was almost too tired to care.

Pulling out a folded cloth, Thea slapped it against my chest. "Seb—you've a nosebleed." She sounded worried. Grabbing my arm, she dragged me with her. Kalax took up the entire front of the cave and fell at once into a deep sleep—only a dragon, or a cat, could sleep like that.

"Let's look at you," Thea said. She pushed me to sit on a boulder and started to run her hands over my head and neck.

I knocked her arm away. "It's just a nosebleed."

Stepping back, she put her hands on her hips. "Just nothing. It was the strain of controlling that many dragons—it could have killed you!"

I nodded and shrugged. She was probably right, but what choice did we have? It was push harder or die.

Right now, my head still spun and an urge for fish lifted in me —I need to fly and fill my belly. I shook my head. Those weren't my thoughts—were they?

Behind us, Kalax yawned and settled deeper into sleep. That was a good idea, but I started to stand. "I should take off her harness and saddles."

"No. We may need to leave quickly. I'll loosen them, but nothing more. You need to rest. Use my cloak. It's not freezing in here, but it's not exactly warm."

She unfastened her cloak and swung it over me. Pushing and shoving, she got me seated on the ground. My body felt numb, occasionally my head felt like a lightning storm was going on inside. But I should do more.

Sleep. Fish. Eat. Drink.

I shook my head. Not my thoughts.

Kalax gave a low laugh. *Dragons know best.*

Yes, we do, I thought back to her.

Sitting in the dark I watched Thea. Kalax's breath began to warm the cave and soon I slept, too, and dreamed of flying, the wind under my wings and the joy of a good fight in my heart.

When I next woke up, it was to the welcome smell of roasting rabbit. For an instant, I thought to stretch my tail and wings, but I remembered the cave—they wouldn't fit. Heart pounding, I sat up and looked around.

I wasn't a dragon.

Hand to my head, I glanced outside.

From the slant of the sun, it was afternoon. I shivered and pulled Thea's cloak tighter. Memories of fangs, talons and fire kept flashing into my head. Kalax, I knew, was near and hunting up stray mountain sheep.

My stomach gurgled and I sat up. I was famished, too.

Thea glanced over at me. "Good, you're up. There's a stream down past the ruins. When you've washed, you can have some breakfast!"

She sounded almost cheerful, but I knew her better than that. Her mouth was set and the lines around her eyes said she was trying to hide her feelings. When she stood, she moved stiffly. She was worried.

About me and everything else.

As well she might be.

I was starting to worry about me, too.

Getting up, I stumbled down to find the swift, clear and cold mountain stream that Thea mentioned. My body felt awkward —too small and no wings or tail to help me balance. I wondered if I hadn't somehow broken the connection with the dragons—was this how I'd always be? A man who felt more like a dragon? Or a dragon who wasn't quite human anymore?

The cold water felt good on my face. I washed off the smoke and grit from my skin and stared at my hands a long time. I also drank down the cold water—it felt good in my belly. Then I sat up and looked at the sky.

Was Torvald really gone?

Were Merik and Varla and the others safe? What of my family —had they gotten out of the city? And Thea's family? Her brothers were with the squadrons, but were her mother and father still alive?

It was all too much to bear thinking about.

Getting up, I walked past the ruins and back to the cave. The world seemed strange to me—every smell seemed vivid and bright. I could hear birds and squirrels and rabbits as I'd never heard them before. I could smell Kalax not far off. I almost sent a thought to her, but decided I needed to watch that just now.

What if I was becoming too much a dragon? I needed to be careful to not let the affinity swallow me.

But why not?

The thought stopped me where I stood.

Why not be more of a dragon? I'd be faster. I'd be stronger. I'd have a family who would never leave me, for were not all dragons one blood? Crossing my arms over my chest, I shook my head. I wasn't going to think that way—but the idea lodged in the back of my mind, ridiculous as it was. I wasn't a dragon —I could never be one. And if I lost my mind thinking that, I'd be no use to anyone.

Heading into the cave, I sat down cross-legged in front of the fire Thea had going. It seemed too small and the cave seemed too cold. She offered me a skinny rabbit leg. I took it and tried to remember not to try and swallow it, bone and all. "I think I have an idea how to find Prince Justin and the others."

"King Justin, now," Thea said, and ate some of the rabbit. She wiped her fingers on her riding leathers. "Do you think even the squadrons will be enough? You saw how many wild dragons Lord Vincent could control—and what he could do at the Winter Ball. He had us all completely witless. If it hadn't been for Kalax..." Thea let her words trail off and shook her head.

I frowned. How had Kalax helped Thea? But then I suddenly knew that Thea had heard Kalax and that had shaken her out of the Memory Stone's control. How could I know that?

I threw the rabbit bones onto the fire even though I really wanted to gulp them down. "If only we'd found the Armour Stone."

Thea stood and walked to the cave entrance. "Ah, yeah, about that...I realized something. Don't be mad at me, but...how much of the battle do you remember?"

I stared at her. "Seriously? As if I could forget any of it." But some bits were...well, they weren't my memories. I could remember swooping down on wild dragons, driving them out of our territory. I could remember thoughts of a dozen dragons —fury, pain, confusion. I remembered having trouble controlling so many minds—the blood and smoke and the utter joy of battle.

Thea reached into one pocket and pulled out a round, black stone. "This was in my saddle bag. It's been there ever since I found it in that small, ruined chapel by the coast where we last searched, remember?"

I nodded. "Yeah...so?"

She hunched down next to me. "Don't you get it, Seb? We shouldn't have survived last night. Kalax was attacked by a wild dragon—that black's claws were out. And what...she got...bumped."

I shook my head. "We were lucky."

"An arrow hit Kalax—I thought it hit a buckle, but now I'm thinking back, it bounced off us because of this." She put the stone into my hand.

It seemed ordinary. A dull black. Smooth, as if worn by water over a long time. It didn't sparkle or shine or anything. It didn't even feel special. I looked at Thea again. "I thought you'd know the Armour Stone as soon as you saw it."

She stood up, walked away and walked back. "I...well, I kept getting these weird headaches every time I sensed the Memory Stone. I thought the Armour Stone would be like that—that it would give me headaches. But this..." She waved at the stone. "It makes me feel calm—and I think it was this stone that helped Kalax break through the Memory Stone's spell."

The Dragon eggs grow in those they touch.

Kalax's thoughts whispered in my head, and I knew Thea had heard her, too.

I also understood Kalax better. The power of the stones was stronger in those who had been touched by the stones. I held up the black stone. "How do we really know this is the Armour Stone?"

"Only one way," Thea said. And she swung her knife at me.

I wanted to twist and lash out with my tail, and that urge held me still. The knife flashed fast and simply skimmed over my arm as if it had struck real armour. It hadn't even cut my flying leathers. Face hot, I stared up at Thea. "Are you trying to kill me?"

She nodded and tucked her knife back in its sheath. "That's the Armour Stone. That's the proof of it."

"I thought there'd be...well, more to it. A flash of light, a sense of power, something like the Dragon Affinity."

Thea nodded. "Me, too. But...well, it just makes me feel calmer. And, well, I don't get those headaches. But I also don't get the same sense I did from any other stone. It's weird that way. It's almost like...well, like it has its own armour to help it stay hidden." She sat down in front of the fire again. "We almost died several times last night, Seb. I know we didn't in part to your navigation and partly due to Kalax being as brave as she was." I felt a deep, rumbling purr from Kalax. Thea waved at the Armour Stone. "But we got a lot of help from the Armour Stone."

I held out the stone. "Here, you should keep it with you—you found it after all."

You're chosen by a dragon, not a dragon's egg! Kalax huffed the thought into my mind. I kept pushing the stone at Thea. "It'll keep you safe. I have the Dragon Affinity, after all."

She glanced at the stone as if she wasn't sure she wanted it, but after a moment, she reached out and grabbed it. "I'll leave it with Kalax in the bag on my saddle. But...now what do we do? You said you had an idea about finding the...the king."

I stood up. "With the Armour Stone, we have a chance again. And I think Kalax can find the other dragons."

⚜

Kalax tried scenting for dragons, but either the wind wasn't blowing the right way or we were too far away. I couldn't sense dragons, either, except for a few who had left the enclosure to stay with the people of Torvald, who'd fled into the mountains. We were guessing about where to go, but since the commander had been mapping the south, I figured that was as good a place as any. A black haze marked where Torvald stood, and I kept shifting my gaze away from that. Worry for my folks chewed at me, but I knew we needed more help. Rushing back on Kalax wouldn't get us anything, except maybe into another battle or captured.

Several times, Kalax would swoop down into the valleys and settle under the trees. I knew why—I could sense the wild, black dragons, too. And I knew they were coming from miles away. The wild dragons were always fighting with each other, bickering like kids.

Our dragons were way more confident—more like adults.

Because we have a home and family, Kalax thought to me.

I knew that was right—and I liked that same sense of security. It was one of the best things about being a dragon. But I had to shake off that thought several times. One thing became clear, however. The hold that the Darkening had on the wild dragons seemed to be weaker just here. The wild dragons out here were starting to act more like they were wild, darting across the sky, chasing each other, getting distracted by prey on the ground.

I remembered how, last night, they'd seemed more like a swarm—the Darkening had been directing them. I shelved that information in the back of my mind, wondering if we could make use of it in the future.

We flew on through the day and into early evening. The land-scape below had turned from mottled greens and browns to the tan of the desert. In that empty landscape, the pinpricks of firelight easily stood out. I called out to Thea, "Does that look like a camp to you?"

At the same time, Kalax chirruped and was answered by a brief, muted call.

Brothers and sisters, she thought.

I could sense the other dragons too, but that only left me uneasy.

"The rest of the riders," Thea said excitement in her voice.

Kalax glided down toward to ground. At closer range, we could see not just campfires but the white tents of Dragon Riders. The dragons were spread out near a river. It looked like the squadrons hadn't been in the air in days.

Some training exercise, I thought.

Kalax called to the other dragons as she chose her landing spot, a little away from the others. I started to wonder why the squadrons hadn't come to Torvald's aid. From this distance they wouldn't have heard the Dragon Horn, but they must have sensed the enclosure dragons taking flight.

Uneasy now, I stayed on Kalax until she'd landed then slipped from the saddle.

Kalax sniffed the air and suddenly recoiled. "Kalax? What is it?" I asked.

Sickness. There is sickness on this camp.

I could smell it too, now. A dry, dusty smell. Something off like a flower that was wilting and smelled bad. Kalax sprang upwards into the air and flew a few lazy circles around the camp. I wanted to go with her. She landed again at a spot upwind from the main camp, near the fast flowing stream and a sheltering cliff.

Kalax will not sleep with sickness.

Wise girl, I thought to her. I started to think the same to Thea, then remembered I needed to use words.

When I told her about the sickness and its smell, and she gave me a long, hard look as if she wasn't sure how I knew all this, but I just told her, "We need to see what we can do to help."

Heading into camp, the sky dark overhead and fires twinkling ahead of us, I wanted to run and find the commander. But the feelings I was getting from the dragons around us wasn't good. It seemed like they were wheezing—having trouble even just breathing.

"What's wrong with them?" Thea asked.

I shook my head. "It's not Dragon Sickness, that much is sure. They're…they're tired. But…I know they haven't been flying. Not for days."

It was odd, walking past slumbering dragons and what looked like weary riders. It felt to me like we were walking through a house of the sick or a strange sort of statue garden. I should be able to feel the dragon's natural inquisitiveness as they snuffed the air and sought to find out who I was and why I was so close —but the dragons didn't care. And in large groups of Dragon Riders like this, there should be games being played or wrestling matches being held. Someone should have out a flute or someone should be singing. Dragon Riders lived a hard life —but also knew to relax when given the chance.

None of that was going on.

I shared a look with Thea. She seemed as nervous as I felt.

The riders we saw were huddled near their fires. Everyone looked…well, as if the sickness was in the riders not just the dragons.

We neared one of the larger campfires. Just as I'd started to wonder why didn't they have guards posted, a man called out, "Who goes there?"

I'd seen this rider before, at the Troll's Head. Dafyd. He was big and broad, and an older rider like Thea's brothers.

Thea stepped forward. "It's good to find you—we've come from the academy."

Dafyd scowled at us. "How do we know you're not some bandits?"

I saw Thea's fists bunch, so I stepped forward now. "Dafyd, friend. It's Seb. Surely you can recognize a Dragon Rider's uniform?" But I wasn't sure he could. Our uniforms looked filthy from the battle and still smelled of smoke and sweat.

Dafyd's frown didn't lift. "They look old to me. Who are you —deserters?"

"How dare you!" Thea pushed in front of the other rider. "Do you not recognize me? I'm a Flamma and a Dragon Rider, and if you call me a deserter again I'll make you eat your words. Now where's Commander Hegarty? Where are my brothers, Ryan and Reynalt?"

Scrubbing a hand over his face, Dafyd seemed to shake off some of his addled wits. He muttered, "Vagabonds." But he gave a shrug and waved us forward. "Okay, let's just see what the commander has to say about you."

"That's all we ask," I said, walking ahead of him and pulling Thea with me into the main camp.

To my great relief, I saw Commander Hegarty standing in front of the command tents. They were at least set up properly, in a rough circle in the center of camp. A bonfire glowed brighter as someone tossed wood onto it. They'd been out to collect wood, food and water—but why did all the dragons seem to be grounded.

Heading toward him, I called out, "Commander! It's me, Seb. And Thea!" He turned and I thought he'd break into one of his sharp grins.

Instead, he turned and stared at us, eyes narrowed and his mustache twitching. "What do you think you are doing, sneaking around my camp? Why are you here? I should have you clapped in irons for leaving your post."

Mouth open I could only stare. Was this an act of some kind? A ploy like the one he'd arranged so we could meet his brother?"

He stepped forward. "If you don't answer me, I'll have you whipped."

I had never seen him like this—actually losing his temper. Commander Hegarty had always preferred a quiet word to correct anyone.

Thea elbowed her way past Dafyd. "Commander, we have no post left."

Hegarty opened his mouth to say something, but another voice called out, "Commander?"

Turning, I saw three men step from one of the command tents. I knew them by sight—Thea's older brothers and Prince...no, King Justin.

"Ryan!" Thea said the relief leaking into her voice. "Reynalt!"

I shifted on my feet, still uneasy. Ryan I knew, was a few years older than Thea and was the prince's navigator. Reynalt commanded the aerial squadrons, and it was he who had spoken.

He hurried the Thea's side and caught her in a hug. Stepping back, he said, "I'm sorry, little sister." He glanced at Dafyd, and the Dragon Rider fell back into the shadows. Turning to Thea, Reynalt said, his voice sounding tired, "We've been having a terrible time. First the dragons got sick, and then fights broke out amongst the men." Reynalt's stare seemed to fade for a moment and I wondered if he, too, was struggling with the illness.

I glanced at the commander who was now staring at the ground and frowning. Ryan also seemed unfocused and tired, his shoulders slumped and his face lined with stress.

But Justin stepped forward. He wore the small, silver circlet of the Prince of Torvald, and I wondered now if we should have brought him the king's crown.

Tears glittered in Thea's eyes, but she stiffened her back and said, "Justin—Your Majesty, I have terrible news.

"You should hear about this nightmare," Justin said irritably, before his voice petered. He rubbed a hand over his face. I saw then in the firelight that he'd worn new lines around his mouth and eyes. For a moment, silence held us all. I heard only the snap of wood in the fire and the wheeze of dragons with labored breathing. That dry, dusty smell wasn't so bad here, I thought.

No one else seemed able to move, so I did.

Going down on one bent knee, I bowed my head to our new monarch. "The king is dead. Long live the king. All hail King Justin."

Beside me, Thea did the same. More silence—a stunned one, I thought—followed the words, and then Justin...well, the king...looked from me to Thea. "What? My father?" The words came out in a strangled whisper and I knew then that he had cared for his father as more than just his king.

Thea looked up at Ryan and Reynalt. Their skin seemed to pale in the flickering firelight. Commander Hegarty went down on one knee, then Ryan and Reynalt and the air echoed with their voices.

"The king is dead. Long live the king. All hail King Justin of Torvald!"

"It cannot be." King Justin staggered for a step and I thought he would fall. Not the best omen as the first act of a new king. But the commander stood and held out a hand. King Justin caught his grip and swayed. I could hear the word spreading through the camp—soft mutters followed by the creak of leather armour. I glanced around to see the Dragon Riders starting to ring the command tents. They all knelt and a few echoed the same words, "All hail King Justin."

Thea stood up, as did I. I could see tears glimmering unshed in the new king's eyes. But he let go of the commander's hand, glanced around, then stepped to where the firelight would better show him. He looked more a Dragon Rider than a king—he wore the same armour we wore, with only a little extra gold and silver threads to show his family banner on his chest.

Lifting his hands, he cleared his throat and called out, "Dragon Riders. Arise and await further orders."

Slowly, the other riders stood and headed back to their camp fires. King Justin turned to Thea, "What happened? You must tell us. Was it a peaceful passing? An accident?"

Thea shook her head, glanced at me, and then took a deep breath. "It was treachery. Torvald has fallen, Your Majesty. Lord Vincent—the Darkening—attacked the citadel while the squadrons were away. A poisoned arrow struck down your father."

The king was shaking his head slowly, not with disbelief but as if to clear something from his mind. He brushed his fingers over his eyes. "Lord who? Wasn't he from the Southern Realm? Or did he have lands in the north?" His eyes clouded. "It cannot be."

Thea wet her lips, but she glanced away as if she couldn't bear to see the king like this—or as if she was thinking too much of how King Durance died.

Stepping forward, I took up the report. "The Darkening, Your Majesty. The same evil we fought in King's Village just a little over a year ago, sire. The Darkening is back. Torvald is burnt, and the palace is in ruins."

The king stared at me. My heart sank—he was still under the influence of the Memory Stone and we needed to find a way to break that.

Reynalt gave a nod. "Deep Wood and Hillars Pass. Both towns have vanished. We were about to follow reports of yet a third, but it seems they might have been meant to divert us from Torvald. The whole city gone you say?"

Turning away, the king headed for his tent. "I—I must have a moment. Time to think." Rubbing his forehead, he disappeared into his tent.

Thea turned to her brother. "Ryan, shouldn't you go with him?"

Ryan shook his head. "I will in a bit, but first I need to hear what happened." He glanced from me to Thea. He looked older now than when I'd last seen him. His blue eyes darkened with worry. "What, exactly, do you mean Torvald has fallen—that it's burnt?"

Slapping a hand on Ryan's shoulder, Reynalt shook his head and said to Commander Hegarty. "Let us hear the story in comfort."

He started to turn to his tent but that dry smell was getting stronger again. I wanted to get away from here. I was already starting to feel tired, as if I could hardly move. Stepping in front of Reynalt, Ryan and Commander Hegarty, I said, "If you don't mind, I can give a better report over by Kalax—we're camped just a little bit over."

The three men swapped glances. Already their shoulders were slumping again. But I needed to get them away from this smell —to fresh air. I had to get them out of this foul sickness, and I was determined to make it harder for them to resist me than it was for them to come with me.

It took a lot more talking, but Thea pushed too and we got the commander, Reynalt and Ryan to come with us to a small camp near Kalax. I didn't want to burn any wood—I had a feeling it was the fumes from the fires that were making everyone tired.

Thea and I took turns telling what had happened since the squadrons left, and talking about the battle. We left out the part about meeting with Commander Hegarty's brother, Jodreth— and the Armour Stone. As we talked, Commander Hegarty's stare sharpened, Ryan's eyes seemed to brighten and Reynalt stopped looking as hunched over as an old man. I could hear the rattle and snores of riders and dragons outside our small circle and I wondered if we'd be able to get everyone away from this spot.

"So all our people are hiding in the countryside?" Hegarty scratched his chin. "Terrible business this, terrible!" Hegarty still looked depressed and defeated.

I glanced at Thea, then asked, "Commander, what's happened here? Tell us about the illness?"

Hegarty glanced at me, his eyes sharpening slightly. I gave him a small nod, and wondered if he understood that I was trying to tell him we'd done as he'd asked and had met his brother. He straightened where he sat on the sandy ground. "Yes, well, we got reports, didn't we, captain?" He glanced at Ryan.

Ryan nodded. "Villages disappearing."

The commander let out a breath. "The prince ordered a prompt investigation. It…I remember asking the…well, the king now, if he thought this wise to take all the squadrons. Why not just a few. But he was adamant." He shook his head. "It is hard to find evidence of something that should be there but isn't."

"And the sickness?" Thea asked. She leaned forward, bracing her elbows on her knees. "What happened to the dragons? Why aren't they flying?"

Reynalt shifted and answered her. "That happened soon after we arrived. It's this place. We had to camp, and a night's rest made it worse rather than better. We couldn't rouse them. We've tried feeding them, but they're not interested, not even in fish. Perhaps one more night…We'll see how they are in the morning."

A chill spread over my skin. How long had he been saying this very same thing, over and over again. "How long do you think you've been here?" I glanced up at the dark cliffs and hills around us and asked the dragons the same question. I got back a confused blur of time from them that left my head spinning.

Reynalt shook his head and glanced at his brother. Ryan yawned. "Not long."

"Caught here while Torvald burned." I said the words louder than I'd intended. Anger burned hot inside me and pushed the words out with a sharp bite.

Commander Hegarty stood. "We should get back. We'll rally the riders in the morning at first light." Ryan and Reynalt stood, too. All of them looked better, but I wasn't sure if it was because they had been away from the fires, or something else that might be helping them.

I glanced at Thea and slowly climbed to my feet as she did the same.

Ryan asked her, "There's an extra cot in the command tent if you wish it."

She glanced at me and shook her head. "My place is with my navigator and my dragon."

He shrugged, and the three men headed back to the camp.

I turned to Thea. "We can't stay here. Whatever's making them sick, I felt it earlier, too. But now I don't feel so bad."

Thea nodded. "I think…well, I think the Armour Stone's helping to protect us. That's why they got better, here, too—the stone is still in Kalax's saddlebag. I sent a thought to Kalax and found she was only lightly resting—she didn't like the feeling here, either.

I put a hand on her side. "The Armour Stone won't protect everyone. If we can't rouse the riders and dragons, we're going to have to find some other way to stop the Darkening."

Thea shivered, and I remembered we were talking about leaving her brothers here with that sickness. "We have to rouse them somehow!"

A sudden idea struck me. "Tomorrow," I promised her. "Commander Hegarty should have the Healing Stone—maybe that can help everyone. And if not...well, maybe we can find Jodreth and he can help us." I knew I sounded a lot braver than I felt.

I was starting to feel that we were as good as dead already.

CHAPTER 18
LONG LIVE THE KING

I was tumbling down into the dark—I was going to die again.

Air rushed past me. Warmth and light vanished.

It was just like that time in the cave.

Panic swept through me, a cold anxiety spreading through my veins. I couldn't breathe, couldn't move.

Give up...let go

A sudden memory of Seb stirred...*Seb staring at me, brown eyes wide. A slow smile curing his wide mouth. Kalax, with her rattle-purr...How could I leave them?*

They need me.

I sat up with a gasp.

Like a flood, visions and memories swamped me.

Mother, looking scared but resolute, as she left to help others flee Torvald. She was brave and she'd sought to do the right thing, even if she didn't particularly want to. I saw my brothers, Ryan and Reynalt, both looking older and their shoulders sagging. What would life be like for them if I just gave up? Merik, Varla, all of my friends at the academy—even Justin. He was a king now and had need of friends around him.

Oddly, I couldn't bring to mind my father's face.

I pushed that idea out of my head.

I won't fall. I won't die.

Getting up, I stared at the dawn. I wasn't falling anymore. No, I would make my stand on solid ground, ready for anything.

Something in me had changed.

"Thea?" Seb's worried voice pulled me from staring at the first rays of dawn.

I turned and saw his face was looking pinched. Behind him, Kalax was raising her great, crimson head to snuff the air. The air seemed light and dusty. I could hear the sounds of snoring and groaning from both dragons and riders in the camp. The air smelled faintly of smoke, with a hint of spices.

Getting up, Seb came over to me. "You okay?"

"Yes, I think I am." I stretched and rubbed my eyes. Was this the Armour Stone making me feel better? Was it protecting me from what Lord Vincent had done to me—or even from the aftereffects of the Healing Stone? Whatever it was, I liked it.

"Well, okay, good." Seb nodded and flashed a tight smile. "I thought I heard you saying 'no' over and over in your sleep."

I slapped his arm. "I'm awake now." We headed to the stream and I washed my face and hands. For the first time in what seemed a year, I felt refreshed, like I was finally getting back to my normal self again. We had some dried meat and very dry bread in the saddlebags and we had that for breakfast. Kalax snorted at that and thought to me that she would hunt after we left this place.

Then Seb and I made plans.

Today, I'd carry the Armour Stone with me. Kalax would fly a short distance away—far enough that she felt safe but close enough that Seb could call her back when we were ready to go. Kalax didn't like the idea of us staying here while she flew to safety, but Seb convinced her that the Armour Stone would look after us. She took off and I watched until she was a small, red dot in the sky. Then we headed into the Dragon Riders' camp again.

If we had thought that what we'd seen last night was bad, this morning—in bright sunlight—was even worse. It made me grit my teeth. I was angry at the riders, and even more angry at what was being done to them.

The dragons weren't really ill, or they didn't seem to be, but they were lethargic, opening an eye or hissing at the air weakly, before collapsing back against the warming sands. They didn't even bother to feed from the buckets of scraps left out for them.

Not bad fish, Kalax whispered to me.

Beside me, Seb flashed a brief smile at me.

I had been worried that perhaps he'd be jealous of Kalax sharing her thoughts with me and not just with him, but he seemed to be pleased about it, like it made us even more of a team. But I was still worried about Seb. He was so close to the dragons, how could this sickness not affect him, too?

Don't need to be a dragon friend to see what is happening, Kalax thought at me.

I frowned and moved closer to Seb, so the Armour Stone might help him, too. Seb glanced at me, his eyebrows lifted. He hadn't heard Kalax that last time—so she really could choose who to talk to and who to argue with.

"Just look at these dragons." I sighed and waved at the huge bulk of lazing dragons. Kalax was right—anyone could see they were suffering from something much more insidious and treacherous than just sickness, and it wasn't due to bad fish.

"I think it's getting worse," Seb said.

In the camp, riders were stumbling out of their tents, some half-dressed and some barely able to walk.

I pulled back and wanted to turn and walk away.

All Dragon Riders lived to fly. We all trained hard, both in the air and on the ground. We were taught to rise before dawn, to keep watch, to eat sparingly and train hard. We were feared and respected—you had to be more than good when there were only two of you piloting a battle dragon. You couldn't afford to be lazy. Every piece of clothing and equipment had to be in the best condition, because one strap could be the difference between life and death when you were up in the clouds. That was why cadets were hammered on with details before they could become riders.

But these didn't even look as good as the rawest of recruits.

Some riders stumbled around, eyes barely opened. Others sat down by unlit fires, staring at the ashes. They didn't even seem interested in food, either. Uniforms looked dirty, and many hadn't bothered to put away their harnesses but had left saddles and leathers out in the open where the weather could ruin them or creatures could chew on them.

Tugging on Seb's sleeve, I told him, "Maybe we should just set out on our own."

He gave a slow nod, but then I heard Ryan's voice and saw him walking from campfire to unlit campfire.

"Riders, get up. Fall in!" Ryan was shouting. Hegarty was with him, looking as if he'd slept in his riding leathers.

"The ... the king orders everyone attend. No, that's not right at all. What was it? Oh, the coronation. Riders, gather!" Ryan lifted a horn and blew a low mournful sound.

Slowly the riders began to stand and stumble toward the command tents following Hegarty and Ryan. All of it would have been funny, were it not for the danger we faced—and fear pulsed under my skin that perhaps there was no way to cure either riders or dragons.

Next to me, Seb kicked at a pebble with his boot. "The king wants his coronation. At least that's a start."

We headed to the circle of command tents to find servants and a few riders were wearily dragging camp chairs out to a cleared area.

Commander Hegarty stood off to one side. Seb nudged me and then headed to the commander's side.

"Commander?" I said and hoped he'd remember us—that he wasn't as bad as yesterday.

He did seem better. He at least nodded and flashed a small smile. "Should be a nice coronation, I hope. A new start for us." His voice started to trail off, but picked again. "We'll get the king back to Torvald, don't you worry."

"Torvald has fallen," I told him again.

He blinked and his mouth pulled down. "Yes, yes, I remember now. But we'll take it back."

A surge of hope flashed through me. This sounded more like the Hegarty I knew. I glanced at Seb, then asked the commander, "Sir, do you have the Healing Stone? Will it help with this...this sickness?"

Hegarty shook his head. "I don't know. I put it someplace safe. It's safe...I think."

Seb leaned closer to the commander and said, his voice quiet, "Sir, we met with your brother."

"My brother?" Hegarty frowned, his forehead tightened with deep lines. "What do you mean?"

I shook my head, but Seb pressed on. "You asked us to watch the cabin, you wanted us to learn about—"

"What?" Hegarty's face suddenly paled. He grabbed Seb's arm and dragged him behind the command tent. I followed. Glancing from Seb to me and back again, Hegarty shook his head. "What are you speaking of?" His eyes narrowed. "Do you think to use him against me? Against us all?"

Seb swapped a worried look with me. I didn't know if I wanted to shout or cry at the pain of seeing the commander like this.

Hegarty still had hold of Seb's arm and was looking around us. "No one must know. Not even me. If the Memory Stone is used on me, I'll tell him. I'll tell him everything. He'll pull it from my mind."

I think that dragon might have already flown, Commander.

Shivering, I wondered if Commander Hegarty even had the Healing Stone still—what if he'd lost it? Or suppose Lord Vincent has taken it? I put a hand on the commander's arm "Sir, the secret is safe with us. But—"

"No buts." A blank look passed over his face. He shook off my hand and scrubbed his fingers over the stubble on his cheeks. "A house…no, a cabin. You were set to watch. You have your orders. Cripple Creek it is. And now there's the king. We must go."

Frowning, I watched Hegarty head back to the circle of command tents. I glanced at Seb. "Wasn't that cabin in Tabbit's Hollow?"

Seb nodded very slowly. The corner of his mouth crooked. "I think the commander just gave us a new clue, which means the real Commander Hegarty is still with us. There's still hope."

We started to skirt the crowd so we could leave, but the new king saw me and waved me closer. A small platform had been created—just rocks piled up, really. Justin stood there, a royal-red cloak over his flying leathers. At least he looked clean and shaven, even if all the other riders looked scruffier than any of Seb's old neighbors.

Reynalt stood beside the king holding the silver circlet of the prince. It was going to have to make do as a crown fit for a king.

Seb started to try and slip away again, but when I tried to follow, Ryan scowled at me and grabbed my arm, making me stay put.

Waving a hand, the king said, "Well, get on with it!"

Everyone could hear him. I winced, but Ryan turned to the assembled riders. At least, Ryan and Reynalt had put on dress uniforms—their leathers gleamed and their armour glinted bright in the sunlight. I felt both underdressed and embarrassed at my battle-worn uniform, but I wasn't half-dressed like most of the riders.

From the look of panic on Ryan's face, however, something which I hadn't seen very often, he'd never planned to crown a king.

"Riders," Ryan called out. Everyone turned to him and the quiet mutterings from the back stilled. "We ask you to gather and stand witnesses to a great event."

Come on, Ryan, you can do this.

"And to this union of—" He broke off and bit his lower lip. I frowned—was he thinking about a wedding? Ryan cleared his throat. "Of man and realm!"

I let out a breath.

Ryan stepped back and held a hand to indicate the new king. "Here before you is Justin, son of Durance, heir to the throne of the Middle Kingdom. Do you recognize him as your new king?"

A few scattered cheers sounded but Ryan suddenly frowned and glanced at the king. "Oh no—that bit comes later, doesn't it?"

"By the First!" Justin sighed and lifted a weary hand. "Does anyone know how the ceremony goes? Anyone?"

"Uh, invocation of right," Reynalt said, sounding unsure. "And then…uh, vows?"

"Vows and then invocation of right," Hegarty called out, stamping his foot as though he was certain. It made sense he would know—he was the only one of us here old enough to recall King Durance's crowning.

"Isn't there something about witnesses?" Reynalt asked. "To act as legal counsel and what-have-you?"

"I thought the audience had been called as witnesses?" Ryan prompted.

Hegarty shrugged, and I was ready to tell them all to just get on with it. Rolling my eyes, I grit my teeth as Ryan went on.

"With great sadness we mourn the passing of King Durance, but celebrate the coming of King Justin!" Ryan said.

"Long live the king," the crowd chanted with less than great enthusiasm. I looked around the faces and thought they all looked as if they were about to fall over.

"King Justin, do you swear by the First Dragon and by your blood to…" Frowning, Ryan glanced at Reynalt, and he hissed back, "To protect the people of the Middle Kingdom?"

"I swear," Justin called out.

"Do you—what else does he have to do? Oh, right—swear to uphold the ancient kinship between dragon and human, as was honored by your father?"

Justin muffled a yawn and straightened. "I swear," he mumbled, and I started to wonder if he was going to stay awake. I edged closer to him, hoping the Armour Stone might help him.

"Do you claim your throne?" Ryan said, his voice stronger now.

I wasn't sure the crowning was supposed to end like that, but everyone was nodding and Reynalt placed the crown on Justin's head.

Voice strong now, Ryan said, "I pronounce you King Justin, Defender of Torvald, Protector of the Middle Kingdom and the Near Islands, Warden of the Leviathan Mountains. Long may you reign!"

The riders cheered. Justin lifted his hands so he could make a speech. I glanced at Seb and told him, "I really can't stand any more of this."

He gave a nod. With all eyes on King Justin, I was able to step back. Ryan and Reynalt didn't seem to see me slip away—they looked exhausted, their faces lined and pale, their shoulders slumping. King Justin was going on and on, saying there were great deeds yet to be done.

Falling into step with Seb, we made for the outskirts of the camp. Seb glanced back over his shoulder. "Do you think Hegarty gave the Healing Stone to his brother?"

I nodded, then shrugged. "It would make sense. If Jodreth knows how to slip away from a dragon, well…he's not an ordinary person, is he? One way or another, we need help."

Seb nodded and looked up into the sky. "Then let's go find Cripple Creek."

CHAPTER 19
JODRETH

T hea and I waited for Kalax on the edge of camp. Once Kalax returned for us, she couldn't get away from the rider camp fast enough. It was as if she wanted to wash her whole body with the clean air. I could sense the tiny sliver of fear she kept trying to bury at what she had seen and felt down there.

From my seat behind her neck, I told her, *that won't happen to you. Ever. And we'll find a way to help the others.*

Kalax remained stubbornly silent. She focused on flying faster, heading toward the line of tall mountains that split the Middle Kingdom almost in two and which bounded the fiercer, wild lands to the north. Kalax had seen in my mind the name Cripple Creek on the maps I had once studied in the now-destroyed map room. It was the name of a narrow, winding creek that ran through the mountains. It was spring-fed and year-round water, so it was a good place to water a dragon. I remembered Merik telling me that and the memory made me wonder how he was doing. Was he with the others from Torvald? Was he okay? Was he with Varla and...

I cut off the thoughts. If I kept thinking about those I missed, those I worried about, I'd only worry more.

It took us almost to mid-day to get to the thin mountain stream that cut deeply through the foothills.

Kalax landed. We dismounted and stared at the splashing creek.

"No house," Thea said. She put her hands on her hips and swept her stare up and down the length of the visible creek. "The commander got it wrong—or did we get it wrong?"

It was my worst fear—that whatever magic had been laid upon the commander had mixed up his memories about his brother and the Healing Stone. Despair hovered over me, dark, and starting to drag at me.

Tucking one hand into my belt, I turned and stared at Kalax. She stared back at me. Thea nudged me in the side. "What is it?"

"Kalax," I said.

Stepping in front of me, Thea put her hands on my shoulders. "I need words. Stop thinking at her and talk to me."

I waved a hand at our dragon. "Kalax took us to Jodreth. She liked him. Maybe she'll be able to smell his scent."

Dropping her hands, Thea gave me a sideways look.

"It's true. Kalax could even smell the spices of the Southern Realm. And dragons seem to have a connection to...to more."

Thea waved a hand. "It sounds like we're clutching at straws, but if that's the best option that we have, let's try it."

I reached out to Kalax. *Can you find the commander's brother —the one we met in the cabin we watched?*

Salted fish! Kalax purred happily at the memory. *Dragons never forget who has fed them.*

That set me wondering. Were dragons connected to everyone they liked, no matter the distance? That opened up new possibilities.

I held my breath and sensed Kalax reaching out with her own mind. A distant pressure built inside my head and chest. It was as if somewhere in the depths of Kalax's mind and soul a fine harp string had been plucked and was vibrating. I followed that thread, but Kalax pushed me—a gentle nudge—and the sensation vanished.

Humans aren't ready for that. Back to your own body.

Kalax nudged me again, closing our connection.

Frustrated, with nothing better to do, I mounted the saddle again. Thea did as well. Kalax remained on the ground.

"Has she got it? Has she got the scent of him?" Thea asked.

The answer was Kalax launching us into the air again.

Dragons!

Kalax's warning sounded in my mind just as I sensed the other dragons too.

We were flying low over the tall pines. Kalax shifted and landed just under an overhang in cliffs above the trees. It was late in the day and we had been flying long enough for my legs and back to be tired. Kalax's enthusiasm, however, was unmistakable. She kept thinking about salted fish and it was making me hungry.

"What is it?" Thea asked, leaning forward to scan the skies.

I glanced around. "Kalax sensed other dragons, but she wouldn't hide unless...there!" I pointed to where, far to the south of us, a dozen dragons flew. They were not like the wild, black dragons, but seemed to be a sandy-orange colour with long tails and very wide wings. "Southern dragons?" I was guessing I knew, but the description matched some of what I'd read in the books at the academy. "What are they doing up here?"

"Do you think they've come to the aid of King Justin?" Thea asked hopefully. It was good to see her looking on the bright side of things again.

I shook my head. "I don't think so—you saw how the king and the others were. How could they have sent word all the way to the Southern Realm, and even if they had, why wouldn't the dragons be flying to him? But...the commander had maps in his study. I think he was searching for southern dragons. It could be that Lord Vincent took advantage of what he knew?"

Thea shook her head and pushed up her flying goggles so they sat on her helmet. "It feels too much like a slice of good luck for dragons to suddenly appear out of the south at just the time that our own have been scattered."

I agreed, and we watched the orange dragons disappear across the horizon. A longing lifted in my chest to fly off with them— to ask them were they were going and go with them. I was so focused on the orange dragons that I didn't notice the wild, black dragons overhead until the air filled with their screaming and shrill cries.

"Watch out!" Thea called out.

A flight of the smaller, wild dragons—barely half the size of Kalax—screamed off in the same direction as the southern dragons. Another, much larger wild black, bigger than Kalax, with a mane of spines all around her neck and a multiple-barbed tail, followed.

"A brood mother," I breathed.

I could feel Kalax's nervous jitters. She was eager to be away from so many dragons, and so was I, but I willed her to be still. *Let them pass. Let them pass,* I breathed at her, but it was no good.

The brood dragon shrieked, jerking her head to stare at where we were hidden. I was afraid she'd caught me talking to Kalax.

There was no time to think. Kalax let go of the cliff overhang. She dropped down low, skimming the treetops. With three, powerful bursts of her wings, she soared upwards toward clouds that were gathering around the mountain top.

The brood dragon bellowed a challenge, followed by the smaller yips and shrieks of her children.

Thea drew her bow and notched an arrow, twisting to look back at the blacks.

"Wait, Thea, wait," I yelled. "We'll use the clouds as cover, maybe sneak away from the whole pack without having to fight."

Something hit Kalax's side and we tumbled through the clouds. It was the wild, brood dragon. She had emerged like a mountain through the clouds and had scraped a claw over Kalax's side. The blow was meant to gut Kalax, but she seemed unharmed. The Armour Stone was still working for us.

"Thea, hold on!" I shouted. I urged Kalax into a tumbling fall. At the last moment, she spread her wings to slow her descent. The brood dragon fell almost on top of us, and Kalax flared out her legs in a vicious, scratching frenzy. Kalax drew blood from the black. The brood dragon backed off, but the smaller dragons swarmed around us.

"Seb," Thea shouted, standing up in her saddle to throw a short javelin at the nearest black dragon, where it tangled with the dragon's wings, sending it spiraling to the ground. That left three more, closing in on us, and the wounded mother still circling.

Leaning back in my harness and saddle, I threw my arms wide, closed my eyes and opened myself to the dragons.

The thoughts of the wild dragons filled me; full of hate and anger.

Beyond the steadier thoughts of their brood mother I sensed something else. A feeling that didn't feel like it came from a dragon's mind.

I could hear the summons Lord Vincent had sent out, an awkward command that had annoyed the dragons, even though they couldn't resist. I could see a pale man—Lord Vincent—but he was surrounded, consumed by a dark cloud, something evil and rank. The blackness behind him was not just a thing—it had intelligence, I knew. I could feel it returning my curiosity. The dragons shrank in fear from that presence, as did I.

The world shifted as I saw the world from the eyes of the smaller dragons. Kalax was swiping her tail and claws to keep them at bay. Because of the Armour Stone, they wouldn't be able to harm us, but they were delaying us.

Reaching out, I told them, *Find Rest. Tired. Sleep. This dragon is too big for you.*

The wild dragons shuddered as if hit by a wave of cold, but were still coming.

I poured all my strength through the link, becoming a dragon myself, calling to them with a dragon's mind.

The brood dragon called out, gathering her smaller dragons and turning tail. Kalax snarled at them—as did I.

For a moment, my mind held with the black dragons. I would fly with them—go with them. Rest. Sleep.

The slap of Thea's hand on my shoulder shook me from the link.

I opened my eyes, but I was dizzy and exhausted.

Found your Jodreth, Kalax told me.

Glancing down, I saw a foothill with scrubby mountain grass and goats that were scattering, running from Kalax. A small, stone-block house was built half into the side of the hill itself. From afar, it looked like another pile of rocks, but a lone figure with a dirty grey cloak stood outside the door, leaning on a staff.

"You found him, Kalax! It's Jodreth!" Thea said and slapped my shoulder enthusiastically.

The sorcerer—that's what the wild, brood dragon had called him.

I caught that last bit of memory from my connection to the wild dragons. So they knew him as well. That was odd. Slumping in my saddle, I was almost too tired to even fly Kalax. She swooped down to land on her own, folding her wings around the small stone-built goat shed for warmth as Thea jumped from the saddle and I climbed down like an old man.

"Seb, Agathea." Jodreth nodded at us. "The skies are thick with the enemy." He shot me a curious look, but waved us inside.

I hesitated. "But what about Kalax? We…I mean she can't just sit out here!"

"No," Thea agreed. "The Darkening will spot her."

Jodreth bowed his head. "A little patience, please. Now go inside!" He gave us a push inside with his staff.

On the other side of the simple wooden door we found a tiny cottage very similar to the cabin, except this cabin seemed made more of stone and dirt.

Leaning over to Thea, I said, "I wonder how many of these little bolt-holes he has." She shrugged and moved away to run her fingers over a shelf of scrolls and what looked like potions in glass bottles, and a lot of what looked like junk to me, but Merik would have loved it. Stubs of waxy candles had dripped all over the wooden workbenches. Dried herbs hung from the hooks in the walls and from the ceiling, giving the room a faintly spicy smell. I didn't see a bed, but fire burned low in a small hearth and an iron kettle sat bubbling over the flames.

"Seb, is that normal?" Thea pointed out of the one, deep window that looked out from the rock house. The world seemed to have disappeared into a milky-white fog.

Jodreth came back into the cottage, throwing back his hood. "It won't last for long, but will give us enough time for a short chat. You are both in grave danger." He turned to us.

"I think we guessed that already." Thea faced him, her arms crossed over her chest.

One eyebrow arched high, Jodreth shook his head. "I don't think you understand. It's cost me greatly to gain such news— and no, I will not tell you my means—but I've learned that Lord Vincent has gone further than any of us thought. He is not only just using the Memory Stone to control the wild dragons and has awakened not just the Darkening, but he has called up the ancient prince himself."

My stomach lurched. "The old king of the north?" I asked, remembering that dark presence I'd felt behind the dragon's mind just earlier.

"Yes." Jodreth looked at me again, his gaze steady and unsettling. It felt as if he could see more than I wanted him to know. "You've felt it, haven't you?" He took a sudden step toward me and I thought he was about to seize me by the neck. "You—you have it, don't you?"

It took everything not to step back, away from him. His eyes sparked and I wasn't certain if it was anger or something else in his eyes. Was he speaking of the Armour Stone? I resisted looking at Thea and kept my stare on Jodreth. "Have what?"

"The affinity." Jodreth threw his arms wide. Overhead, the herbs swayed. "You are what they call a dragon friend—one of those of the old blood, just as he was."

My throat tightened. I had to swallow hard, then I asked, even though I knew what he was speaking of, "He?"

"The ancient prince. He inherited his blood from his mother, and with it came a connection to the dragons—the ability to link human and dragon minds. That was the gate that he used to grow stronger and to allow darkness into the world." Jodreth was visibly paler. He stepped back and stroked his beard. "I knew it. When I saw what you did earlier—with the wild dragon—I knew."

Heart pounding, I faced him. "But...but the affinity...it's a good thing." I shook my head. I didn't want to hear what Jodreth might say against my connection to dragons. "It's saved me and Thea on more than one occasion, including just now."

"And it saved a lot of people at the fall of Torvald," Thea said, glaring at Jodreth.

He nodded, and then shook his head. "Yes, it can be used for good or ill, but it is a danger. If you cannot control it, the Darkening will use it to control you, to command your mind like a puppet. Don't lie now. You caught a glimpse of that ancient prince—did you not? You saw true evil."

I swallowed, but I couldn't speak. Looking away, face burning, I couldn't meet his stare, or Thea's. Was this what had started to happen of late? Was the Darkening starting to turn me into more of a dragon—a person it could control and use?

I heard Thea's boots scuff against the wooden floor. Looking up, I saw she'd put herself in front of Jodreth. "Your brother trusts Seb. Commander Hegarty believed Seb could use his powers to help us all—that he had to use his powers. We need Seb, and we need his affinity. And he's strong—more than strong enough to resist the Darkening! He didn't give into the illness—and we need the Healing Stone now to help others."

I'd never heard Thea speak like that...as if she really believed in me.

But I also wasn't sure she was right. I wasn't sure I really could resist the ancient prince. The affinity was growing stronger in me.

Jodreth met her stare, and then looked at me. "I am sorry, young Seb. Perhaps I misspoke out of too much concern." He glanced at Thea again. "This illness, describe it to me."

I stayed quiet while Thea told him what we'd seen and felt at the Dragon Riders' camp—including how the riders were becoming lazier, depressed and despondent.

Jodreth listened for a time, then shook his head. "You're right, it is not Dragon Sickness. It is the Darkening, working through the influence of the Memory Stone in Lord Vincent's hands, sucking the very life and will from the dragons and all whom it comes near. That energy is being used to power the Darkening itself, to make it even more powerful. The Healing Stone will do little—and it is not in my hands."

I sucked in a sharp breath. "Commander Hegarty didn't remember where he put it."

Jodreth nodded sadly. "It may well be that the only thing that can help us is the Dragon Stone itself."

"That's just a myth," Thea said, but she didn't sound all that certain.

Jodreth chuckled. "After all I've told you and all you have seen, you can still say that? Just as the Memory, the Healing and the Armour Stones are real, so is the one stone that brings them all together."

"But...what about the Armour Stone?" Thea said, her hand moving to her pouch and, before I could say anything, she drew out the rounded lump of black rock crystal.

Blinking, Jodreth gave a sharp laugh. "Not only is one of you a dragon friend, but you have found the Armour Stone again?" A wide grin cracked his features. "No wonder the same enchantment could not reach you. The Armour Stone protects not just from physical injuries but magic as well."

The monk made a quick set of movements in the air, and I saw the air between him and Thea ripple like a heat wave. And then I felt it, a wave of force that pushed me back, setting aside the tables and papers like a powerful blast of cold air. When I staggered to my feet once more, Thea was still standing in the same spot as she had done before, but the rest of the room around her was in disarray.

"You see. It protected you!" Jodreth grinned. He glanced at me. "You two are also linked through your dragon, otherwise, you would have a very sore head right about now."

Thea's mouth tightened. She tucked the Armour Stone back in a pocket. "Can't we extend the Armour Stone protection to all of the dragons and riders?"

Jodreth frowned and pulled at his beard. "I've never heard of such a thing, but if Thea is connected to you, and you were connected to every other dragon there—"

"And every dragon is connected to their own rider," Thea continued. She turned to me, hope shining in her eyes. "We could do it, Seb."

I wasn't as certain as she was. What if I connected to all those dragons and lost myself? What if that was all the Darkening needed to gain control over me?

I started to list the reasons this wouldn't work, but in my mind Kalax almost shouted, *dragon approaching!*

The cottage rafters rattled as she uncoiled herself from around the scrubby stone buildings.

Kalax was roaring as we ran out of the cottage. The fog that Jodreth had summoned was being torn apart by strong air currents.

"I'll try to hold it! Go now!" Jodreth shouted, raising his staff to the skies. White fog lifted from the grass, but swirled up and disappeared.

Thea grabbed her bow from off Kalax.

They must have sensed me.

I knew that was the truth. The affinity was proving to be as much of a problem as it was a help. I scrambled up into the saddle. I only had enough time to fasten the essentials of my harness.

I heard Jodreth groan through clenched teeth. The fog he was trying to weave around us billowed and was pushed back by a chill wind. A shadow fell over us, almost turning the day into night. A deep roar echoed.

It sounds big, I thought as Kalax leapt into the air.

"I can't find a target," Thea shouted. She was trying to track the shadow that appeared and then slipped away again into the fog. Looking down, I glimpsed Jodreth fling fog and then clouds up into the sky.

With a roar, a black shape swept down on us. I'd never seen a wild dragon so big—it was easily three times the size of Kalax! For a moment, I thought it was the brood mother come back— but this black was even bigger.

The fog cleared and then I saw the black had a single rider on its back—a tall, thin man with a narrow face and black hair. He turned and stared at me—it was Lord Vincent.

"Fly," Jodreth shouted at us. He swung his staff up in a circle over his head, throwing a gale at Lord Vincent. The black dragon was pushed back, but swept its huge wings up and down as it struggled to maintain control.

I heard the twang of Thea releasing an arrow. It flashed in the air and hit Lord Vincent.

I saw Vincent twist and slump in the saddle. The huge dragon lurched to one side, suddenly confused by no longer having a rider in command. *Oh no.* It did the only thing that wild predators knew how to do when confused and attacked—it went after the nearest target.

The black swooped down on Jodreth, claws extended.

I screamed and tried to reach out with my mind to stop the dragon, but it was all over with much too fast. The black caught up Jodreth. The air shuddered and Jodreth's magic slammed into the black dragon, sending it tumbling down the mountainside.

"He's—he's dead," Thea said. "Jodreth is gone."

"Come on, if Lord Vincent has the Healing Stone, we're not safe yet. Let's at least honor Jodreth's memory by saving his brother." I wheeled the agitated and cawing Kalax around to fly as fast as she could back to the Dragon Riders' camp.

CHAPTER 20
TOGETHER, SAFE

S eb was leaning forward, not talking, just concentrating. Just like at the battle of Torvald, I could tell that he was using every bit of strength he had. I could even feel the thrum of energy off him, that echo of his Dragon Affinity that I shared with him through Kalax. And I was worried for him. Because Kalax was worried too.

Behind us, the fog that Jodreth raised still clung to the edge of the mountains, forming a deep haze as we flew over the ravines and forests and out to the desert and the Dragon Riders' camp. I really wanted to fly there and find out that King Justin had managed to rally the troops to fly back to Torvald—but I knew better. Jodreth was gone, the Dragon Riders were still ill, and we were in trouble.

But we have the Armour Stone…and a plan now.

It seemed to take hours to fly back. I pulled out a little of the dried meat and bread from our supplies—there wasn't much of it left. We were going to need to find better food and a place to sleep—a safe place. It hit me again that the academy might be gone. It had become our home, but now…now it might be just another ruin. I shivered and pulled my cloak tighter.

At last, Seb pointed down to the smoldering campfires, most of them unlit. The camp really hadn't changed from when we'd left. The dragons still looked ill as they lay on the sands, and I hoped none of them had died. The riders' tents were starting to look at little wind-battered. I really hoped we'd be able to shake everyone out of this daze.

Seb started to bring Kalax down, urging her to land closer than she had before. I could tell she was uneasy—I was, too. We were protected right now by the Armour Stone, but we had to find a way to spread that protection over everyone.

I looked at Seb to see how he wanted to handle this, but he wouldn't meet my eyes. He wouldn't talk to me at all. By the time we'd landed and alighted, his jaw looked clenched tight and he was frowning.

"Seb, what is it?" I said. "We're here now—we have a chance."

He turned and stared at me, his eyes dark. He pulled off his dragon helmet and shook his head. "You heard what Jodreth said. The affinity…I felt the Darkening through the mind of that wild dragon. The Darkening, Lord Vincent, or whatever it is behind him—they got to Jodreth because of me. They found him because of me. I'm becoming the biggest danger around here. And I'm going to end up getting you in trouble again."

He started to turn away, but I grabbed his arm and swung him back around so he had to face me. "No, Seb. It could have been this that the Darkening sensed." I drew out the Armour Stone, holding it between us to remind him of our duty. "Jodreth died trying to protect us so we could bring this here and save his brother. Don't take that away from him. You heard what he said—we need the Dragon Stone if we are going to win!" I held out the Armour Stone. "But first we have to save the king and our friends."

Seb shook his head again. He opened his mouth like he was going to protest even more. Instead, he slowly put his hand on mine, closing his fist around the Armour Stone. He pushed the stone back to me. "You keep it. You need to stay safe."

All stay safe, together.

Kalax unfolded her long wings and wrapped them around us, and I knew she was seeking to stop our arguing. For one moment, I felt infinitely warm, protected and secure. Almost at peace. I was leaning against the warm belly of our strong dragon, and in front of me I could feel Seb's hand on mine, on the Armour Stone.

Together, I thought, and heard that same feeling echo from Kalax to Seb, to Kalax, and back to me again.

A shiver, like an electric spark passed between us, a pulse of power like Seb's Dragon Affinity, but this time it was coming from the Armour Stone.

Seb's eyes widened. "What the…? Did you?"

Together. Safe. Kalax repeated.

If I concentrated, I could feel the ripple of whatever had happened start to expand beyond our tiny circle. It was spreading out like a strong wind, flowing over the camp of Dragon Riders. I could almost sense them starting to remember their duties and who they were.

Looking up in wonder, I watched Kalax stretch up and turn to the nearest dragon—a green who started to snort and cough, as if waking from a long dream.

Yes, Kalax said in my mind. *But not enough. Many still need to heal.*

I turned to nod at Seb. "We are going to do it! We're going to free the Dragon Riders."

I put my other hand on the Armour Stone—Seb did as well. The hum of power seemed to surge. This was what I'd expected to feel from the Armour Stone. The stone seemed to warm in my fingers. I could feel Seb making a connection with Kalax—and with other dragons. But I also sensed he was holding back a little. It was as if he was afraid now to use his Dragon Affinity.

"Seb—concentrate!" I told him.

He snapped back, "I am."

The flow of energy from the Armour Stone seemed to waver—and then something odd happened.

I felt the flow shift—as if something else was pulling at the power. I shivered, remembering how Jodreth had said that Seb's affinity could be a bad thing—it could link him too strongly to the Darkening. Was that happening now?

Opening my eyes, I glanced around. It seemed to me the dragons around us were waking up. They were all starting to stand or rise and stretch. I could hear a low hum of voices from the camp, too—the riders were starting to come out of whatever had been draining them.

But something was still pulling at the Armour Stone.

I tried to follow that tugging thread—and glanced at the mountains that stood next to the camp.

The mountains rose up a dusty rose colour, near enough to see the scrub trees and rocky outcropping. Something was stirring in the mountain—I could feel it. A vibration started in the Armour Stone and spread up my arms.

"Seb?" The word came out of me with caution—were we doing something wrong? I wasn't sure, but Seb seemed totally caught up in the Armour Stone and connecting it to our dragons and the riders.

The ground started to shake under my boots. Heart pounding, I glanced around again, wondering what was happening. "Seb—did we do something wrong."

His eyes popped open and for an instant, he almost seemed more dragon than human. His eyes had that swirl of colour I'd seen in dragon eyes. He blinked and it vanished, leaving me thinking I must have imagined it.

He also turned to stare at the cliffs above us.

The mountain looked like it was shaking as if a giant had hold of it. Rocks tumbled down the side, loosened by whatever was happening. What was happening? Great spouts of dust burst from the mountain. I could still feel the Armour Stone—it was straining now, shaking in my hand as well, as if something had hold of it and was trying to drain its power.

"Seb, that's no earthquake," I said, taking a step back and breaking the connection with Seb.

At once, the pull on the Armour Stone stopped. I could hear dragons around us, stirring, roaring. Kalax roared as well, a challenging call that I knew was one she only gave if a strange dragon came near.

Seb was staring at the mountain as if he couldn't look away, as if he was caught somehow by something there.

Grabbing his arm, I shook him. "Seb? What is it?"

He didn't react. I clutched the Armour Stone tighter and thought to Kalax, *What do you sense?*

Danger comes.

She was right. I looked around us. The camp had at last come alive again. Riders were grabbing saddles and harness and throwing on their leathers and clothes. Someone blew a horn, sounding the call to mount. I could hear shouts—Ryan, it sounded like to me—yells to get into the sky.

Under my boots, the ground still shook. The mountain nearest us seemed to be changing—or was that cracking apart? I couldn't really tell, but dirt kept shifting and now rocks spit past us. I had to duck as one shot past like an arrow. The scrub trees were sliding down the slope, and as I watched, two large caves near the mountain top seemed to collapse into the mountain. It was as if the mountain was coming alive.

I glanced down at the Armour Stone as it rested in my palm—it was cool again and I no longer felt the tug on it. But something, I knew, had reached out to pull energy from the stone. A lot of energy. Had the Darkening connected to it through Seb? If so, he'd been right to worry.

"Seb, we need to get to Kalax, to get in the air," I told him. Grabbing his arm, I pulled at him. He seemed stuck now, like the riders had been. He could only stare at the hillside. "Seb!" I shouted at him.

Around us, riders hurried to their dragons, which were bellowing now and stretching their wings. After so many days on the ground, the dragons needed time to loosen stiff muscles, I knew. Riders were throwing saddles in place. Tents were forgotten, as was everything else except the need to get into the skies.

Muttering an oath, I grabbed Seb and dragged him with me to Kalax's side. But I couldn't very well throw him up in the saddle. I took his shoulders and shook him. "Seb!"

"It comes," he muttered. "It comes."

"Yeah, well, we'd better go."

Dirt had been pushed into the air. The ground shook again, and the side of the mountain was sliding down. The camp wasn't so close to the base of the mountain that it was in any danger, but all that moving ground pushed even more dust into the air. I coughed and pulled my flying goggles into place. Stuffing the Armour Stone into my glove, I turned to Kalax. "Can you get Seb to mount up?"

But Kalax wasn't looking at me either.

In fact, all the dragons were now staring at the mountain, roaring and calling out like another dragon was coming at them. For an instant, it seemed to me that the side of the mountain bulged out—like something was pushing to get out. The features of the mountainside shifted and I stared, my mouth dry and my heart pounding. It couldn't be. But I knew it was. Those irregular features—the angular head, the horns, and the spiny back— those were something every Dragon Rider knew by heart.

A dragon was coming out of that mountain.

But it was a dragon larger than any anyone had ever seen before—bigger even than the black Lord Vincent had been riding.

It was like it was being hatched from the stone—as if it had been growing unnaturally inside the hill. Was this why the Dragon Riders had been lured here? To see this monster's birth. Or to be here as food for the beast?

More rock shifted and trees slid as the huge dragon began to climb from its hatching ground. The beast shook itself free from the ruined rock and earth, clutching at the ground and hauling itself up. I saw then that it wasn't like any dragon I knew.

Six horribly mutated limbs and four wings lifted into the air as it roared at the sky. It was mottled black and its tiny red eyes glittered as it swung its head around.

Grabbing Seb's arm, I shook him again. "Seb, we have to go!" Around us a few other dragons launched into the sky, their riders clinging to their saddles and harness. The air seemed filled with dragon roars and dust. The huge dragon from the mountain bellowed a roar that shook the air and vibrated in my chest.

I knew Lord Vincent would be near—he'd want to see his beast come to life. This has to be some monster of the Darkening. I searched the sky, looking for Lord Vincent or his wild, black dragon. But what I really needed was to get Seb into the saddle.

Fumbling to pull the Armour Stone out of my glove, I called out to Kalax, "Be ready to fly."

I pulled the Armour Stone free and pushed it into Seb's hand, closing his cold fingers around the stone. "Hold it tight," I told him.

For two heartbeats nothing happened, but then Seb blinked and his eyes focused again. "Seb, let's go. That monster over there —if he's like any newly-hatched dragon—it's going to be hungry."

At last Seb's eyes focused on me. He nodded and then glanced at the huge dragon now stretching its wings over the crumbling mountaintop.

I was hoping we could stretch the Armour Stone again to shield the rest of the camp, and maybe we could keep this monster from destroying all of us. But I wasn't sure that would work. The stone seemed cool in my hand as I took it from Seb and clutched it.

Not dragon kin! Kalax hissed. She was right, it wasn't. It was a creature larger than the size of an entire castle, larger than the entire academy and Torvald put together.

Kalax bent her forelegs to make it easier for us to mount our saddles. Seb climbed into his harness as if he were an old man. I vaulted into the saddle, but my harness would need to wait. We had to be in the air.

Hearing a screech overhead, I looked up to see a wild, black dragon. Seb was in the saddle, so I shouted, "Kalax, fly!"

She took off so fast, I clutched at the saddle to stay on. The black kept coming at us and I knew we'd collide.

Kalax had to turn and bank as the huge dragon from the mountain reached out with a long claw toward her. That monster-dragon had a reach longer than any river I'd seen. Kalax turned … the wild dragon hit her side.

For an instant I held on, but I had the Armour Stone in one hand and my grip on the saddle leather began to slip. With a cry, my fingers gave way.

I spun into the air and fell, landing on my back. The breath whooshed out of me in a gasp and I lay there, dizzy—the Armour Stone had saved me from a deadly fall. But as I struggled to sit up again, I saw the black Armour Stone had slipped from my grasp.

I reached for it, but the wild, black dragon swooped down on me, and I froze as I stared up into the narrow, pale and gloating face of Lord Vincent.

CHAPTER 21
THE DARKENING

"She's okay!" I called to Kalax.

I'd seen Thea lying flat on the ground and for an instant my heart seemed to stop. It was as if my worst dreams had come true—Thea had fallen from the saddle. That was the fear of every rider—that we'd fall and our dragon would be unable to save us. I had felt the dragon slam into Kalax and had known another dragon must have hit us, but I was having trouble focusing. It was as if my mind was split between my own thoughts and those of the panic-stricken dragons below us. Their fear was mine. My heart thudded fast like theirs. My breaths came in shallow gasps. I wanted to fly—to run. But then Thea fell and I could only think of her.

She moved and I let out a long breath. The Armour Stone had saved her from a deadly fall. A roar put both Kalax and me on alert. I looked up to see the monster-dragon from the mountain swing around, its two tails sweeping over the hills and scattering anything it touched. Kalax had to veer and bank out of the way. Air rushed past us, pushed by that huge dragon's movements. Below me, dragons launched into the sky with their riders. The monster-dragon's tail swept down into the camp, smashing tents flat. I heard some screams then the dust rose up, hiding the destruction below. I needed to get back to Thea.

I could hear riders still on the ground, calling to their dragons and dragons answering with shrill cries that sounded on the verge of all-out panic. How many would get away? How many would be caught by the thing that had exploded from the hillside?

The monster-dragon was now flapping its many wings, still testing its strength and skills as would any young dragon. It lifted up on its haunches and bellowed, fire shot from its mouth. This beast was not like our dragons. I could sense only evil from it—an urge not to hunt for food, but to spill blood and destroy. It was a mindless thing, a pure beast with nothing more to it.

Our dragons had at least been given brief moments of clarity thanks to the Armour Stone—those that were not already in the sky and flying were screeching as they picked up their riders in their claws and launched themselves into the air and to safety. Once they were away, I knew they'd gain in strength. Maybe I could give them just a little more time.

The dust from the mountain's destruction was making it hard to see, but Kalax swung around and rode the air currents back to where Thea had fallen. I'd need her help if we were going to distract the huge dragon from our riders.

A terrible screech pulled my stare, and I saw the big, black dragon again. This time I glimpsed Lord Vincent in the saddle. He had swept down from the clouds. I should have known he would follow us here—or had he set this trap for all of us?

Haven't we been here before, boy?

I heard his voice in my head—a dark sneer. The air around him pulsed and shimmered—the Darkening and the ancient prince working through him. Now I could see them like a black shadow that clung to Lord Vincent in an almost transparent cape. I shivered and called to Kalax for more speed.

I would not allow him near Thea.

But the wild black dragon Lord Vincent rode was fast.

His laugh echoed in my head, and I thought back to him, *that monster is your doing…and I'll see you die with it.*

His wild dragon darted down, wings folded tight in a dive. My heart stopped as the dragon headed for Thea. But it swerved up again, and Lord Vincent lifted a hand to me—he held the Armour Stone itself. He had snatched it from Thea—or from where it had fallen from her grip.

I could see into his thoughts and I knew he now intended to see his giant dragon kill us all.

"No!" I shouted.

Kalax bellowed beside me, joining in my efforts.

I'll never see Thea fall again—not to you.

Closing my eyes, I gave myself utterly to my Dragon Affinity. I had no choice. It was that, or perish. I slipped into Kalax's mind and then into our dragons'. I pushed out and caught the thoughts of the wild black dragon—who hated the beast Lord Vincent had created as much as did our dragons.

Sweat popped on my brow and slicked my shirt to my back. My head felt as if it would explode, but I had to go on. I focused on our dragons—and then turned my thoughts to the monstrous beast Lord Vincent had created.

I screamed—and so did the dragons.

Spreading my wings, I would soar with them, and I told them, *free—we will be free!*

Freedom of flight—freedom to hunt as we wish, to have the friends we want. The sky, I called to them. *Fly. We must fly!*

I heard the shriek from the wild dragon Lord Vincent was riding. He might hold the Armour Stone, but his dragon was no longer his. I cut the ties between the Darkening—pushed myself between it and all dragons.

The huge dragon from the mountain stopped and stared at the sky.

Fly...

Wind whipped past my face. I soared and spun.

The huge beast blinked and I opened my eyes. For an instant, our stares met. I looked into dark eyes that seemed to be endless. It wanted to destroy—to kill. It was made to be a tool of the Darkening, but somewhere in there was a dragon's heart. I reached for that small part of it that was still a dragon—the part that had to be there.

It gave a rumbling roar and I thought it would reach out and swat Kalax and myself from the sky.

Dragon friend, I thought at it. Dragons…not the Darkening.

I severed the last ties to myself and fell utterly into the dragon's mind—*for Thea*, I thought. *For all Dragon Riders. For Torvald.*

At first, darkness swallowed me. Hate. Evil. Destroy. I wound myself deeper, pushing into that beast's mind, putting myself there. No…not destroy. Be a dragon. Be free of Darkening. It's not my ruler. It's not my kin. It's not me!

I was free…I was a dragon so mighty none could stop me.

A roar echoed from my throat, vast and shaking the earth. I lifted up into the sky, spread my wings and turned toward the warm south—to the vast heat of the ground, to the open wind. I would fly. I was a dragon.

Seb?

No Seb…dragon!

"Seb?" The word echoed not just in my head but in my ears. I blinked open my eyes. I lay on the ground, staring up at blue sky. Kalax lay curled around me, holding me with her tail. Had she just called my name?

Thea's hand tightened on my arm. "Seb?" she said again.

I blinked—for an instant I knew I could stay as a dragon.

I could live inside that huge dragon's mind and be one with it. I could soar forever. I could hunt and live as a dragon. I'd be the ruler of the skies—a dragon so mighty none could harm me.

Something wet splashed on my face. I looked up to see tears spilling from Thea's eyes. Reluctantly, I let my connection with the dragons slip—first from the huge dragon now flying south, then from our dragons who seemed to be scattered everywhere, and then from the wild, black dragon that had thrown Lord Vincent. I couldn't sense Lord Vincent near—but I knew he had the stones. I could feel that power pulsing around me, and I shut down even that thread of connection.

Good, Kalax thought at me. *Seb dragon friend, not dragon.*

Just before the connection vanished, Lord Vincent's thoughts swept into mine—dark and swirling and angry. I knew he's used the powers of the Darkening to make his escape. But he sent me one gloating thought.

The Memory Stone, the Healing Stone, and the Armour Stone— the perfect tools to take apart your entire, wretched world.

I didn't remember much of what happened after that. I had some memories of how Kalax flew me back to Thea. I knew I'd managed to save her—and the Dragon Riders—but I wasn't sure how, except I'd been a dragon. I'd been all dragons—for a brief time. And I'd left a small part of myself in that huge dragon that the Darkening created—it was no longer a mindless thing meant to kill. It had in it somewhere deep a connection to us—but I wasn't sure that would be enough if we ever had to face it again.

I also wasn't sure I could ever do that—become a dragon—again and come back to being just myself. Thinking about it left me cold inside.

Thea, however, hovered next to me.

The Dragon Riders' camp was a mess—utterly destroyed by that monster-dragon. Tents had been knocked over and dragged over the sand. Some riders had been buried—I could hear the keening of the dragons who had lost riders. A few dragons and riders got away, and a few had stayed to try and fight.

But I worried we were in a bad spot still—at least the one good thing was that the illness that had affected everyone was gone.

Just before nightfall, I got out of bed, dressed and stepped out of the tent.

The camp was getting ready to move. Dragon Riders were taking down tents and saddling dragons and packing up anything that was still worth taking—food, weapons and water. Dragons were calling with impatient cries to their riders—they didn't want to stay here and I didn't blame them. I resisted dipping into any dragon's thoughts

In the light of a rising, full moon, the ruined mountain was now just a scarred hunk of land—it looked as if the top had been wrenched off by a giant hand.

With the giant dragon no longer here—and Kalax told me that dragon had been pulling at everyone's life force just by being here—riders were now acting like riders again and the dragons all sounded by their calls eager to get into the skies.

I knew we were going to need to be strong for whatever came next. The Darkening and Lord Vincent had all the Dragon Stones—but we had one, thin hope left.

Cold now, I knew I should go in and put on a cloak. We would be in the skies soon. Thea came over to me and slapped my arm. "About time you woke."

I nodded.

She kept staring at me. "Any dreams?"

I shrugged and lifted a hand. They weren't anything I would ever tell her. How did you tell someone you knew what it was to soar above clouds—that you longed to have the wind on your face again and the power of huge wings? "I'm hungry."

She grinned and led me over to friends she had made who shared the fish they'd just caught. It was the only campfire burning, and it was soon put out and the order came to assemble and fly.

We were, I thought, a poor collection of Dragon Riders. Some of the riders had borrowed dead friends' armour. Others were missing helmets. Some of the dragon harnesses had been mended with ropes. But the faces were all set and the weapons gleamed in the moonlight.

Kalax bellowed a roar and as soon as the order came, she lifted into the air faster than any other dragon. I clung to the saddle and let her do the flying. With all the other dragons, we couldn't get lost.

But where were we going?

We flew north—or that's what I started to notice. I couldn't help it. I was a navigator and the stars told the story of the direction we set. Glancing around, I saw fewer dragons than I would have wished for—the squadrons had been scattered. I knew that Thea had been looking for her brothers and the king, but we hadn't seen them. My hope was that they'd gotten away early.

It grew chill as the night deepened, but I welcomed the cold. I was done with desert heat—a faint bit of it lurked in my mind. The huge dragon from the mountain had found a toasty spot in the Southern Realm. I cut off the connection and tried to focus more on the stars.

And then I saw it.

A flash. A faint one on the horizon. It looked like the reflection of light on a pane of glass. I tried to ignore it, thinking it must be one of the roaming bands of Wildmen or bandits setting alight to another village. The Darkening at work in other parts of the kingdom. But the flashes settled into a regular order. My heart lifted and I called out to Thea, "Signals!"

The flashes were the signaling code of the Dragon Riders—the one that every navigator knew by heart. Whoever was signaling had to be up very high for us to see them. And just one word repeated over and over again.

Gather.

No one needed to give the order. All the dragons shifted and headed for that light.

We flew, all of us, in a ragged group. I realized then that I hadn't seen Commander Hegarty, and I hoped he'd made it out early too.

We followed the signals to the eastern part of the Leviathan Mountains. In the bright moonlight I glimpsed a secluded valley edged by deep trees with a waterfall that gleamed silver and what looked like inky, deep pools on the other side of the falls. And I saw the best thing I could have seen.

The valley opened out, safe and green and sheltered—and there were campfires and dragons.

I saw Ferdinania first, so I figured Merik and Varla had made it here. That meant this tiny valley sheltered those from Torvald, too—my folks might be here. My heart leaped, but I told myself not to hope too much or too hard.

A dragon swept down at us, both taking a closer look and welcoming us. Jensen and Wil waved and shouted at us from Dellos—they'd been flying patrol.

Kalax landed us down in the valley. We tried to keep some order to our scrappy group, but soon everyone split up in the search for friends and family. I gave a nod to Thea, and she slipped away, no doubt looking for her parents. I went looking for my folks.

It took me longer to find them than I would have wanted—my heart kept jumping at the sight of every small group huddled around a fire. But it was the clang of a hammer on an anvil that pulled me to them.

Da had brought his anvil on a cart—and my stepmother and sister were there, too. They had a tent at the edge of the clearing. A lean-to, really, set up next to the cart. My stepmother gave a cry when she saw me, my sister ran over to hug me and my da just said, "And where have you been?" As if I'd been lazing or day dreaming. I could only grin.

They tried to push dinner on me, but I knew I needed to report back to whoever was in charge.

They let me go with hugs, and my da shook my hand and said, "I'm pounding out swords if you need a new one." I reached down to my side. I still had my sword on me, but it seemed a tiny thing now compared with a dragon's claw that could have easily speared a cow.

Heading toward the Dragon Rider tents that were set up near the waterfalls, I came across Merik and Varla. Varla thumped my back, she'd been hanging out too much with Thea. Merik pulled me aside. "I saved some of the maps, but not all of them. What happened to you?"

I shook my head. "We'll talk after we eat. Have you seen Thea?"

They had. I found her outside the king's tent—King Justin had survived. His dragon, with Reynalt, had been one the first off the ground, but once in the air, the dragon wouldn't go back to face that monster. *That was a smart dragon,* I thought.

Commander Hegarty was there. I tried to get him alone from the others to tell him of his brother, but when I said I had something to tell him, he shook his head and smoothed his mustache. He had shaved his cheeks, and if his uniform was still a little worn, it had had the dust shaken off and the greaves polished. "We'll talk of losses later."

I nodded and my throat thickened. He knew, then, about Jodreth. I wondered if there had been a special tie between them. Would I know if my da died—or my sister? Or did he assume the worst because he'd not heard anything from Jodreth?

I wasn't sure, but I saw Thea heading back from the other tents. She came to my side, smelling like roses. I pulled back and stared at her. She made a face. "Mother," she said. "Somehow she managed to trade for a few comforts, including perfume. My father thinks she ought to have held out for a bed."

"They safe?" I asked. But how safe were any of us?

Thea nodded, and wrapped her arms around herself. "Father took a knock on the head. He's going to have quite the scar and he's spitting mad that he had to leave. He's certain our house didn't burn, but I'm not so sure. I found Reynalt, too. We're to sit in at the king's council, which—by the way—comes after dinner."

I realized then that I was starving.

Dinner turned out, however, to just be hunks of bread and cheese. Kalax thought to me that she would bring me fish in the morning, and I had to grin. The idea of raw fish for breakfast didn't sound that good—so maybe I was going to be all right after all.

I saw Instructor Mordecai at the council fire which was held outside the king's tent—there wasn't enough room to fit us all inside. He gave me a nod, and for the first time it felt as if he thought of me as a true Dragon Rider.

The council meeting went on most of the night, and it was a good thing there was plenty of wood to keep the fire burning. Those from Torvald told their story first—the flight from the palace and the city—and how they'd been harassed by Wildmen and bandits. Beris and Jensen spoke next for the Dragon Riders from the academy. It was the first time I'd ever heard Beris talk without boasting, about how hard it had been to defend those fleeing the fall of Torvald. Merchants spoke up, asking for help from the king. All the Dragon Riders just swapped looks at that.

Reynalt, Ryan and Commander Hegarty talked about what had happened with the squadrons. Then Thea was called on to speak.

I noticed she didn't say anything about the Armour Stone.

A touch of anger stirred in me.

It was past time to stop acting like these old stories had to be held back. That hadn't done anyone any good. I was tired of the idea that just a few could protect everyone. That wasn't true. I thought of my father, making swords for anyone who would pick one up. That's what we needed.

So when Thea sat down, I stood and said, "The Darkening—it knows how to warp a dragon's mind to its will. I know because I've felt it. I can feel a dragon's thoughts." A mutter went around the circle. I swept my stare around it, daring anyone to say anything. The muttering died. "We can fight back. However, right now the Darkening thinks it will win. It's created a monster and will do worse. But we have a chance still."

Stares were swapped. King Justin looked again more like the young man I had first met. He shook his head and said, "I'm not even sure what happened to us."

I was tired of him not knowing how to be a king. It was time he learned. Voice strong, I said, "What matters now is that we must find the Dragon Stone, the one that combines all of the powers. It exists. And it can defeat the Darkening."

A murmur went around the circle again, then Reynalt stood and asked, "But how? Who knows where such a thing could even be now? It's a thing of legend."

"I know one person who might have known." I said, looking northwards, and thinking about a small, ruined stone cottage built into the side of a mountain, and a brave man who'd done more than any of us here. "And he will have left clues for us—to help us."

"Jodreth?" Thea said, the word very quietly. She pushed up to her feet and stood next to me, bumping my shoulder with hers.

I turned back to the circle of firelight and the worried, grimy faces of my friends. The commander sat here, and the king, and the leaders of Torvald and of the Dragon Riders. But I'd been a dragon. I didn't fear them—they didn't know what real power was.

Behind them, the enclosure dragons—Kalax included—had spiraled themselves into knots about each other, taking satisfaction just in being alive and having each other. For tonight, I was sure they had the right idea.

"Tomorrow," I said with quiet certainty. Amazingly, all the Dragon Riders, the merchants and even the king himself seemed ready to listen to me. But I knew it was because I was talking like a dragon. I knew how to speak with true power now. I smiled. "For tonight, let us just remember the joy of life. Tomorrow we start to take back what has been stolen from us."

One by one, the faces around me hardened with determination. I saw nodding heads and faces brighten. Thea bumped my shoulder and gave me a grin that was more about her wanting to get back into the fight to give Lord Vincent what he deserved.

In the shadows outside the firelight, I caught her fingers with mine.

Between us, the sparks of the camp fire spiraled up to kiss the star-strewn sky. And I regretted—just a little—my choice to be human and not to be a dragon that could soar into that darkness. But only just a little.

THE END OF DRAGON LEGENDS
BY AVA RICHARDSON

Book three, **Dragon Bonds**, is out now.

Keep reading for an exclusive extract!

THANK YOU!

I hope you enjoyed this book! If you'd like to let other readers know this is a book they won't want to miss out on, please leave a review :)

Receive free books, exclusive excerpts and be kept up to date on all of my new releases, when you sign up to my mailing list at AvaRichardsonBooks.com/mailing-list

Stay in touch! I'd also love to connect with you on:

Facebook: www.facebook.com/AvaRichardsonBooks

Goodreads:
www.goodreads.com/author/show/8167514.Ava_Richardson

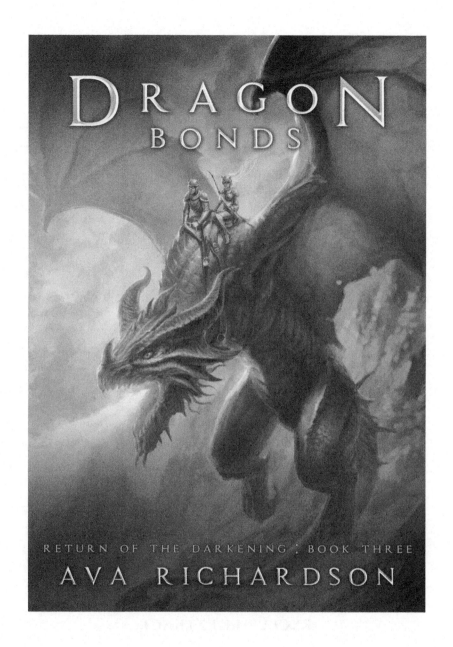

DRAGON
BONDS

RETURN OF THE DARKENING : BOOK THREE
AVA RICHARDSON

BLURB

The Darkening has risen...

Agathea Flamma and Sebastian Smith now face an overwhelming enemy. The rapid spread of the Darkening, a threat arising from the mists of legend, looms over the entire land. With both their families torn apart by the conflict and betrayal lurking around every corner, one mistake could doom the kingdom.

They'll have to decide where to put their faith: blood ties or newfound friends?

After the destruction of the Dragon Academy, it's up to Thea and Seb to gather their loyal comrades—and forge uneasy new alliances—to quell the ancient menace and face the evil Lord Vincent. With civil war raging, the Dragon Riders must race against time to find the legendary Dragon Stone, the only tool they have to fight against the endless darkness that threatens to swallow them all.

Download your copy of Dragon Bonds here!

EXCLUSIVE EXTRACT

"Dobbett? Is that you?" A rustling and snuffling in the darkness ahead put me on alert, and I set a hand on my sword.

Since the attack on Torvald, things had changed in the Flamma household. Luckily, most of the house had been spared from direct damage—but that didn't mean that any of it was safe. Bands of Wildmen could be heard in the streets, and the Darkening-controlled wild dragons flew overhead, passing like a shadow and swooping down on anything that moved.

Not as many as there were.

Ten days ago, Prince—no wait—*King* Justin had ordered us back to the city to help anyone we could find. We couldn't approach the mountain; the air was so thick with the vicious, black wild dragons controlled by Lord Vincent. They'd torn apart the city, their claws scraping away roofs and their snouts breaking apart grain houses, inns and homes. But the wild dragons were growing tired of destruction—most had left. There were only so many cobblestones even a feral dragon can eat before it's had its fill. And only so many orders they could take before their wild nature took over again and they headed back to the wilds.

Perhaps it cost too much to control them all?

I didn't know, but I needed to find out.

Pausing outside my family's sweeping staircase—the one that had once led to my own bedroom— I could see the window was thankfully unbroken. My parent's had returned to Torvald so they might salvage what they could. Now I just wanted to get them out of the house and gone from the city. The view looking down over the different tiers of the city was a sad one. Smoke still drifted up from several fires, and I could see the ruinous smears of crumbled buildings, bridges and walls. No movement in the sky today. I remembered how Seb had suffered when he had been trying to control the wild dragons. He'd been exhausted, too tired to even speak afterward. How much energy must it have cost Lord Vincent to control so many wild dragons?

How much willpower does the Darkening have?

A huff and a snarl from the darkened room ahead of me snapped my attention back to the present. Just what on earth was wrong with me? You would have thought I would be at least a little wary of where I was about to set foot in such an uncertain situation.

I tried to breathe, remembering the mental exercises I'd been taught at the Dragon Academy, taking time to flex my hand around the hilt of my short sword, draw it without a sound and feel its weight as I edged closer to the darkened, half-open door.

What was I about to find? A Wildman, a raider from the South or some other horror?

"Thea?" The word came out a worried hiss from behind me. I looked down to see my mother, the Lady Flamma, standing at the bottom of the stairs, brandishing a heavy iron skillet. *That is probably the very first time she has ever had to pick up one of those.* Guilt for being a little unkind bit at me. I could see the fear in my mother's pinched face—she just wasn't used to this kind of thing. And yet she still had gone off to find the biggest, heaviest thing she could use to help her daughter.

As if I still need protecting.

I was the one who'd had training as a fighter—just as all Flamma children had been trained. My oldest brother, Reynalt, was now commander of the Dragon Riders, and Ryan was the King's Navigator. I was a Dragon Rider, too, along with Seb, my navigator. But, to be honest, I didn't know which, if any of us, I would put money on winning in a fight against the Lady Flamma when she was armed with an iron skillet and an iron will. The events of the past few days had marked her—I had heard of hair turning white overnight, but I had never seen it before, and Mother's hair had done just that. She had given up elaborate hair dressings and now wore her silver-white locks in a simple braid. Her gown was simple, too—blue wool with no decorations. Her hair and dress made her blue eyes seem even brighter. They glittered right now with a battle lust.

Flapping at her with one free hand, I whispered as loud as I dared, "Go back. Father needs you to keep him safe."

My mother frowned, and I was sure she was about to refuse. Amazingly, she turned and left, hurrying back to the drawing room where she had left her husband.

"First time for everything," I muttered. But I felt strangely sad, instead of pleased. It was odd not to have Mother fussing over me like I was still a girl. Not that I wanted Mother to spend the rest of her life trying to get me married to a nice, wealthy boy —far from it. Besides, there probably weren't many nice boys left.

That thought was still too sharp even for me. I veered away from what that actually meant for the many noble suitors I might have once had. Even the Westerforth boys, Terence and Tomas, horrible as they were, didn't deserve to be eaten by a dragon. But was a dragon hiding here?

Something snuffled and growled inside my old room. It was now or never.

With a yell, I kicked aside the door and swept in, my short sword low. Something small, wiry and fanged barked and snuffled. The furry white land-pig growled, snapped and got caught in the ruined bed sheet.

A wave of relief crashed through me. It felt like years since I'd last seen her. "Dobbett, where have you been? Have you been up here this whole time?" I sheathed my sword and extricated her from the voluminous white sheets that had once been part of my bed.

She excitedly licked my hand and tried to snuff at my face.

"They thought you had run away!" I scolded the land-pig, who looked a little like a cross between a small, pug-nosed dog and a fluffy cushion. Her big, rolling eyes regarded me with the love and undying admiration that only a pet can give. I sat down, sighed and allowed Dobbett to climb up onto my lap with snuffles, snouts and sneezes.

"There, girl." I patted her thick fur as I had done a hundred times before in this very room.

But it had looked quite a bit better than this.

The wooden board windows to the balcony had been left or blown open, allowing the winds to ravage the small room. Smoke tainted the air and even a few leaves littered the floor. A wardrobe had been overturned, spilling out a collection of sugary dresses and blue robes, jerkins of fine fawn and a mass of shoes. They looked like they belonged to someone else and to a very different time.

My old writing desk had fallen over and had deep gashes on its surface—doubtless from Dobbett's scrabbling and not from a dragon. The wall hangings and blankets were spread around the room and pulled from the walls. Despite all the destruction, what struck me the most was how the room seemed too much space for anyone.

Have I changed so much? Have the years of cramped living at the Dragon Academy, sharing a room with Varla, changed me so much?

Small, finely-embroidered cushions lay scattered over the floor. They'd been made by a great craftsman from the Gabbon Heights. They were still nice to look at, but they were useless. *They'll keep my father warm, at least.* I gathered them up in a blanket that was still mildly clean.

On a still-standing bedside cabinet, I saw my small dragon figurines, baring fangs or in noble stances. They had been carved by a master woodsman from the South and although they had certain elegance it was clear the carver had never ridden a dragon.

These are the sorts of things people carve when they think about dragons and Dragon Riders.

I picked one up, looking at its fierce snarl, with one claw raised high. "Kalax doesn't look like that, does she, Dobbett?" I asked the land-pig, who had closed her eyes and was wuffling happily. A *really* fierce dragon didn't bother to strike a pose before it struck.

"I was such a stupid little girl," I told Dobbett, who agreed with a pleased whine. She started to make a husky, almost purring snore. I urged her up to follow me, stepping over a spilled pile of dresses, breeches and other old clothes.

Growing up as the only girl with two big brothers, one couldn't help but be a bit rough around the edges. But I had also been the darling daughter of Lord and Lady Flamma and therefore had been expected to dance, recite poetry, play a musical instrument and practice the art of dressing well.

I much preferred my Dragon Academy jerkin, the tunic, breeches and heavy riding boots. I cringed when I thought back to the girl I had been. I must have been so naïve, so arrogant. What must Seb and the others have thought of me when they'd first met me?

Another fearful whisper rose up from the stairs below. "Thea?"

Sweeping up Dobbett under one arm and clutching the cushions and blanket under the other, I stepped out to the landing. "It's just Dobbett, Mother."

"Oh, by the First Dragon!" Mother swore while shaking her head. "You gave me a fright. Come back to the drawing room. Your father has almost decided."

"And I bet I know *what* he has decided," I muttered, trying to keep it under my breath but to no use. Mother had always had *very* sharp hearing.

"Agathea, that is no way to talk about your father."

I hung my head. She was right, of course. My father had been through enough without having a disobedient daughter as well. They had seen their home and the city of Torvald destroyed, the old king was dead, and now most of the land was in the hands of an enemy. The Darkening had returned. A good portion of the population was presumed dead, and still others were under the strange effects of the Memory Stone and had forgotten almost everything that had once mattered to them.

If there was *anything* that we could give thanks for, it was that Lord Vincent had other things occupying his mind than individually controlling the ordinary citizens of Torvald.

Most of those affected by the Memory Stone had been left where they stood, to be taken away by friends, neighbors and family to be looked after. Lord Vincent and the Darkening had other battles to fight. Now, I needed Father and Mother to come with me and join the refugees heading to the king's camp. Ryan, I knew, would have been saying the very same thing to them.

"Come on, you'll catch a chill out here that will be the death of you!" Mother's voice took on a stern tone. I headed down the stairs.

Without the servants or any supplies, my mother had seemed mortified that we couldn't keep the house heated or even clear up the mess from the recent battle.

I clambered past our small barricade of tables and chairs and slipped into the room.

Believe me, Mother, the very last thing anyone should worry over is dying from a cold.

Download your copy of Dragon Bonds here!

Made in United States
Orlando, FL
08 August 2022